KARAH
QUINNEY

THE SEEKING STAR

(Book One)

K/P

ISBN-10: 0989263819

ISBN-13: 978-0-9892638-1-8

THE SEEKING STAR

KENNEDY PUBLISHING

Published in the United States by Kennedy Publishing.

Library of Congress Cataloging-in-Publication Data

Quinney, Karah

The Seeking Star: a novel/Karah Quinney.

KENNEDY PUBLISHING
TITLES BY KARAH QUINNEY:

The Whale Hunter
Pillar of Fire (Book One)
Sacred Fire (Book Two)
Sacred Path (Book Three)

The Great Land
The Seeking Star (Book One)
Shadow of the Moon (Book Two)
Light of the Sun (Book Three)

Sundancer
Legend of the Sundancer (Book One)
The Last Sundancer (Book Two)

Warrior
The Warrior's Way
Daughters of the Sun
The Cloud Forest – New Release

License Statement:
This book is licensed for your personal enjoyment only. This book may not be re-sold or given away to other people. If you would like to share this book with another person, please purchase an additional copy for each reader. Thank you for respecting the hard work of this author.

CHAPTER ONE

Thousands of years ago….

The hunt was long and arduous, but the skill of the hunters brought success to the men that followed the bison. The men moved as one, walking in a single line across the gently blowing grass. Their arms were thick with corded muscle and their backs were slightly bowed under the weight that they carried. Stalking such large herds often proved dangerous and patience was needed to choose the right place to take a stand and make a kill.

Cahil led the hunt and the men of his village looked to him for guidance. He was the eldest son of Kusug, the leader of their village and his younger brother, Makiye, shared the responsibility of the hunt. They stalked the giant longhorn steppe bison over several days, having traveled a great distance from their village to find the herd. The men were painted for the hunt, wearing the white color of newly driven snow upon their arms and faces. Their near naked bodies glistened in the sunlight as they kept pace with the herd. Each hunter knew that the timing of the hunt must be done together, as one.

The strength of one hunter's spear was not enough to stop the thundering bison and they would risk life and limb if they were not careful. Cahil waited for the right moment to drive the herd into a natural enclosure provided by the land. He could sense the tension in the air and he was relieved to see that the herd continued to graze without concern as they crept closer, moving like shadows upon the land. Just as Cahil lifted his voice in a deafening shout, he saw his brother break free from the tall grass that hid them and race toward the running herd with a young man at his side.

Cahil's heart thundered as Makiye dipped into the herd of bison, along with Anuk, a young man barely past his first kill. The other hunters took up the charge, shouting and whistling as they herded the bison toward the hillside enclosure. The men knew better than to slaughter the bison at random. Dark plumes of rolling dust thickened the air as Cahil plunged forward, eager to see to the welfare of Makiye and Anuk. He silently cursed his brother for distracting him when his sole focus should be upon leading a successful hunt. The bison herd moved as one, there hooves thundering over the ground as they unknowingly ran toward the location where several would meet their end.

He caught sight of Makiye as his brother drove his spear through the side of a buffalo with a cry that was ripe with triumph. Anuk stood beside him as a large male bore down upon him. Cahil's breath caught in his throat as he saw that Makiye was focused completely upon making his kill and Anuk would surely be trampled. He ran with the full strength of his legs, but he knew that he would be too late. He shouted and several of the men threw their spears as the buffalo bellowed in agony. Anuk finally regained his senses as Cahil reached him, while the rest of the herd thundered past as the men combined their efforts to bring the giant buffalo down. It took several spears along with raw strength to subdue the large animals and the work itself was bloody and strenuous.

They spent the rest of the day butchering the buffalo and dividing the meat amongst the men. Cahil worked to skin one of the buffalo with the help of several men. He used his full strength to cut along the back of the animal to get to the tender meat beneath the surface. The other men worked without speaking, honoring the life of the buffalo as they removed the legs and shoulder blades. Steam rose into the air as the internal organs were exposed and a collective sigh of appreciation came from the men as Makiye called their attention.

Cahil turned to see that his brother was the first to hold up the bladder as a great cheer came from the other men. All together they took three buffalo from the herd and it was more than enough to satisfy the people of their village. The skins of the buffalo were invaluable in a land that was often filled with snow and ice.

At midday, Cahil led the men back to their village as his heart pounded in triumph. He saw that his brother's chest rose and fell with pride, for they would be well praised for the success of the hunt. As the distant mountains came into view, Cahil thought of the calamity that could have befallen Anuk if the other men failed to step in.

Unbidden, anger arrowed through him as he thought of the risks that Makiye had taken so that they would return to their village triumphant. He would have been angry if his younger brother risked his own life, but he was furious because Makiye put someone else in harm's way.

"Our father will be well pleased." Makiye hoped to quiet the anger that he sensed in his brother.

Cahil glanced over his shoulder with a grimace. "Our father will be well pleased, but what will he say about the actions that you took this day?"

"He will say nothing, because you will not tell him."

"You are a man fully grown and yet your selfishness has become a burden that you wish to throw upon the other men." Cahil narrowed his eyes as Makiye struggled to find a response. "Do you deny it?"

"I know only what I can see, touch and feel. Look at the burden of meat that we carry, fresh meat that will be cooked over the fires by the women of our village. Kusug will hold his head high and strength will return to his limbs. Strength given to him from our hunt."

Cahil shook his head as his brother's words whispered on the wind, like oil and water; they did not mix with all that they learned at their father's knee.

"You should be glad," Makiye continued, despite the dark look upon his brother's face. "You will offer Delak's parents a portion of the meat brought in from our hunt and they will allow you to take her as your lifemate."

Thoughts of Delak swirled within Cahil's mind even as he recognized that his brother sought to manipulate him. As a strong hunter of their band, he took his time choosing the right young woman as a wife. Delak stirred his blood and she incited his male hunger with the lowering of her lashes and the coy glances that she tossed about. He enjoyed the scent of her hair and the sensuous way that she moved, as if she floated over the ground.

He did not share his plans to take Delak as his wife, but as always, Makiye was observant. He must have watched them sneak away from the village fire after the hunting ceremony, which took place only a few days ago.

Cahil never laid claim to Delak's body. She would allow him to touch and stroke her when they shared a blanket, but she would not allow anything further until they were joined as husband and wife. While he understood her hesitant nature, he wondered if she feared the mating act or simply lacked the burning desire to join their bodies as one.

When he mentioned his concerns to her, tears formed in her eyes and her full lips turned down as she looked up at him. If she was not pleased with his actions, her tears always ripped an apology from him. It was simply the way of things between them.

"You cannot persuade me to avoid talking to our father about your behavior. Anuk could have been killed. You are a skilled hunter and yet you take unnecessary risks, Makiye." Cahil spoke of the way that Makiye rushed into the buffalo herd, eager to spear one of the largest males. It was obvious to all that the fatherless boy would do anything to win their approval and Makiye always found a way to force Anuk to prove his loyalty. It did not matter to Makiye that the youth was like a younger brother in Cahil's eyes.

"I would not do anything to purposely harm Anuk." Makiye cast a glance over his shoulder toward the youth in question.

Anuk carried a large burden of the buffalo meat upon a travois. Earlier, he waved away their offer of help, once again seeking to prove himself to them.

Cahil took several steps forward, so that his brother was forced to keep up with him, while the other men gave them space, easily sensing the discord that existed between them. "You are wrong, Makiye. Anuk is willing to follow you wherever you lead, that is a burden that you must learn to bear. If not for the other men, Anuk would have been crushed by the charging male that targeted him because of your inability to exercise patience."

Cahil's eyes darkened as he speared his brother with a seething glare.

"I will not always be able to watch out for you, whether it is during a hunt or in a skirmish with other men. You must learn to evoke loyalty from the men that we lead."

"We?" Makiye scoffed, having heard nothing of Cahil's warning except what he wanted to hear. "You are our father's eldest son and as such, it is your responsibility to lead our village."

"Our father still lives. Even in his old age, he is strong." Cahil did not like to think of the time when their father would not be present to hold tight the bond between his two sons. "You and I have been burdened with the responsibility of leading the men on the hunt. You will either learn to put others before yourself or suffer the agony that comes from being responsible for the death of another."

"I am not like you, Cahil." Makiye's dark brown eyes were shadowed as he held Cahil's gaze before turning away. "I no longer wish to hear your words of doom. Our father will be delighted with our efforts and he will not want to hear talk of guilt and death."

"Makiye!" Cahil called after his brother as Makiye walked ahead, but his brother would not turn back. The other men carried most of the burden while Makiye walked free, except for his hunting spear and other weapons.

Concern over his brother's unwillingness to listen weighed heavily upon his shoulders as he went to help the other men. He knew that Makiye wished to be the first to enter their village with the good news of a successful hunt.

His brother would reap the glory heaped upon him by their people and he would forget all that passed between them this day, but Cahil would not forget. He was determined to speak to their father as soon as possible. If he failed to do so, then he alone would be responsible for those that suffered because of Makiye's reckless behavior.

"Yi! Yi! Yi!" The call of triumph carried to the men as they entered the Ula'tuk village. With tired smiles and aching backs they handed over the fresh meat that would feed their village for many days to come.

"Makiye has told us of the success of your hunt! You are to be honored over the village fire at sunset." Women, young and old, rushed forward to help with the meat brought in by their husbands, brothers and sons. Several of the men would rest and return to the hunting site to recover the necks and heads of the animals, which was removed intact. Their village held ten hands of people and they were still growing in size. Naked children ran underfoot, eager to win a raw scrap of meat from the hunters before it hit the cooking fires. The women discussed how they would make use of the buffalo skins and the men teased and accepted the praise that came their way.

A soft voice from behind caused Cahil to turn in heady anticipation. He was not disappointed to hear his name spoken by the woman that would become his lifemate.

"Cahil, you have returned from a successful hunt."

He took in the sight of Delak as she watched him knowingly out of shining eyes. A fur trimmed deerskin dress displayed her curves to perfection and her dark hair swung free, gathering around her shoulders as she walked toward him. She bent to speak to one of the village children and her motion drew his eyes to her hips and trim waist.

"Delak." He opened his arms as she returned her attention to him and stepped lightly into his embrace. Her lips brushed over his cheek and she stroked one hand over the long braid that hung down his back.

"You should sheer your hair so that you look more like your father." Delak chided as she glanced over her shoulder toward Kusug.

Cahil saw that his father and brother stood with their heads bent close together. It was obvious to him that Makiye was the image of their father; both men were lean of form with dark eyes, sloped noses and wide mouths. Kusug's back and shoulders were bowed from the passage of time and he often walked with a limp as a result of an old injury, but Makiye stood just like their father, though his stance was enhanced only by the proud bearing of his youth.

Cahil was slightly taller than his father and brother, while his angular features were much sharper, as if cut from stone. He preferred to wear his hair long and uncut and even as a young boy he never allowed anyone to cut away the length.

Most of the men of their village wore their hair sheared above the shoulders, but this was not his preference.

"Cahil." Delak pouted prettily as he returned his attention to her. "Will you speak to your father? He has been ill in your absence and he will need you now more than ever."

Concern arrowed through Cahil as he removed his hands from Delak's shoulders and walked over to his father.

"Father." Cahil waited until his father turned to face him and he was rewarded with an approving glance.

Kusug spoke in a voice that was aged and worn. "You have been successful in your hunt. Makiye told me that it was not easy. The buffalo herds have begun to shift from their former trails. You have done well, my son." Kusug nodded approvingly as his gaze slid back to Makiye. "You will be honored at the feasting ceremony tonight."

Cahil did not know why he felt as if his father often weighed his actions against the bond that they shared as father and son, but it was simply the way of things. He brushed aside the swelling emptiness that often caught him unaware as his father continued speaking.

"Makiye has already told me how he acted bravely, saving Anuk from almost certain injury. He said that your attention was with the men, as it should have been, but he remained focused on his young companion." Kusug's eyes gleamed with pride as he slapped one hand upon Makiye's shoulder.

Cahil inhaled sharply as Makiye looked at him in silent challenge. He could remain silent or tell his father that Makiye not only lied, but sought to cover over his rash actions which almost brought injury to another. Cahil expected his brother to seek glory over the hunt, but he never anticipated this unlikely turn of events. Makiye's foolish actions placed him in an untenable position. If he denied his brother's words, it would become a matter that their entire village would need to review. The deep, echoing cough that racked his father's frame caused him to lift his head in concern.

"Father?" Cahil immediately placed his hand upon his father's back, but Kusug continued to cough without let up. Makiye's brow furrowed in concern as his father struggled to catch his breath.

"He has been ill, just as I have said." Delak stepped between them and ushered Kusug toward his lodge. Their father leaned heavily upon the young woman as he struggled to catch his breath.

Cahil started to join them, but Makiye placed a bracing hand upon his shoulder. "I can see in your eyes that you thought to tell our father about your concerns."

"I would have told him the truth and let him judge the matter for himself."

Makiye's wide smile was at odds with the anger shimmering in his eyes. "I thought that you were my friend as well as my brother, but I see that I was wrong."

"I am your friend, Makiye, but you will kill an innocent man if you do not change your ways." Cahil did not look away from the glimmer of anger that he saw in his brother's eyes.

Makiye's anger shifted into a triumphant smile. "Have no fear, Cahil. I will be more careful in the future. For now, let us enjoy the celebration that is to take place. We have heaped honor upon our father's name, have we not?"

Makiye walked away with his shoulders thrust back in undisguised pride as their people deferred to him. He left Cahil staring after him, wondering how often his brother manipulated others with such apparent ease. Concern for their father overrode everything else as with a last glance, he turned his back upon his brother.

CHAPTER TWO

The scent of dried herbs was heavy within Kusug's lodge. Cahil did not expect to find his father resting upon his sleeping furs in the middle of the day, despite the racking cough that rattled his lungs. His father was a strong man capable of defeating any foe.

"Father?" Cahil edged forward as Kusug turned shadowed eyes toward him.

"You are my son." Kusug looked at Cahil strangely as he spoke with possessive force and then closed his eyes. Cahil watched as sleep claimed his father and he turned his attention to Delak.

"How long has he had this cough?" Cahil spoke in low tones as Delak watched him.

"He was sick from the day that you left our village on the hunt and it has only worsened since that time."

Cahil was thankful that Delak took it upon herself to care for his father, even though there were other women in the village that might have done so. He smiled as he looked at the young woman that would become his lifemate. Her eyes flashed as she watched him. Her gaze was bold, as it often was when they were surrounded by others or at times when he was unable to act on the longing that she sought to stir within him. He was uncomfortable with her attempts to draw his attention at a time when his sole focus should be upon his father's wellbeing. She demurely lowered her eyes and he told himself that he was being unreasonable simply because of his earlier discussion with Makiye.

"Thank you for watching over him, Delak."

"You are welcome, Cahil." Delak's voice was breathless as her breasts rose and fell. She arched her back as she stretched prettily and moved to stand.

Cahil clasped her small hand in his and felt the startling lack of calluses that spoke of her high standing within their village as nothing else could. The other women worked to skin and soften animal hides, scraping away blood and flesh with a sharp stone, while Delak took care of their children. The other women sat by the fire at night to sew and stitch clothing, while Delak saw to the preparation of her family's meal. Delak's father was a close companion of Kusug and as such, he was deeply respected within their village. Her parents had once been friends with his mother, long ago, before sickness took her from them. He could barely remember the woman with the sad eyes that pressed kisses over his face when he was a young boy.

Delak slid her lithe form provocatively against him as she edged toward the entrance of the lodge. "You know where to find me if I am needed. My mother prepared a healing brew for your father and it will quiet his cough and make him sleep for a time."

"I will remain with him." Cahil enjoyed the warm press of Delak's body and he called himself a fool for ignoring her earlier advances. He wanted to inspire passion in the woman that he took as his wife and Delak's eyes spoke of hidden passion that was as yet untouched.

"One day, you will make a great leader of our people and I will be at your side, ready to offer my support." Delak's fervent vow was spoken in a low murmur, so as not to wake Kusug. Cahil narrowed his eyes as he considered her furtive demeanor, but the innocence in her gaze belied any harmful intent. With a deep breath, Cahil took a step away from her, putting distance between them.

"My father will lead our people far into the future Delak, have no fear." As they exited the lodge, Cahil leaned close to whisper in her ear. "Meet me after the ceremony tonight, by the boulders that mark our village. I have longed for the sweetness of your touch and the warmth of your embrace."

A flicker of alarm passed over Delak's upturned face and Cahil drew back in concern. "Delak, I wish only to hold you close during the moonrise, is that too much to ask?"

"No, of course not, Cahil. I am concerned that my parents will notice my absence, that is all. I will find a way to meet you tonight in our secret place."

An unaccustomed feeling of shame cooled his irritation and Cahil immediately retracted his request that they meet in secret. He bent to touch her lips in a brief kiss that she fervently returned. A movement from inside the lodge drew his attention and Cahil reluctantly broke away from her as she cast one coy glance over a softly rounded shoulder before hurrying away.

"Cahil, you must escort me to the feasting ceremony. I can hear the beat of the drums and I know that our people will wait on my arrival." Kusug donned a warm fur parka, stitched with painstaking care and made from sealskin.

He wore dark brown buckskin leggings and warm foot coverings edged in gray fur as well as the traditional headdress worn by the leaders of their village since time beyond memory. The headdress was crafted by the hunters of their village and as such, it was endowed with honor signified by feathers of various colors, which adorned the stitched band while an array of beadwork rimmed the headpiece.

In full raiment, Kusug appeared to be a strong leader of a growing village, but in truth, he was far more ill than Cahil expected. He was alarmed to learn that his father coughed up blood, combined with dark green mucus that caused his chest to rattle.

His father once told him that he carried a similar chest sickness in his youth, but each cold season that approached brought the sickness back to him with a heavier burden. There was a sense of finality in Kusug's voice that caused Cahil to lift his head in concern.

"You are strong, Father. Long have you led our village with a firm hand and you will continue to do so far into the future."

"Cahil, you speak as if you can will strength into my lungs. You should listen and hear what it is that I have to say."

"I am listening." Cahil struggled with the need to tell his father that Makiye not only lied to him, but also risked the lives of others in pursuit of honor and glory. He set thoughts of the hunt aside as he gave his full attention to his father.

"I have decided to choose a leader to walk in my place and I will announce my decision tonight after the feasting ceremony." Kusug's eyes were full of shadows as he looked at his eldest son.

Cahil always proved to be trustworthy and deserving of respect. He could ask nothing more of the young man that sat proudly before him.

It pained him greatly that he would not live long enough to continue to guide his village, but old age and the weathered shell of his body spoke to him as nothing else could. The time left was reduced, this he knew well.

Cahil started to speak, but Kusug held up a staying hand.

"Go and find your brother, there is something that I must say to both of you. He should be here, next to me where he belongs." Kusug began to prepare for the ceremony ahead and he dismissed his eldest son with a flick of his wrist.

Cahil was accustomed to the way that his father shifted from doting parent to village leader and he did not take offense when Kusug dismissed him as easily as one would an errant child, though he was a man in his thirtieth season. The implications of his father's request lingered with him as he caught sight of Makiye, surrounded by several men and women.

"Makiye, our father would like to see both of us, before the ceremony this evening." Cahil thought that his brother would have sought their father's lodge earlier in the day. Like him, Makiye witnessed their father's coughing fit and subsequent departure, yet he sat with his friends, surrounded by women that were eager for his attention and young men that wished to share in the glory of the hunt.

"I will be there shortly, but first I have to finish telling the others about the hunt. They will not let me go with you now." Makiye laughed when a young woman sat upon his lap and whispered in his ear. "This one says that she will not let me go, ever."

"Makiye!" Cahil's voice held a warning, but if his brother heard the irritation in his tone, he chose to ignore it. "Our father is ill."

"He is not ill, he is simply old. Old ones have aching bones and rattling coughs, this is nothing new." Makiye laughed over his response as the others joined him.

A muscle tightened in Cahil's jaw as he lunged forward and lifted Makiye to his feet. The woman shrieked as she slid off his lap and Makiye rounded upon him with a sneer. "You have overstepped your place."

Cahil heard the derision in Makiye's voice, but he could not find justification for it. With a deep breath, he struggled to remain calm. "Makiye, I am concerned about our father, his chest fairly rattles the lodge each time that he coughs."

Makiye glanced longingly back toward the fire as Cahil gestured for him to come along. "He coughs up blood, Makiye."

This brought his brother's head around and Makiye stared at him for a long time before speaking. "Then he truly is ill."

Before Cahil could respond, Makiye stalked forward with angry steps. Laughter from the fire faded into the background as Cahil returned to his father's lodge, trailing after his brother with shoulders that were heavy with concern.

Kusug was not unaware that his time upon the great land was coming to a close. He could sense the end of his life, though at times he held death at bay by the strength of will that served him well as a young man. Yet he was no longer a young man and he regretted some of the decisions that he made in the days of his youth when he was filled with vigor and vitality.

Long kept secrets caused him great pain, adding a drawn and withered appearance to his features. He should have listened to his wife, Anatti, when she pled with him to reconsider the decision that changed the course of their lives. Long ago, he simply wanted to move forward and put the past behind them.

He was currently faced with a decision that would shape the future of the Ula'tuk village, a village built with the strength of his hands. His every decision threatened to bring calamity or a renewal of life and hope to the people of his shared blood.

His sons were his legacy and they would live on long after he breathed his last breath.

"Ah, but to return to the days of my youth." Kusug looked up as one of his oldest companions came forward. Atsuq had been with him when his life spiraled out of control and he advised him to end the feud that threatened to steal his sanity. "I should have listened to you long ago."

Atsuq smiled as he stroked one hand over his shoulder length white hair. "We are old men now, my friend. You cannot continue to live with regrets resting in your heart."

Kusug's smile was grim as he met Atsuq's intuitive gaze. They were friends as well as brothers of the hunt. "I not only hold regrets in my heart, but secrets, perhaps that is the reason why my bones grow weak and my breath remains short. I can barely find the strength to draw air into my lungs."

Atsuq's eyes flashed with understanding, but he could not offer Kusug the one thing that he needed. Forgiveness for the mistakes of the past.

"Long ago, what happened to you was a grievous thing."

"Yet, what I did in return, was that not also a grievous thing?" Kusug knew that his friend would not lie to him, not now when they were old and gray, wise enough to know that they would have made different decisions in the past if they had been able to peer into the distant future.

"What can I do?" Kusug asked as he lowered his head. "Simply tell me and I will listen to your wise counsel."

The silence grew between the two men as they remembered their youth. They each carried regrets, but Kusug was burdened with his past actions, which were driven by grief, but wrong nonetheless.

"You must set things right." Atsuq finally spoke. "Do this and you can live the rest of your life with a measure of peace."

Atsuq left Kusug to stare at the distant mountains that towered over the foothills and tundra. Kusug remained standing in one place as he wrestled with the past and struggled to inhale the fragrant scent of the great land.

Cahil and Makiye knelt before their father in the lengthening silence of his lodge. Kusug set a bundle of sage to burn over the low fire and the scent permeated the air. The strengthening brew given to their father by Delak's mother seemed to have helped him regain his strength.

"You know that I have battled sickness each time that the cold season approaches and yet this time, I can feel in my bones that I might not survive."

"Father, no." Cahil did not care to hear his father speak of his death. It seemed impossible that he was discussing the end of his life with such apparent ease.

"I will do everything that I can to prolong my life, but I will not rest easy until my son sits as the leader of this village." Kusug's eyes drifted over Cahil and Makiye. Heaviness filled his heart as he considered his next words carefully. "My rightful son."

"What do you mean?" Makiye's eyes lit with interest, whereas before, his face held an appropriately solemn expression.

"You are my son, the son of my blood and your brother, he is the son of my heart." Kusug watched Makiye for a moment and then turned his attention to Cahil. "I am your father in all the ways that matter, but you are not of our shared blood and as such, you will never be allowed to lead our village."

"Father?" Cahil struggled to make sense of his father's words.

"What of our mother? I can barely remember her, but if Cahil is her son by birth then his blood is the same as any other man in our village." Makiye struggled to come to terms with the truth in his father's eyes.

With a grievous sigh, Kusug addressed Makiye's question. "Your mother suffered through a difficult birth before you were born. That child, a son, lived until he was four seasons of age. He was named as my firstborn son and he later died at the hands of my enemy. Cahil came to our hearth shortly after our firstborn son was killed. Your mother gave birth to you thereafter."

Cahil felt as if the world shifted and collapsed around him. "My mother was not my mother and you are not my true father."

"I am your true father!" Kusug shouted as his chest heaved and he coughed roughly, covering his mouth with a softened piece of hide that was flecked with blood.

"I am sorry that you lost your first son." Cahil took a deep breath as he met his father's eyes. "You raised me to be a man that leads other men. You raised me to lead our village and yet, now you have said that I will never be accepted as the village leader. Why did you fail to tell me who I was as a child?"

Kusug was silent for a moment as his eyes filled with regret and he set his mouth in a hard line. When he next spoke, his voice was firm.

"I choose Makiye, the son of my blood to lead this village. I will make the announcement tonight at the feasting ceremony. Your brother will become a strong leader and he will walk the same path that I have walked. You would do well to offer him your support."

"Who am I?" Cahil's dark eyes were wide open with shock as a coughing fit racked Kusug's frame and for the first time he saw the differences in their features. His father's hands were smaller and his lean arms were shorter. His eyes and nose were different as well, although they were a close match to Makiye's features, but not his. He could not remember any other parents, but if his father's words were true, then he would have been about four seasons of age when he was brought to Kusug and Anatti to sit at their hearth. Old enough to remember the past, yet as he struggled to do so, he found nothing but a dark void.

"Who am I, truly?" Cahil asked again as his father turned watery eyes upon him.

"You are Cahil, the son of Kusug, the brother of Makiye." Kusug recovered his breath and spoke boldly with eyes that told Cahil to accept his words.

"I am Makiye, the true son of Kusug and I am the next leader of this village." Makiye's eyes glittered with excitement as he considered his good fortune. He always walked in his older brother's shadow and while Cahil never harmed him, he coveted his brother's position as the eldest son.

Cahil ignored Makiye's pronouncement as he stared at Kusug. "If I am truly your son, then why would you choose a man that is unfit to lead our people as the next leader of this village?"

Kusug looked into Cahil's eyes and saw that he was deeply hurt, betrayed on a visceral level that would not easily heal. Regret touched his heart, but he knew that he made the only decision that their village would accept. "You did not speak ill of your brother until this day."

"I held my tongue for your sake. I would have spoken of the matter long before now if you would have told me that Makiye would stand in your place one day. Do not choose me, if I am truly not of your shared blood, but whatever you decide, you must choose anyone other than Makiye." Cahil's voice was firm and he saw by the rigid set of his father's spine and the glitter of anger in Makiye's eyes that he had been duly heard.

"I have made my choice known." Kusug's voice was cold as he spoke in dismissal. He would not allow Cahil to question his decision. He was finished with the matter.

"I will not remain here to see our people decimated by Makiye's poor decision making and quest for glory."

"Then go, if that is your wish!" Kusug looked as if he would call the words back, but Cahil reared back as if struck and before Kusug could speak, Cahil inclined his head and abruptly left the lodge.

"Father, I am honored by your decision and you will not live to regret it." Makiye did not pity Cahil. He was glad that his father set the matter right. "Give me your blessing and I will lead our village just as you have said."

Kusug ran his tongue over his teeth as he considered his son's words. Makiye was correct, Kusug knew that he would not live to see the outcome if he was wrong and Makiye failed their people.

His failure to inform Cahil of his origins was the reason that his eldest son reacted in anger and confusion. The fault was his and he refused to believe that Cahil truly saw something vital lacking in his brother.

"Makiye, you have my blessing as I live and breathe. You will be the next leader of the Ula'tuk village." Kusug did not see the glimmering excitement in Makiye's eyes as the young man dutifully bowed his head.

He watched his youngest son leave the lodge with a proud cast to his shoulders and he was reminded of himself as a young man. By sacred ceremony Makiye would become the leader of their village before the night ended. He would see that it was just as he said and nothing would change his mind.

CHAPTER THREE

Wild fury grabbed hold of Cahil as he left the village behind and walked toward the swift flowing river that carried icy water down from the mountains. Although his mind raced with anger and sadness, he took the time to don his warm weather parka and leggings, along with foot coverings that were well made and edged in fur. Wearing suitable clothing in the cold weather was second nature to him and he thought nothing of it, other than the need to escape his surroundings.

A soft voice carried to him on the chill wind and Cahil glanced over his shoulder with a growl of warning lodged in his throat. He was surprised to see Delak standing along the pathway to their village and he saw at once that her eyes were wide and uncertain.

"Cahil?"

"Yes, it is me, Delak." Cahil stepped closer so that she could see him in the fading darkness, but she remained still and uncertain. "Is anything wrong?"

Delak glanced toward the village and then met his gaze. "Nothing is wrong. I followed you out of the village. I hoped to find you alone."

Cahil closed his eyes for a moment as Delak's words settled over him, calming the raging fire in his soul. He should have known that she would watch for him and even come after him if he left his father's lodge.

Delak expected him to offer a gift to her father's lodge before the evening ceremony. However, with the unwelcome tidings shared by his father, he could not concentrate on anything else.

The tradition of their village was to accept a new leader only after the death of the last, but his father's declining health changed everything. He felt obligated to warn Delak of what was to come.

"My father has chosen to name a new leader of our village at the ceremony tonight." Cahil almost choked on the words, but he forced himself to speak, despite his confusion and disbelief.

Delak came closer as her eyes lit with excitement. Her hopeful expression was enough to make him reconsider warning her, but the need to confide in someone else forced him to speak. "He will choose Makiye as the leader of our village."

"Makiye?" Delak laughed softly as if Cahil sought to tease her. "What foolishness is this that you speak?"

"It is not foolishness. I speak the truth."

"Why would your father do such a thing?" Delak's expression was incredulous and a part of him was glad that she was shocked on his behalf. He needed her comforting words and he craved the gentleness of her touch to soothe the raging storm inside of him.

"He has told me that I am the son of his hearth, but not the son of his shared blood." Cahil clenched his fists in renewed anger as he spoke the hated words.

"If you are not his son, then why did my parents agree to our future union?" Delak's expression of alarm should have come as no surprise to Cahil, but her statement confused him.

"Why would they disagree?" It was true that Cahil would not take the respected position of leadership, but he was a strong warrior, a skilled hunter and an able-bodied man that held Delak in high esteem.

Delak laughed bitterly and the unkind edge to her laughter caused him to look at her with new eyes.

"I am untouched by any man and my father holds a position of status within our village. He is Kusug's trusted companion. Surely, if my father knew that you were not Kusug's blood son, he would not have approved of our plans for the future."

"What plans for the future?" Cahil's question was cruel, but Delak's scathing words cut him to the quick.

"I would have become your wife."

"Would have?" Cahil's eyes narrowed as Delak took a step back.

His stormy expression must have frightened her because she flinched when he reached out to her. He looked into her face and saw that her eyes were filled with tears that threatened to spill onto her cheeks at any moment. He must have been wrong to believe that she would sway in her desire to become his mate.

He clutched her shoulders as he spoke. "Delak, you must know that I would never harm you."

When she settled into his arms in a familiar manner, he was soothed.

"You must understand that this is very confusing for me." Delak spoke through muffled sobs as Cahil tried to comfort her. Yet, a distant part of him realized that his spirit was reduced to ash and cinder while Delak spoke of her confusion and frustration.

Cahil laughed roughly and Delak jerked away from him. His very soul bled and she spoke of her own troubles, her own pain.

"Cahil, you must plead with your father to reconsider his decision."

"Never." Cahil's answer was abrupt and final. Kusug's decision was firm.

"But what of our future together?" Tears trailed down Delak's cheeks as she waited for him to agree with her, just as he relaxed his stance in the past when she used tears as a weapon against him.

"Nothing has changed between us, Delak." Cahil could no longer deny the need to break free and wander the distant land around him. The looming rock mass and mountainous peaks offered more comfort than he would find within Delak's arms.

As if sensing his withdrawal, Delak's voice turned bitter and waspish. "You will seek out the high places and the mountains that hold your attention and you will leave me to suffer the consequences of your foolish need to wander."

Delak looked as if she would call back the angry accusation as soon it formed, but Cahil took a step away and she lifted her chin in defiance.

"Delak," Cahil sighed as he looked back and pressed a brief kiss against her lips, watching her expression all the while. He saw that her eyes were wide open and she did not bother to return the intimate gesture. With a sigh of regret, he stepped away from her.

"Return to the village and set the matter straight with your father. Tell him that you will do anything if he will simply choose you as the leader of our village." Delak's gaze was pleading and anger caused her voice to tremble.

"My father has made his choice." Cahil waited for Delak to accept the truth, but she merely shook her head in denial. "Wait for me and I will return for you."

She would have responded, but Cahil did not give her a chance to speak. Instead, he took off at a lope toward the distant mountains.

She did not watch as he faded into the distance.

The darkening shadows around her lengthened as she set her chin at a defiant angle and walked with measured steps and swaying hips toward their village.

"Anuk, why have you followed me?" Cahil circled around the youth to find him sleeping in a tree. Anuk almost fell when Cahil's loud voice suddenly interrupted his slumber.

"Cahil!" Anuk righted himself and slid to the ground with the uncoordinated movements of the very young.

"You followed me and I asked for an answer." Cahil's jaw ticked as Anuk gulped and stared at him with wide eyes.

"Yesterday, after the feasting ceremony your father announced to the entire village that Makiye would become our leader." Anuk swallowed and his throat moved uncomfortably as he took a few shuffling steps forward. "I wanted to let you know what occurred so that you could set things right."

"I already know that Kusug chose Makiye to lead our village." Cahil appreciated the youth's efforts to warn him of his father's decision. It was not a small thing to trail a man in the cold and dark as he wandered into the mountains.

"You already know?" Anuk's maturing voice shifted a few octaves as he ran a hand through his hair. The youth's short, straight black hair always stood on end, despite his attempts to tame it, giving him an expression of suspended surprise.

"You can return to our village now that you have delivered your message." Cahil glanced around as he considered returning to the village simply to ensure Anuk's safe arrival. He dismissed the idea when the mere thought of seeing his father caused his fingers to clench in anger.

"But what about you, Cahil?" Anuk ran to keep up when he saw that Cahil dismissed him. "I see that you have set your footsteps along the path to the land that is forbidden. Have you no fear of the spirits that dwell there?"

Cahil stopped and turned dark eyes upon Anuk. "A man only fears that which he can see, touch and feel. I do not fear the spirit world."

"Just so." Anuk gulped again and then ran his fingers through his hair. His efforts did nothing to arrange the short black strands which stood out at all angles. Anuk held up his spear and pointed toward the tree. "I brought your spear and an extra waterskin."

Cahil grimaced as Anuk returned to the tree and retrieved the weapon and empty waterskin before handing them over. "I planned to return soon. Anuk, you should go back to the village before you are missed."

"There is no one to miss me."

Anuk's quick reply elicited a familiar pang of sympathy from Cahil. Anuk's mother died shortly after childbirth and he was a fatherless boy that lived on the mercy of their village. He was too clumsy and accident prone to be accepted by the families in their village, so he stayed in the hunters' lodge from the day that he made his first kill until now. At thirteen seasons he wore the appearance of an overgrown cub, with arms and legs that were too long for his thin frame. It occurred to Cahil that Anuk was not viewed as a boy, but a man of their village.

"You fear the spirit world and yet, I seek it out. Go back to our village while you still can." Cahil's threat was harmless, but the youth's face lost all color before he turned his head away. Anuk was deeply afraid of the workings of the spirit world. At times, his fear of the unknown was a thing of amusement to Cahil, but he used it now to pressure Anuk to leave him alone. "I cannot be responsible for you. There are times when a man needs to be left alone."

Cahil told himself that he wanted to be alone in the great expanse set out before him. He was plagued by questions that he could not answer. He wondered who his father was and if he still lived. He wanted to know about his mother and whether or not she mourned deeply or gone on with her life as if the loss of a son was insignificant. The thought of brothers and sisters that were not aware of his existence crossed his mind and suddenly it was too much to contemplate. The mountains loomed ahead and the land fell away in eddying waves wherever his eyes drifted.

"You should return to our village." Loneliness weighed heavily upon his shoulders and his voice did not hold enough force to ring true. He was almost glad to see that Anuk ignored him.

Cahil took one step forward and Anuk kept step with him. In this way, they continued walking together as the land changed from rugged terrain to glistening rock and stone.

CHAPTER FOUR

"Cahil, we are close to the high places that are forbidden to us." Anuk finally spoke after remaining silent during their long walk. The sun rose over the mountains, lighting the land around them in glorious splendor.

Cahil continued to put one foot in front of the other as if he could leave the painful memories behind with every step that he took over the rocky foothills that led to the mountains. At the sound of Anuk's voice, his stride lengthened so that the youth was forced to run at his side.

Down below, he could see a creek which ran like a narrow ribbon over large boulders and rock. To his left he saw the mountainous region that was forbidden to them and he admitted to himself that he was deeply intrigued.

Since the time of his youth, the people of the Ula'tuk village were forbidden from exploring the high places that were said to be sacred. Kusug had never given them a valid reason not to seek out the high places and the yearning that Cahil felt deep inside begged to be answered. He questioned everything that he was once told and everything that he knew to be true hung in the balance.

"You should turn back now." Cahil warned.

"Tell me that you do not intend to travel to the forbidden high places and I will remain with you." Anuk peered over at Cahil and what he saw must have frightened him greatly. "Cahil?"

Instead of answering, Cahil used the blunt end of his spear as a walking stick as he turned to survey the land in question. Each mountainous peak was dusted with a light covering of snow and Cahil breathed deeply, inhaling the clean, crisp air that renewed his spirit. A column of white rose into the air and he turned his attention toward the unwelcome sign that people dwelled nearby. From his vantage point, he saw dark specs moving in the distance and his thoughts were confirmed.

He did not need the distraction of others while he sought to explore the forbidden high places. Sound echoed in the mountains and just as he turned to issue a warning to Anuk, the young man lifted a hand and pointed to the smoke. "Aiee!"

"Quiet!"

Cahil responded immediately, but it was too late, Anuk's shout of excitement echoed into the distance.

If there were other men about or hunters searching for game, they would know that there were newcomers in the area. Duly chastised, Anuk shook his head in silent apology, but Cahil ignored the gesture. It was too late for regret, whether for good or bad, their presence was made known to those that dwelled below.

Lily's heart beat with excitement as she watched the two newcomers walk forward. Her uncle and the other men were wary, as they should be, but other than the size and form of the larger male, the strangers did not act in a threatening manner.

"We bid you welcome."

Lily stood silently by as her uncle, Simoi, greeted both men, though his eyes drifted back to the larger male. The youth at the man's side, stared at them with a curious expression upon his face, but if violence or danger came from anyone, she expected it to come from the man that responded to Simoi's greeting with a mere inclination of his head.

Cahil took in his surroundings with a critical eye. There were two young women standing behind three men of various ages. The women wore fringed buckskin dresses that fell below the knees and their feet were covered with moccasins that were well stitched and warm. The men were adorned in warm weather parkas similar to the one that he wore, though he noticed that they went without leggings.

"I simply wish to pass through this place. I mean no harm." Cahil saw the relief that flickered in the man's eyes as he kept his

34

spear carefully pointed toward the ground. "We would have brought a gift to honor you if we knew that you lived here."

Simoi was impressed with the man's direct gaze and easy manner. While they spoke the same language, the stranger's use of their words was elongated and flowing. Simoi glanced over his shoulder at his niece and he saw that Lily watched the proceedings with avid curiosity, while her friend, Saghani, kept her eyes lowered.

"You are welcome to partake of our meal. We have only just returned from fishing and we have enough halibut to share." It was a large boast for Simoi and he knew that his companions, Gisik and Nimiuq would not be pleased by his offer.

Cahil began to decline as Anuk's stomach rumbled loudly and all eyes centered upon the youth. His face turned an alarming shade of red as he smiled in embarrassment, showing crooked teeth that only added to his youthful charm. "Ah, a strong son with hollow legs, this is the way of young men, is it not?"

"It is, although Anuk is not my son." Cahil was eager to be on his way, but he grudgingly agreed to join Simoi's band for a meal.

"My niece is named Lily and she will see to our meal while you will sit and tell us of your travels. Yes?" Simoi gestured to the low burning fire as he introduced Gisik and Nimiuq. "As you can see, we are a small band, but the mountain has been good to us and we withstood the warm season without calamity."

Cahil knew that for a small band, to survive the bitter cold and lack of hunting was a great success. "Then you have been richly blessed."

Gisik said very little, but his eyes were ever watchful and Cahil was careful not to offend the large man. Nimiuq was small of stature and much older than the other two men. His face was weathered by time and age and his expressive eyes were wise.

Cahil sent Anuk a stern glare when the young man opened his mouth to speak. He did not want Anuk to share the details of their travels and Anuk settled upon a blanket near the fire as they accepted wooden platters of food from the women.

In most bands and villages it was considered disrespectful to stare at a woman, but Cahil found himself gazing into a pair of remarkable brown eyes as the young woman extended a steaming platter to him. Lily's black hair swept over her shoulders with each graceful movement and the sweet scent of her sun warmed skin caused his nostrils to flare. Anuk gulped loudly as the women modestly offered food to them and Cahil forced himself to turn away, but the warmth that he found dancing Lily's eyes did not dissipate.

"Cahil, Nimiuq has heard of your name before from a band near the seeking star."

"The seeking star?" Anuk asked as Cahil returned his attention to the conversation at hand.

"Yes. Even now, we make ready to join the ceremonial procession that must take place if we are to survive another cold season. We will journey to the encampment of the Krahnan band where we will hunt and celebrate the renewal of life."

"You do not dwell within these mountains?"

"Only for a short time this season. Although, we have remained here during the worst of the cold season in the past. Look and see, this small passage is protected on four sides by the towering peaks capped with snow. During the cold season, our band is safe, though hunting is scarce. We seek to follow the old ways by returning to the Krahnan band before the cold season begins." Simoi watched as Cahil took in the protected valley and saw for himself that their skin lodges could easily be erected and dismantled. "Is it the same way in your band?"

"My people remain in one place season over season." Cahil thought of his village and he did not know that shadows filled his eyes as he met Simoi's gaze.

"Tell me, what has brought you to travel away from your people, with only a youth as your companion?"

Cahil glanced at Anuk, but the young man was busy devouring the tasty meal. He chewed without swallowing and barely avoided choking as he shoved food into his mouth with his fingertips.

"I did not intend to travel so far, but the mountains call to me."

Cahil never intended to reveal so much about himself, but there was something about Simoi's calm manner that invited openness.

"This is the way that the land called to me long ago. We came here when my niece was a mere child." Simoi replied.

"Just so." Gisik nodded.

A woman's voice intruded into the conversation and all eyes turned her way. "Will you stay with us to hunt for a time or will you return to your village?"

"Saghani!" Nimiuq warned in a sharp voice, but the young woman's eyes merely sparkled with interest. Her grandfather spoke quietly to her and with a meek expression of apology she turned away.

Cahil looked at her companion and he saw that Lily smiled shyly, even as quiet amusement over her friend's forward nature caused her eyes to dance with hidden laughter.

"We cannot stay." Anuk volunteered when the men returned their attention to them.

Before Cahil could remind Anuk to keep silent, the youth spoke through a mouth that was still full. "Cahil seeks the high places that are forbidden to us."

CHAPTER FIVE

"You cannot go near the high places. They are protected by the spirit world." Simoi's gaze widened as he looked at Cahil with new eyes. The man carried the strength of a warrior and the muscular build of a hunter, but if he sought the high places then he was not of sound mind.

"No one goes there." Nimiuq shook his head in dismay as Cahil stared into the distance.

"Why not?" The question came from Cahil and it was directed at Nimiuq.

"I traveled there once, in the hopes of following a herd of bison that went where man should not tread. Hunger drove me to ignore the warnings given to us by those that have lived upon this land since time beyond memory. I cannot say for a certainty that you will walk away with your life. I can only remember hearing the screaming of the wind from the moment that I laid eyes upon the high places until I stumbled away."

"He was gone for three days." Saghani ignored her grandfather's glare as she once again spoke without invitation. The worry in her voice caused her grandfather to overlook the unwelcome intrusion.

"Time passed in mere moments, but many days elapsed before I was able to regain my senses and return to our band."

"We feared for his life." Simoi remembered that dark time and since that day, he and Gisik chose to hunt while Nimiuq remained nearby to protect Lily and Saghani.

Lily watched Cahil shift his shoulders and she thought that it was like watching the mountains stand up and sit down again. She caught sight of the torment in his eyes and wondered what caused it. She found his appearance pleasing as she noticed the dark eyebrows that sat like raven's wings above his eyes, which were long and fringed with black lashes. An aquiline nose gave way to a mouth that hinted at fullness. His face was a study of rugged plains and angles, while a muscle clenched in his jaw and his hands slid into fists at his sides. Her eyes widened as she saw that he watched her over the fire.

"Uncle, allow me to give you and our guests something warm to drink." Lily offered an earthenware vessel to Simoi who accepted it gratefully.

"My niece is ever thoughtful." Simoi drank deeply and passed the vessel to Anuk. The young man sniffed the contents of the vessel and took a cautious sip. His eyes widened and then he drank deeply before sheepishly handing the almost empty gourd to Cahil.

It was impolite to refuse an offering and Cahil would not have done so since the young woman went to such lengths to prepare a meal for strangers. He inhaled sharply before testing the warm liquid on his tongue. He could not identify all of the ingredients, but he recognized the last berries of the warm season. He swallowed appreciatively as the images of warm sun and rain washed over him.

"It is good." Simoi announced as he thanked the women for their efforts.

Cahil handed the empty vessel back to Lily and in the fading light their fingers touched. Her eyes widened slightly as she accepted the gourd. Cahil's attention was drawn back to Simoi and Nimiuq, but he could not forget the moment of awareness that went unnoticed by the others. The young woman was lovely and it was only natural that she might draw his interest, but he remained loyal to Delak in his thoughts and actions. A heavy weight settled deep in his chest as he considered the reasons that he walked away from his village in the dark of night.

By now, his brother was the leader of their village. Everything in his life was forever changed and nothing would ever be the same again.

"It is foolish to travel where others have warned you not to go." Nimiuq spoke in protest as Anuk followed at their heels. They walked at the base of the valley, shortening the distance between their position and the high places.

Cahil nodded in understanding but he continued onward, lengthening his stride so that Nimiuq was forced to gather his breath before speaking. The older man was used to the towering heights, but Cahil and Anuk struggled for each breath.

"Very soon we will hear the screaming of souls and you will know that you have erred." Nimiuq's voice trembled in warning and Cahil could not determine if it was the chill of the morning air or fear that caused the elderly man's voice to quake.

Cahil would have preferred to explore the high places by himself, in silence, but Simoi granted him permission to go only if he took Nimiuq with him.

"It is for your own safety. Only Nimiuq has returned from the high places with his life, you would do well to heed his advice." Simoi declined Cahil's offer to help with the hunt that they planned. "We have hunted on our own before now and we will continue to do so after you leave."

There was no censure in Simoi's words, but Cahil still felt as if he let the other man down. The concern in Lily's gaze almost weakened his resolve. He did not know why the young woman affected him so strongly, but he kept his distance from her even though she called to him like a new sunrise. It did not sit well with him that he and Anuk accepted the hospitality of Simoi's band, but offered nothing in return. He decided to find a way to repay their kindness.

Nimiuq grumbled under his breath as he led the way. "Watch your step, Anuk. If you stumble and break a leg you will be helpless to run for your life when the time comes."

Anuk glanced fearfully at Cahil and he almost missed a step that would have caused him to slide down the rock strewn embankment that they climbed.

"Nimiuq, with respect, I ask that you refrain from trying to frighten the boy."

"I thought he was a man of your band, well prepared for all that you have put in front of him."

"By right of the first hunt, I am a man." Anuk reminded Cahil as he lifted his chin.

"You are right, Anuk. I will refer to you as a young man from now on. It is simply that I think of you as my younger brother." Cahil saw Anuk puff out his chest in response to his words and he was surprised to discover that he almost wanted to smile.

He could well remember how it was to be a callow youth with dreams of manhood shining in his eyes. Ordinarily, he would have given Anuk the appropriate amount of respect, but he spoke without thinking. He did not believe that the high places held any danger. For him, the path that they walked was like a long forgotten memory and each step toward his goal filled his soul with a keen sense of wonder.

"It is said that a band of people that have long since left these mountains behind once dwelled here."

"Truly?" Cahil wanted Nimiuq to continue, but as if sensing that he held the upper hand, the contrary man kept silent.

"Are their restless spirits here?" Anuk glanced around with fear evident upon his face, but one glance at Cahil caused him to stiffen his spine.

"Restless spirits?" Nimiuq tilted his head at an angle as they reached a plateau and the wind suddenly picked up strength. A slight whistling sound strengthened until the wind began to screech as it swept past. "As I said, the screaming of lost souls will greet us."

Cahil felt a chill shiver over his backbone as Nimiuq turned unfocused eyes upon him. "We can turn back before it is too late."

"Yes, let us return to the safety of the fire and join Simoi and Gisik in the hunt that they have planned." Anuk offered hopefully.

"Turn back if you please, but I must continue." Cahil knew without a doubt that he needed to see what was around the next overhang. His heartbeat sped up within his chest as he clenched his spear and walked forward. Anuk's terrified groan rang in his ears as Nimiuq muttered an incantation that begged the spirit world for their safekeeping though they trespassed on sacred ground.

CHAPTER SIX

Lily sat with her legs folded as she worked the deerskin with skilled hands. Her uncle and Gisik were successful with their early morning hunt and they would have venison to see them through the end of the warm season. Saghani, named for the black bird that flew over the land, raised her hand to shade her eyes as she looked into the distance.

"You will not find them returning so soon, Saghani." Lily said as she gestured toward the deerskin. "Help me with the task at hand and the time will pass by quickly."

Saghani gracefully fell to her knees as she turned inquisitive eyes toward her friend. "How is it that you do not worry over the stranger and the young man with him? I have every reason to worry about my grandfather."

"I care about Nimiuq as if he was also my grandfather. This you know well." Lily did not give in to her friend's prying gaze. Her feelings about Cahil were new and she did not wish to share her thoughts with anyone. However, she and Saghani had been friends since they were young girls, they were as close as sisters and she should have expected her friend to pry.

"I sat at the same fire as you last night and I saw the way that you watched the one called Cahil. He is a strong hunter, I can tell by the cast of his shoulders." Saghani peeked at Lily from under the fall of her lashes and Lily gave in to laughter.

"You seek to know my innermost thoughts."

"Yes, I do. So you must tell me quickly, before the men return." Saghani's reasoning was faultless and Lily shook her head in amusement.

"I do not know Cahil or his reasons for visiting our band." Lily thought of the turmoil in Cahil's stormy eyes. She ached for him even though he never intended to incite her interest. "It is likely that he has a wife and little ones waiting on his return."

"Do you think that Anuk is his son?"

"If so, then Cahil's face does not tell his true age, besides he said that the young man was not his son." Lily shook her head at the notion. "What man would not claim a strong son?"

"Very true." Saghani did not truly believe that Cahil was Anuk's father, but she sought to keep Lily talking.

"You are struggling to find something to say that will keep my attention fixed upon Cahil."

Saghani's eyes widened expressively before she ducked her head in renewed mirth. "I like the way that you say his name."

"Whose name?" Simoi approached on silent feet as both women glanced up with expressions of surprise on their faces.

"We were speaking of Cahil." Saghani lowered her eyes as Simoi knelt beside them to examine the deerskin.

"This will make a fitting garment for one of you, if you are able to finish it quickly." Lily and Saghani smiled appreciatively as they returned to their work with no more words said between them.

For his part, Simoi noticed the interest in his niece's eyes as she glanced toward the high places that were forbidden to all. Cahil and Anuk were fine young men and in his estimation they chased after the wrong things altogether.

Yet, he was a man that did not interfere in the dealings of others. It was not his place to tell Cahil the right and wrong of his decision to visit the high places. He could only hope that Nimiuq did not meet with any harm.

Cahil glanced back at Nimiuq and Anuk. They refused to go any farther and he could not convince them to do otherwise. He could see the forbidden high places, covered in rich, vibrant green grass, surrounded by scattered rocks. The pattern of rocks appeared haphazard and tossed about by hands far greater than those of man.

"Wait here," Cahil turned to Anuk and Nimiuq. "I will not be long."

Nimiuq's tone was grim, but he appeared relieved to remain where he was and Anuk wore a similarly mollified expression. "Do not disturb anything and perhaps you should offer a prayer of forgiveness for intruding in a place where you are not welcome."

Cahil considered Nimiuq's words, but when he reached into the place where his spirit dwelled, he did not feel a need to beg forgiveness. Instead, he felt the land spread before him in welcome. He walked around a large boulder as the wind whipped his long hair around his face and the necklace that he always wore around his neck slipped free. The leather thong held an image carved from ivory and though Cahil did not know the meaning of the image or the origin of the necklace, he wore it always.

He decided to leave his spear with Anuk. It seemed wrong somehow to walk upon the high places with his weapon in his hand. He could not say why this was so, but he trusted his instincts which never failed him.

To his surprise, the high places held mounds of grass, rock and soil that were of various sizes, but they were all formed in similar shapes. As he walked amongst the mounds he realized that the formations were not natural, but crafted by the hands of man. Cahil inhaled sharply as he realized that he was surrounded by a burial ground.

It was not the way of his people to bury their dead deep underground. The ground was often frozen solid and did not unthaw until the warm season and even then, it was difficult to dig deep down into the soil.

The people of his village buried their dead under piles of large stones on the surface of the land. But here it was evident that the mounds were ritualistic burial places, well constructed and protected on all sides by the natural rock formations.

He wondered about the people covered reverently by their loved ones. He did not have to see their weapons and the many cherished items that were buried with them to know that their precious belongings rested against drying bones. He could feel the presence of the proud people that lived and died under the shadow of the moon and he knew without clear understanding that he was somehow connected to them.

Once again, his hand drifted to the familiar necklace, a treasured token from his childhood that always gave him strength. He touched the three interlocking oval spheres and ran his fingers along the ridged markings.

A memory of a woman's smile and soft, gentle hands came to mind as he closed his eyes and the screeching wind ceased. Confusing thoughts drifted behind his eyes as he remembered the sound of a man's angry voice and a woman's terrifying screams. The wind howled with renewed vigor and he opened his eyes as he looked once more at the sacred mounds.

Without knowing the reason why he did so, he set his palms against a nearby rock wall and lifted himself up until he found a handhold. He climbed higher and higher until he could look down at the sacred mounds and his breath caught in his throat as he saw that the rocks were not scattered about without reason. They formed an unmistakable pattern that was both familiar and disturbing. With one hand he lifted the pendant at his neck and compared it to the rocks below.

"It is the same." Cahil's breath shuddered in his lungs as he tried to comprehend the enormity of his discovery.

"What is that in your hand?" Nimiuq's eyes narrowed in suspicion as he caught sight of Cahil walking toward them with a necklace clasped in his hand. Cahil did not speak until he was close enough to be heard clearly and as Nimiuq and Anuk looked closely at him, they were surprised to see that he wore a stunned expression upon his face.

"This is a necklace that I have worn since I was a child." Cahil stared at Nimiuq as the man suddenly began to tremble in fear.

"You took something from the sacred burial mounds!" Nimiuq shouted in accusation as he looked wildly around.

"No. I took nothing from the burial mounds. This is the same necklace that I have always worn." Cahil held up his necklace so that Nimiuq could see the image clearly, but the older man cringed in fear and fell back.

"Let the spirits protect me!" Nimiuq was fearful beyond reason as the screaming wind took up a high keening pitch which caused him to tremble and shake. "Only the men that once belonged to a sacred bloodline have worn that image upon their chests. If you are an angry spirit sent to trick me then tell me now. I beg you!"

Nimiuq fell to his knees as Anuk gaped at them and Cahil reached out to the trembling man.

"Nimiuq." Cahil touched Nimiuq's shoulder, but he jerked away, moving much faster than Cahil anticipated.

Cahil glanced at Anuk, but he could see that the young man was deeply fearful. As always, any mention of the spirit world caused Anuk to freeze with fear and Nimiuq's behavior only made matters worse. The youth often visibly shuddered when one of the men mistakenly mentioned their ancestors by name. Cahil observed the old ways and he did not speak the names of the dead, but Anuk harbored a deep fear of the spirit world that often caused others to heap ridicule upon him. Cahil noticed that the older man stared fearfully at his necklace as his lips moved without sound.

"Nimiuq," Anuk intervened, swallowing audibly as he tried to aid the older man. "The necklace belongs to Cahil. He has worn it since I was a child and I can promise you that he is a man of flesh and blood."

"If you speak with deceit upon your tongue, you have placed yourself in danger." Nimiuq declared as he raised his hands against Cahil, as if to ward off evil. "If you have cursed our band, I will seek you out and place my hunter's knife between your ribs."

Cahil was taken aback by Nimiuq's bold threat. "I have not cursed your band. You were right, the high places are much more than they appear to be from a distance. They hold sacred mounds, the burial grounds of a band that once dwelled here."

"Of course they do!" Nimiuq looked about wildly as if bracing for an attack. "No one should walk upon such a sacred place. The spirit of a great band of people dwells here upon the high places. You insisted on seeing the high places for yourself, but that does not explain how you came into possession of the necklace that you claim is yours."

"It is mine." Cahil wondered if Nimiuq was aware of the image which marked the sacred mounds. He held the three interlocked spheres up for Nimiuq's inspection. "What do you know about this image?"

"I know that it is worn only by those who have the right of leadership over an ancient band of great strength and might, those that belong to a sacred bloodline. Long ago, they buried their dead here, but they no longer reside in this place." Nimiuq glanced fearfully over his shoulder as the shrieking wind died down.

Cahil felt overwhelming sorrow for the band of people that once dwelled upon the mountain and he was deeply saddened to learn that they no longer lived. "Nimiuq, the necklace is mine."

"If the necklace is truly yours, then these were once your people and you belong to them. Until this day, we thought that the sacred bloodline was no more, yet you exist."

Anuk trembled in place as Cahil threw a narrow glance his way. "Be calm, Anuk."

"He should not be calm!" Nimiuq replied. "We walked on sacred ground. He should run down the mountain screaming for his life. That is what I would do, if I was not an old man with weak legs that tremble in fear. I would run for my life!" Nimiuq's eyes grew wide as Anuk glanced fearfully over his shoulder.

"Nothing stands behind you, Anuk."

"Nothing that you can see." Nimiuq inserted as he silently mouthed to Anuk that he should run while he could still escape.

Anuk's teeth chattered as he looked between the two men.

Cahil was at the end of his patience. He could not make sense of Nimiuq's mutterings, but he wanted to know more about the people that once lived upon the mountain. Instead of receiving answers, he was left with unanswered questions that plagued his every thought.

CHAPTER SEVEN

Lily saw three figures approach from the direction of the sacred mounds as the sun bled over their sheltered valley and she breathed a sigh of relief. Her fingers trembled as she quickly placed long strips of venison upon rocks heated at the edge of the fire. She did not announce the return of the men to her uncle, simply because she knew that he was already aware of their presence.

Simoi stood as the men approached and he clapped Nimiuq on the shoulder in greeting, but the older man waved him away. Anuk's eyes were wide, but he readily accepted a waterskin and the offering of warm food.

As Lily met Cahil's eyes, warmth flooded through her body and she almost turned away. Cahil reached for the food that she offered and she was plagued by a feeling of loss when he avoided making contact with her hands.

"Thank you."

Lily accepted his thanks even as she noticed that there was something different about his eyes. They were alight with a spark that wasn't there at the outset of his journey.

Cahil watched as the wind lifted a tendril of Lily's long hair, where it drifted about her shoulders like a dark cloud before settling into place.

"You have returned whole." Simoi spoke to Cahil over the low burning fire. "This is good."

"We heard the screaming of souls, just as Nimiuq warned." Anuk responded as he licked his fingers clean.

"Just so." Nimiuq came to rest beside Anuk and grunted in appreciation as he saw that Lily cooked thin slices of venison rolled with wild greens which were slowly roasted over the fire. "Cahil carries the image of the sacred mounds upon the pendant that he wears around his neck."

"Grandfather, truly?" Saghani's eyes widened as Nimiuq nodded gravely.

"I wear a necklace that I have worn since childhood. It holds the same image as the one set in stone around the sacred mounds." Cahil clarified. "The people that are buried at the sacred mounds are my people."

Shocked silence greeted him as the others digested his words. Cahil shifted uncomfortably as he struggled to comprehend his lost past.

"Did you offend the spirits with your presence?" Simoi was concerned. He recognized that Cahil appeared to know nothing of the spirit world or the ways of such things, whereas Simoi was a deeply spiritual man and he did not wish to offend the heavens.

"We did not." Cahil felt welcomed and at ease upon the high places, though filled with sorrow that he never knew the brave men and women that were buried nearby.

"You do not know if that is the case." Nimiuq complained as he looked to Simoi with an angry glare. "You should not have allowed them to travel to the sacred mounds."

"I am not the keeper of that place. You and I both know that it needs no keeper, it is protected in its own right." Simoi understood Nimiuq's concern, but he could not have stopped Cahil except by the use of brute strength.

He recognized that Cahil was not a man to rule over from the moment that he caught sight of him until now. It was their good fortune that Cahil did not intend them any harm. Simoi would have protected his niece and the others, but blood would have been shed and one or more of them would have died, of this he was certain.

"I wish to know more about the people that once lived upon the high places where the sacred mounds now rest." Cahil looked to Nimiuq as he held up his necklace. "If they lived and died together, who buried them? Who placed the stones upon their bodies and left the image upon the ground?"

"We know very little about them." Nimiuq responded sharply.

"I need answers." Cahil's voice was grave and confused. "I need to know more about my lost past."

"I would imagine so." Simoi responded.

"Tomorrow, I will return to my village, but you should expect my return. I must bring a gift to you in appreciation for the kindness that you have shown us." Cahil addressed Simoi in turn, before nodding to Gisik and Nimiuq.

"You owe us nothing." Simoi responded, speaking over the muttering of Nimiuq.

"Even so, it will be just as I have said."

"We appreciate your kindness." Lily replied when Simoi merely nodded.

"Do you have a wife and children waiting for you in your village?" Saghani appeared at Lily's side as she gave voice to the impertinent question.

Cahil glanced up sharply as he broke contact with Lily's wide gaze and noticed that Saghani looked at him much like a hungry bear eyeing newly spawned salmon. "Not yet."

His answer invited no further inquiry and Saghani simply murmured under her breath as Lily took her place beside Simoi.

"We will leave this place shortly to meet those that take up the old ways by sacred ceremony. The warm season has come to an end and we must leave this place and travel for many days to reach the ceremonial hunting grounds known to our band. You are welcome to join us. If you are related to the people that once dwelled in these mountains you will find more of their kind at the end of our journey. You carry the necklace worn by those who once led their band. Perhaps you might even find the answers to your questions at the encampment of the Krahnan band if their village elders still live."

Cahil was taken aback by Simoi's gracious offer and he was intrigued to learn that relatives of those that perished might still exist. Simoi did not know him fully and yet, he offered him a place within his band, even if only for a time.

"Their elders still live," Nimiuq inserted. "I would know in my spirit if my friends no longer walked the great land."

Anuk gulped audibly and for a moment, all eyes turned toward him before returning to Cahil.

"I must return to the Ula'tuk village. I have much that I left unfinished and my discovery here has only left me with more questions than answers. I must speak to my father in the hopes of obtaining the truth of my past."

"My offer remains the same." Simoi responded.

"My bones ache from the cold wind or perhaps an angry spirit has taken to lashing me all over because we disturbed the sacred mounds. Who can say?" Nimiuq raised his voice in complaint as Saghani ushered him toward his lodge. She draped a warm cape over his narrow shoulders as he growled and muttered loud enough for the others to hear.

After a time, Simoi and Gisik sought the comfort of their skin lodges as Cahil remained near the fire. Anuk was already asleep and Cahil was instantly alert as he heard the sound of light footsteps.

He was surprised when Lily returned with two warm sleeping furs. She handed one to him without a word spoken between them. He was captivated by her slight form and the quiet strength that resided in her eyes.

The urge to keep Lily with him, if only for a moment caused him to speak. "It was kind of your uncle to invite us to travel with your band."

Cahil searched for something to say to the intriguing young woman. He saw at a glance that she knew nothing of the enticing postures and coy glances that he was used to with Delak. Her gaze was direct and her eyes were wide with innocence.

"You seek answers, but you will not share the reason that you hold questions in your heart." Lily was surprised by her own boldness, but Cahil's very presence spoke to her.

"I am the son of the leader of my village, yet I lead no one." Cahil would have called the words back if he could. He expected Lily to tell him to fight for the position of leadership, but she simply sat across from him and allowed silence to rest between them. "My father led me to believe that I would one day stand as the leader of our village, but he chose my brother to stand in his place."

"Then let him lead. I am angry with your father on your behalf. It was wrong to mislead you, but your brother has found his place, now you must find your place." Lily sensed that Cahil struggled within himself and she hoped that she could ease some of the turmoil that dwelled within him. "My mother once told me that to find true happiness in life we must be strong like a reed, willing to bend when life blows in various directions."

"Is it that simple?" Cahil was stunned that Lily would summon anger on his behalf, though she urged him to move forward.

"We must all find our place and we must learn to bend so that we do not break." Lily's natural radiance called to him and though he told himself that he was not tempted, the desire to keep her nearby overrode common sense.

"Lily," Cahil sounded out her name on his tongue. "What does your name mean?"

Her voice was breathless when she answered. "It is the name of a vibrant flower found in the land of my birth."

Cahil thought that her name was fitting. She was a vibrant creature, fragile and feminine, yet he sensed a core of strength inside of her. "You were not born here in the mountains that edge the great land?"

"No. My uncle brought me with him on a long journey over the mountains when I was a young child."

"What happened to your first band?" Cahil asked as Lily hesitated and glanced back at her uncle's lodge.

"They went the way of many bands, since time beyond memory. Sickness plagued our people and my parents entrusted my care to Simoi. He has been kind to me and now he is the only father that I can remember."

"But you were taken from your parents."

"It was their wish." Lily responded and her voice held acceptance and understanding. "Many died and I remember them even now. My parents knew that my uncle would watch over me and knowing this, they left me in his care."

"You will travel with your uncle to the ceremonial hunting grounds that he mentioned earlier?"

"We will go together. It is a good time to ask for a blessing or seek guidance. Our band is small, but we have survived the cold season once more and if we keep the old ways, we will do so again." Lily bit her bottom lip as she considered asking Cahil what he discovered when he went to the sacred mounds. "We follow the seeking star."

Cahil was intrigued by both the tone of Lily's voice and the glimpse of the unknown. "What is the seeking star?"

Lily lifted her face to the dark sky and searched the heavens until she found the bright luminary that hung overhead. "It is there, by the shadow of the moon, do you see it."

"I see it." Cahil's eyes drifted toward the bright luminary hanging in the sky and then back to Lily's upturned face. Her features were limned in the glow of the fading fire and her voice was whisper soft, filled with awe. He was startled to realize that her very presence comforted him more than the mountains surrounding them.

"Are you certain that you do not wish to go with us?"

Cahil was surprised at the sense of yearning that filled him when he thought of traveling with Simoi and his band to reach fertile hunting grounds outside of the reach of his village. However, honor was sounded down into his heart and he could not turn away from his responsibilities. His future with Delak weighed heavily upon him, even now and he was certain that she was anxiously awaiting his return. Even though he did not understand all that occurred in the past, he owed it to Kusug to be there for him when he was ill.

"I admit that I am intrigued by your uncle's offer, but I will return to my village. My father is ill and I must see to his welfare. Perhaps he will be able to give me the answers that I seek."

"I wish good health to your father. You are a strong son and he will find comfort in your presence." Lily recognized coiled power hidden within Cahil's striking gaze. "I must return to my uncle's lodge, but know that I wish you well."

Cahil remained awake long into the night as the stars drifted overhead and the fire died down to glowing red coals.

The sun rested below the mountain peaks when Cahil and Anuk took their leave. They accepted a small portion of food and fresh water from Saghani and Lily.

Anuk's throat moved as Saghani stepped forward and wrapped her arms around him in a warm embrace. "You are like the younger brother that I have never had the chance to torment."

"Thank you." Anuk's eyes were wide as Nimiuq spoke of his granddaughter's impulsive nature.

Gisik stepped forward and cleared his throat. Cahil waited for the large man to speak and when instead he simply nodded toward the waiting mountain pass, he coughed to cover his amusement.

"Cahil, we will not be here when you return." Simoi said. "Even now, Gisik and Nimiuq have begun to break down their lodges. We will travel a far distance to reach the ceremonial grounds that we seek."

Simoi was certain that Cahil would return with a gift if he did not warn him of their departure. He did not need a long acquaintance with the man to know that he honored his promises.

"Safe travels." Nimiuq urged them on their way as he kept a watchful eye on Saghani.

Lily's heart beat rapidly as Cahil glanced her way, but he made no move to speak to her and she told herself that she was foolish to hope for anything more. She would treasure the memory of sitting by the fire with him and she would never forget their time together, however brief. Only she knew that her dreams were full of the handsome young warrior that befriended her band and stole a piece of her heart.

Cahil glanced back at Simoi's band and thought to himself that they were exceedingly vulnerable in comparison to the strength of his village. Three men and two women against the wide expanse of land around them. Yet, Simoi also possessed a rare type of freedom that he envied.

Anuk drew his attention and Cahil slowed his steps so that he could catch up.

"That woman wrapped her arms around me." Anuk's voice squeaked on the last word as Cahil hid his amusement.

"It was a gesture of farewell."

If Cahil would have glanced over his shoulder, he might have noticed that while the others turned away, Lily continued to watch until they faded from view.

CHAPTER EIGHT

The need to return to his village wore upon Cahil until he hurried his footsteps and Anuk panted at his side. The young man did not complain as they traveled as fast as their legs could carry them. They did not stop to rest and when at last they reached the boundaries of their village, Cahil breathed a sigh of relief.

At first glance, everything appeared to be exactly as it should be. The lodges of his people were well kept and neatly arranged. The village central fire was unlit, but it was late evening and not uncommon that their people should seek their rest. As Cahil walked to his father's lodge the scent of ash caused his nostrils to flare and he stood still and unmoving.

Ash was spread in a circle around several of the lodges and he knew that it could mean only one thing. Someone in their village recently died. Grief caused his throat to ache as he thought of his brother, Makiye.

"Father?" Cahil called out as he scratched at the entrance to his father's lodge and then entered only to find the familiar dwelling empty.

Cahil exited the lodge as he called out to the others of his village. They were slow to emerge from their dwellings and he saw that their faces were drawn with grief.

"What has happened?" Cahil spoke to those that approached him with outstretched hands.

A voice from behind, sent relief surging through his body.

"Cahil, you have returned."

"Makiye." Cahil spun to face his brother and what he saw shocked him. Makiye's face was gaunt and his eyes were dark pools of sorrow.

Makiye reached out to his brother as the villagers surrounded them. "Cahil, my father has died."

"No." Cahil stumbled and he would have fallen if not for the hands that braced him.

"It is true, Cahil." Makiye wore their father's feathered cape and he displayed the garment to his brother as Cahil stumbled backward.

"Father was ill, but he did not die." Cahil shook his head in disbelief.

"The coughing sickness stole his breath during the night. Delak was with him when he breathed his last breath." Makiye was relentless as he drew closer.

"You wear our father's cape." Cahil could not digest his brother's words.

"He gave it to me, prior to his death. He wanted everyone in the village to see me as their new leader. He must have known that death was near."

"No." Cahil remembered looking into his father's eyes and even though Kusug told him that they were not of shared blood, he was the only father that he could remember. "Father should not have died. He should have survived the chest sickness, just as he always has."

"He should have, but he did not." Makiye's eyes widened with sorrow and Cahil could not determine if his brother's grief was real or feigned. "I am now the leader of our people and as such, you must swear loyalty to me."

"Take me to our father's body!" Grief tore the words from Cahil's lips.

Makiye swept his hand over the gathered crowd as he urged everyone to return to their dwellings before turning back to Cahil. "We both know that he was not your father."

"He was my father just as he was yours." Cahil trembled with anger and disbelief. He closed his eyes as the world around him shifted and he found it difficult to breath.

"Of course he was the only father that you remember, but you and I both know that he was not your blood father. You and I are not brothers, in truth." Makiye was relentless in his desire to make things clear to Cahil.

"Take me to see his body!" Cahil resisted the urge to strike his brother. He knew the heady sense of power that Makiye coveted had already filled his senses to the brim.

"This way." Makiye led the way past the hunters' lodge where Anuk watched them from the shadows. Cahil was numb with grief as he realized that his father, the strong man that led them season over season, was no longer alive.

Makiye pointed to a fresh burial mound, covered completely by rock and stone. Cahil fell to his knees as he took in the evidence of his father's death. Grief swept over him in eddying waves and he could not catch his breath, nor did he try.

"Your grief is still fresh and new. When you have finished here, you must come and greet my new wife." Makiye left as Cahil knelt before their father's burial mound.

Anuk saw the calculating gleam that lit Makiye's face and he also saw the way that Cahil swayed with grief and sorrow. He was confused by Kusug's death, just as Cahil must be, but he could not understand why Makiye chose to marry so quickly. A few of the villagers walked by though they kept their distance as Cahil lifted his voice in grief over the death of his father.

"Where is my brother's lodge?" Cahil could barely speak as grief nearly choked him and his throat was raw from the death song that he sang for his father.

Anger caused his shoulders to tremble. Because of his father, he was lost without any understanding of the past. He no longer knew who he truly was and a part of him wanted to hate Kusug, but his death prevented him from experiencing true hatred. Grief outweighed the anger, giving way to a series of shudders that wracked his lean frame. The sense of loss that he felt was overwhelming. Not only had he lost Kusug, but he also lost any hope of finding the answers that he sought.

Anuk stared at him for a moment, before pointing toward the center of the village.

"How is it that my brother showed no interest in any of the women from our village and now he has taken a wife for himself?"

"I do not know." Anuk answered as his brow knit in confusion.

"Makiye." Cahil's voice was raspy as he scratched at the entrance to his brother's dwelling. He quickly entered and stared at the sight that greeted him.

Makiye was naked upon his sleeping furs and a woman lay underneath him with her legs wrapped around his waist. In the darkness of the lodge he could not see her face, but his brother pulled her to a sitting position as he turned to face him.

"Cahil." Makiye's eyes glittered menacingly as Cahil caught sight of the woman in his arms.

Delak.

A low growl built in his throat as Cahil charged at his brother. Delak screamed and wrapped the sleeping fur around her shoulders, hiding her nakedness.

Rage blinded Cahil as he grabbed hold of Makiye and threw him through the lodge wall, shattering the night with a primal roar.

Makiye landed under Cahil as he struggled to defend himself. Cahil roared and lifted Makiye to his feet. The urge to kill his brother snaked through his belly as he plowed his closed fist into Makiye's stomach.

"Cahil, she is his wife!" Anuk shouted as Cahil stormed toward his brother's coughing form.

The two powerful men grappled for a handhold as they twisted and rolled on the ground, wrestling violently.

"Cahil, stop!" Delak added her voice to Anuk's, but Cahil and Makiye were beyond hearing.

"She is mine to do with as I choose." Makiye ground the words between his teeth as he broke free of his brother's hold.

Cahil's eyes were wild as he glared at Makiye, daring him to raise a weapon against him.

"You have dishonored a woman of this village, for the last time!" In the past, Cahil never approved of the way that Makiye treated the village women. He offered false promises so that the young women would set aside their honor and share their bodies with him. Delak fell under his protection from the moment that he expressed an interest in her. Concern for Delak's wellbeing caused him to glance her way and what he saw shocked him.

Delak moved between them, but she did not go to him. Instead, she turned to Makiye and used the fringe of the blanket wrapped around her naked body to wipe the blood from his mouth.

"Delak?" Cahil struggled to catch his breath as Delak finally turned to face him. "What have you done?"

"It is a great honor to become the wife of the Ula'tuk village leader." Makiye turned anger brightened eyes toward him as he grinned in triumph. "Delak gave her willing consent and she is my wife."

"Never!" Cahil knew that his brother could act with treachery when he chose, but he would not believe that Delak went to him willingly.

"It is true, Cahil." Delak glanced toward the crowd of people that watched them with interest. "My parents wanted me to join with the next leader of our village and I have honored their wishes."

"Delak, no!" Cahil remembered their earlier conversation and her feelings for him appeared to be genuine, but she ducked her head and shifted closer to his brother as if seeking protection. Protection from Cahil.

"It is done." Delak turned her face away and Makiye placed his arm possessively over her shoulders.

"I should have known that you would react badly to losing her to me." Makiye tested his lower lip with his tongue and then stepped forward as he sneered at Cahil. "If you ever attack me again, I will see you dead."

"Cahil." Anuk rushed forward as Cahil lowered his hand to his waist. "You must come with me. You are welcome in the hunters' lodge and you must rest."

"Yes, take him with you." Makiye laughed as he pressed Delak closer and placed his face against the curve her breasts. "I wish to enjoy my wife and already our peace has been disrupted."

"Do not allow him to taunt you, Cahil." Anuk's voice held deep concern as Makiye lifted Delak into his arms and her laughter reached their ears.

CHAPTER NINE

Cahil could not rest. His eyes remained open as the other men in the lodge found comfort in slumber. Anuk fell asleep as soon as he assured himself that Cahil would not murder his brother.

The morning sun was barely up as Cahil stalked from the hunters' lodge with determination shining in his eyes. He was thankful that Anuk stopped him from raising his hunting knife against his brother, but he could not rest until he knew that Delak chose Makiye of her own free will.

He knew where the women went to gather water each morning and he was waiting when Delak walked down the path to the small trickling stream. His footsteps were silent as he stepped forward and caught hold of her arm.

"Delak." Cahil held Delak's shoulders as she flinched in surprise.

"Cahil, you should not be here." Delak glanced over her shoulder, but there was no fear in her expression when she turned to face him.

"Tell me now, if he has forced you." Cahil looked deeply into her eyes as he brushed a long strand of hair away from her upturned face. "I can accept my father's decision to make Makiye the leader of our village. Though I know that Makiye is not a leader of men, it is not my place to say that my father chose the wrong man to lead our village, but I cannot believe that you would willingly give yourself to my brother. This I cannot accept."

Delak sighed heavily as she set her empty basket down. "Cahil, you saw me with your brother. You must have seen enough to know that he did not force me."

The memory of Delak's firm legs wrapped around Makiye's waist was seared into his mind forever. It occurred to him that she never allowed him to touch her intimately, but she welcomed his brother into the heat of her body at the first opportunity. The pain caused by her betrayal burned him to the core.

"You and I were to become husband and wife. Why did you choose to betray me?"

"I never loved you." Delak's eyes narrowed with anger as Cahil pressed her for answers. "My parents demanded that I join with a man that would improve our standing within this village. Who better than the son of our leader? But you were not his true son, were you?"

Cahil felt as if she cut him to the soul. "I would have protected you, all the days of your life, I would have put you first."

"You betrayed me. You did not fight for the position of leadership even when I begged you to do so. You refused to stand before your father and beg him to reconsider his decision."

For the first time in his life, Cahil wanted to strike a woman. He took several steps away from Delak as he noticed the bitter turn of her lips and the haughty gleam in her eyes. She lifted her gaze to meet his and her voice was pitched seductively low when she spoke.

"Cahil, it is not too late. You can choose to fight your brother and the village will stand behind the winner. Kill Makiye and I will take my rightful place as your wife."

"Your rightful place?" Cahil was stunned. "You speak of slaying Makiye, your husband, as if the taking of a life means nothing at all."

"I was forced to choose the man that would offer me all that I deserve." Delak's voice was firm, but her eyes told him that she already regretted her actions.

"You have made your choice and now you regret your decision, but it is too late, Delak. You have shown yourself to be a valueless thing, easily bartered for and fickle of heart."

"You are weak, Cahil." Delak saw that she erred. She could barely stomach Makiye's touch and he did not treat her as kindly as she knew that Cahil would have if she was his wife. The bruising on her thighs was a result of his anger when he learned that his new wife was not untouched. "We once shared something good, if you would simply listen to me—"

"Do not speak!" Cahil's voice was a harsh command and Delak's mouth hung open as she started to speak despite his warning. Rage welled up inside of him, threatening to override his tenuous hold on the last vestiges of his self control. "There is nothing left between us to discuss!"

As she saw the anger in Cahil's eyes, fear lit Delak's gaze and she remained silent.

Cahil faded into the surrounding forest, but he held her in place by the burning heat of his gaze. A few of the village women came along and Delak stared into the shadows before she gathered her carrying basket and followed after them.

Cahil's heart beat like a drum in his chest as he moved through the forest toward a distant clearing. The familiar lodgepole pine trees cloaked his form and the underbrush cushioned the sound of his footsteps as he lengthened his stride and quickly reached the clearing. With a deep sigh, he raised his eyes and caught sight of the nearby mountains. He sought the calm that came to him whenever he turned his eyes toward the familiar heights.

With his hands fisted at his sides, he clenched his teeth together and shouted in agony. The wild cry that rent the air was the sound of a wounded animal. Grief over his father's death, mingled with the shattering betrayal that he suffered at Delak and Makiye's hands threatened to send him to the ground. Cahil bent at the waist as he tried to keep the pain in his chest contained.

Anguish filled his soul.

He never expected Makiye to turn his back upon their bond of brotherhood, no matter that they were not bound by blood ties. He always walked as an older brother to Makiye and he was patient and kind at every turn.

Last night, he blamed his brother for Delak's actions, but in the light of day he could no longer hold Makiye solely responsible.

Delak chose to pursue Makiye from the moment that she learned that he would be chosen as the leader of their village.

"I never loved you."

Her words taunted him, cutting deeper than the edge of a serrated knife. If he remained within the Ula'tuk village, he knew that his blazing anger would one day consume him. If he stayed, he would be forced to see Makiye and Delak together day by day as they passed him in the village.

"I cannot abide it."

His heart was laid upon the ground and it was nothing more than ash and cinder. He remained bowed at the waist, clutching his stomach as the animals of the forest took up their daily tasks.

Whether he wept or shouted in anger, there was no one to hear or see. The wise grey owl and the red ground squirrel were his kindred spirits and if he revealed his pain to them, they would keep his secrets to themselves.

CHAPTER TEN

Light filtered across the sky, bathing the land in a gossamer haze of gray until individual hues began to break free. Cahil approached his village with a heavy heart. He looked at the familiar surroundings with a detached sense of trepidation.

He knelt before his father's burial mound as he tried to find a place deep inside where peace dwelled. With a sigh, he realized that no matter how hard he tried, there was only turmoil and pain. He needed answers and he knew that those answers could not be found within his village. The only one that could have answered his questions was his father and he was gone forever.

"You grieve for a man that did not claim you as his son, not even with his dying breath."

Makiye's face showed signs of their fight, though he did not appear to be severely injured. "Our father claimed me as his firstborn son and this you know well."

"Yet, only a man of the same blood as that which ran in our father's veins is capable of leading this village."

"Then it is a pity that he chose you, instead of a capable man, willing to endure the responsibility of leading so many."

"Endure?" Makiye openly scoffed.

"A true leader must learn to accept the responsibility for the lives that will inevitably be lost."

"You speak of bad tidings and death." Makiye glanced around their village with eyes that gleamed with contentment and satisfaction. "I see a prosperous village filled with strong people who know the land and the dangers that exist season over season."

"They do not know you as I know you, and yet they look to you to lead them."

A flicker of unease passed over Makiye's face, but his earlier bravado quickly returned. "You are welcome to remain in the hunters' lodge with the other men."

Cahil gained his feet in a sudden rush of movement that caused Makiye to draw back. He noticed that his brother carried his spear, even within the safety of their village. Cahil's eyes narrowed as anger burned in his heart.

"I do not need your permission to remain in a place that has always welcomed me."

"This is where you are wrong." Makiye smiled smugly. "If it is my wish, I could order our men to turn their spears against you. You would be driven from our village or killed if I chose to command it."

"Then do as you please, but first tell me, where are the men that you so easily command?" Cahil knew that Makiye sought to anger him, but his brother's callous regard for the life that they formerly knew caused rage to burn within his soul.

"I want you to acknowledge my authority before everyone in our village. There have been rumors that you seek to challenge my position of leadership and I will not rest until you deny such false sayings."

Cahil thought of how his people managed to distance themselves from him ever since the ceremony that named Makiye their leader. Now that they were made aware that he was not their chosen leader, they treated him differently. The women whispered behind their hands and the men did not include him in their plans to hunt game. He was not certain how long he could bear their ostracism.

"Kneel before me now, while all eyes are upon us and I will accept your pledge of loyalty. First, you will cut your hair so that you will look like one of us, even though your origins are unknown." Makiye's eyes glittered in challenge as Cahil watched him. "Keep your eyes upon the ground where they belong!"

Cahil lunged forward suddenly, causing Makiye to rear back. His brother's face flamed with embarrassment as the quiet whispers from the villagers touched his ears. "You carry a spear and yet you fear what I will do to you. Where is your strength, little brother?"

"You are not my brother. You are nothing to me at all."

"If this is the way that you feel, then my choice has been made for me." Over the long night that passed, Cahil considered leaving his village forever and as he looked into his brother's cold eyes, he realized that his future was already decided.

Anuk separated from the crowd, boldly placing his gangly form between the two opposing men. "Cahil, it is good that you have returned. I wanted to speak with you about going on a hunt, but the other men left before daylight. If we hurry we can catch up to them."

"Move aside, Anuk." Makiye's eyes glittered with menace as Anuk's eyes widened fearfully.

"Step back, Anuk." Cahil spoke quietly, but Anuk remained frozen in place and therefore, in danger.

Makiye reared back as he raised his spear against his brother. He was in the act of plunging the weapon forward when Cahil shoved Anuk out of harm's way and ripped the spear from his brother's hands.

"Cahil, no!" Anuk found his voice as Cahil turned the spear upon his brother. He refused to look away as he spoke.

"Go and gather your things from the hunter's lodge, Anuk. Hurry on your way!" He bent close to his brother's ear as Makiye regained his feet. "The next time that you turn your weapon upon me, make the strike count."

Cahil shoved the spear into Makiye's hands as his brother watched him out of eyes that promised dire retribution. "If you leave, then your life is in your hands. I will not come to your aid, nor will you be allowed to return."

"If I stay, then I place my life in the hands of a worthless man that knows nothing about true leadership. Our village has already begun to suffer a slow death, it is a death of the spirit of our people and yet, you are too foolish to see it." With a slashing motion of his hand, Cahil turned his back upon his brother as the people of their village looked on.

By turning his back upon his brother, he openly proclaimed that Makiye's threats were meaningless. Likewise, his brother's threats fell upon deaf ears as Cahil walked away without looking back.

Cahil approached the hunters' lodge where he quickly gathered his things and spoke quietly with Anuk. "You are old enough to make your own decisions. If you choose to stay here, beware of Makiye, for he will not forget that you stood between us today."

"Do I have any other choice?" Anuk's throat bobbed up and down as he looked around fearfully.

"If you choose to follow me, then hurry along. We have a distance to travel before the moon rises and I cannot delay."

"Will we be allowed to leave this village alive?"

Anuk's question was telling, but his actions were even more revealing. He grabbed his sleeping fur and his weapons as well as two empty water skins even as he headed toward the lodge entrance.

"It appears that you are willing to leave with me, regardless of the danger."

"There is nothing for me here, Cahil." Anuk responded.

"Nor is there anything left here for me." Cahil refrained from thinking about Delak. Despite her behavior he found it difficult to harden his heart toward her. Instead, he turned his attention back to Anuk. "Never again stand between two armed men that are ready to battle each other."

Anuk gulped and then one side of his mouth lifted as he said, "You were not armed."

Cahil's voice was stern as he replied. "I cannot make any promises to you, Anuk. Our destination might be worse than what you would have found here under the authority of Makiye."

Anuk glanced back at him and nodded sagely. His face was still rounded with youth and unmarked by time, but he clenched his jaw in determination. "I understand."

"Then stand tall as we leave the Ula'tuk village behind." Cahil brushed past Anuk with his spear in one hand and a hastily constructed carrying pack resting upon his back.

Most of the village gathered outside, but the crowd consisted mainly of women and children, along with a few of the older men. The younger men left at first light to bring back fresh game for their village. He was certain that some of the men considered him a friend as well as a brother of the hunt and it pained him deeply that he would not have the chance to bid farewell to so many of them.

"Cahil, where will you go?" One of the women called out to him as he placed one foot in front of the other.

Anuk almost stumbled into him when he stopped and glanced back at the people of his village. They stood together with a look of uncertainty upon their faces and he felt pity for them. They did not choose Makiye as their leader, but they would live or die based upon his father's choice and his brother's whims.

He lifted his chin and looked toward the distant mountains where he recently found a sense of belonging and serenity unlike anything that he ever experienced before.

"Anyone that wants to go with me is welcome to come along. However, for those that are too fearful to leave the safety of this village, know that I understand and I wish you well."

Sensing the tension in the air one of the youngest children wailed, a bitter litany that struck them all. A few of the women looked away as they gathered their children close. No one dared step forward and follow him and he could not blame them. The great land was both beautiful and dangerous. If he could be certain that Anuk would not be harmed by Makiye, he would have forced the young man to remain within the village.

A man without a band or village was at risk of succumbing to the ways of the land. This he knew well. Yet, Cahil was certain that if he stayed, he would be forced to watch as their village was destroyed from the inside out. His deepest fear was that given enough provocation, he would eventually slay his brother. He could not live with the man that he would become if either disastrous occurrence came to pass and he did not look back as he set a trail leading away from the only home that he could remember.

CHAPTER ELEVEN

Simoi watched his niece out of wise eyes that saw far too much. Lily sat overlooking the foothills with the sky at her back and the land falling away below. "You cannot continue to wait for him."

The surprise on Lily's face failed to hide the sheen of tears in her eyes and the high color in her cheeks as she spun around to face her uncle. She did not bother to deny that she was plagued with many foolish dreams about the tall stranger that came to their band only to leave without a second glance.

Simoi sighed heavily as he settled down next to his niece. "Sometimes we believe that we have found our true mate and life teaches us that it is not so."

"He did not even notice me." Lily took a tremulous breath as she remembered the way that Cahil stirred desire in her heart without even trying. It was not her way to boldly approach a man, nor would she do so if she could relive her time with him.

"Perhaps he thought that I was a mere child." Lily could see with one glance at Saghani's lush figure that she lacked the curves that drew a man's eye.

"All young women blossom at different times. But if a man cannot see past the outer shell to the core of strength and beauty beneath, then he is a man that walks without seeing all the days of his life." Simoi remembered his sister during the days of her youth whenever he looked at Lily. It was true that his niece was slender of form, but she was no less beautiful in his eyes.

Purposely mistaking his meaning, Lily responded in anger before she could give thought to her words. "Even you think that I am only a child."

"You are wrong, Lily. If you think that I see you that way, then you speak of the way that you see yourself." Simoi knew when to push and when to ease away. "You have the look of your mother, my sister appeared fragile and she also looked younger than she was, but as you remember, your mother was a woman of beauty and strength."

Over the past few days, he watched Lily pine after a young man that she might never see again. If he could have done so, he would have taken more time with Cahil before he left, if only to gauge whether or not he was worthy of Lily's young heart.

Despite Lily's desire to find a mate, he did not wish to see his niece leave her place at his hearth before she was ready.

"Uncle." Lily sighed heavily. "I did not mean to speak disrespectfully."

Simoi prolonged the tense moment by stroking his hand over his upper lip. It was a gesture that told the observer that he kept silent so that he would not speak in anger.

Lily's beautiful brown eyes widened in concern and he removed his hand to display a grudging smile, which she quickly returned.

"You would do well to help Saghani gather the items needed to begin our journey."

"Yes, Uncle." Lily scampered away, much like the young girl that she claimed not to be.

Simoi watched her with concern until she returned to the skin lodges that were being dismantled by Nimiuq and Gisik. He protected and watched over Lily since she was a thin young girl with eyes far too large for her small face.

He had been present at her birth and he promised his sister that he would stand as a protective barrier between his niece and the world around them. It was the way of their first band that a woman's brother took the position often delegated to the father in other bands.

In this way, Simoi was the stern disciplinarian and he was also Lily's teacher, offering guidance and direction when needed. He could not find fault with his niece, though as a child she needed a firm hand, as a young woman of seventeen seasons, she was ever obedient and her heart was full of good thoughts toward others.

His decisions thus far kept her safe from harm and content. However, he could not control the yearnings of a youthful heart. He decided that it was time to seek a mate for his niece. He would seek a young man of courage and strength and above all, a man who would hold Lily in high regard, all the days of her life.

Foothills fell away at the base of the mountains, giving way to colors ranging from palest yellow to vibrant green. Life abounded around them, wherever he cast his eyes. The last few days of the warm season were already upon them and yet they were late beginning their journey.

Simoi inhaled the familiar scents of grass and rich soil as he decided that they would leave in the morning to seek out the Krahnan band and those that gathered to observe the hunting ceremonies.

He could not delay the inevitable any longer.

He knew well that the two young women in his care were essentially defenseless without strong men to defend them. The journey would be difficult and the dangers tremendous, but this was simply their way. They would leave at the rising of the sun.

"My grandfather said that Simoi has been behaving strangely ever since we left our encampment yesterday." Saghani moved cautiously over a wet patch of ice and snow. She walked with Lily as Simoi and Nimiuq took the lead with Gisik following close behind.

Lily glanced at her uncle's back even as she considered Saghani's suggestion that Simoi was not himself. Simoi wore a large cape with a fur hood and his feet were encased in warm moccasins. He carried a bone hatchet upon his back while using his walking spear as a staff to aid his footsteps, but there was nothing weak or uncertain about him. Her uncle was a strong man capable of acting as a warrior or hunter depending upon the circumstances that they faced and she didn't see anything odd about his behavior.

"He is most likely worried about the journey ahead, there is much that could go wrong and Simoi carries the weight of that burden."

"This is true, but you must admit that it was strange to see him place a marker at the place where we once raised our lodges."

"I did not think that it was strange." Lily smiled gently as she glanced at her friend. "We will build our lodges in the same place again in the future." Lily surmised that her uncle simply planned ahead, though he never left a marker in the past.

"If you say so, but I think that it is exceedingly strange." Saghani's eyes ventured to Simoi and then she increased her pace when Nimiuq grumbled over their slowness.

"We should focus on collecting green plants that will help season the meat that the men hunt along the way." Lily often grew tired of Saghani's chatter, though she knew that her thoughts were unfair.

The monotony of walking day by day over muddy ground and slush often wore upon her, just as it did Saghani. She should be able to understand that her friend wanted to find something to occupy her mind.

Yet, Lily's heart was torn over the first glimmer of what transpired between a man and woman, something that she sensed when she was in Cahil's presence.

"Do you think that could be what he has planned?" Saghani asked as Lily swung her head around in response.

"What who has planned?" Lily blushed as she realized that her thoughts were so full that she missed most of what was said.

"Do you think that Simoi plans to find a mate for you at the gathering ceremony?"

"A mate for me?" Lily swallowed as she struggled to form a response. "Why would he choose a mate for me now when he has not done so since I became a woman."

"Perhaps because you have not shown any interest in joining with a man until now. Your uncle is stern, but he would not withhold a husband and children from you."

"But if I join with a man outside of our band, I will be forced to remain with him and his family." Lily struggled to imagine a time when she would choose a mate over remaining with her uncle and the others. "You know well that Simoi would prefer the wide open spaces and the quiet of the mountains."

"It is not the need for wide open spaces that keeps Simoi away from others. You do not wish to speak of his bitter enemy, but you and I both know that he will not remain with the other bands because of the one that we will not name."

"Saghani." Lily raised her eyebrows in warning. She did not wish to speak of what transpired between her uncle and Umak, a warrior from a nearby band. The man called himself a leader of men, but was almost the cause of a battle between the men that were loyal to the Krahnan band and those that were loyal to his band, the Mirotuk.

Simoi's anger over Umak's attack upon three women from the Krahnan band sparked a seed of discord between the two bands. Simoi threatened to kill Umak and the other man returned the threat, though both were unable to act simply because it would bring reproach and dishonor upon their names.

Lily knew that her uncle did not make idle threats and she shivered as she thought about the possibility of losing Simoi if he suffered defeat at Umak's hands.

"I will always be grateful to Simoi for saving us from whatever Umak planned." Saghani's voice was serious as she met Lily's gaze.

"As will I and this is something that we must be wary of when we are amongst the Krahnan band again."

Saghani waved her hand as if they could easily dismiss that fateful day. After Umak and his men raped and killed three women, he turned his attention toward two scared little girls that were stunned speechless by the violence that they witnessed. Simoi arrived to find Lily and Saghani huddled together, hiding in the tall grass as Umak advanced toward them.

"Lily, you must know that you will not always remain with your uncle. One day, you will go your way and your uncle will go his way, this is how it must be if you ever want to become a wife and mother."

Saghani lifted her head, sending her long hair cascading over one shoulder. In that moment, she appeared to be a woman fully grown and capable of offering sage advice.

"If you are not ready for a mate, perhaps Simoi can convince my grandfather to search out a husband for me." Saghani's smile widened as Lily glanced her way.

"And what would you look for in a mate?"

"I require a man with broad shoulders and a trim waist. He must not have a fat belly." Saghani made a sour face as Lily laughed. "If he is a good husband, I will feed him fermented seal flipper, but before we become mates, I wish to see him wearing only his loincloth so that I can determine if he will give me big, strong sons."

Lily's face turned scarlet as Saghani laughed in amusement.

"Saghani!" Nimiuq glared at his granddaughter in warning. "You should leave Lily alone. You caused enough trouble with the young men of the various bands the last time that we were there. This time if you are the cause of fighting between the young men, I will see to it that you are given to the man that wins the fight."

"Grandfather!" Saghani gasped as Lily struggled to hide a smile. Nimiuq's eyes twinkled with mirth, but Saghani did not see anything other than his fierce scowl.

"Do not plead with me. I have spoken." Nimiuq gestured with one gnarled hand for the young women to keep pace with him as he turned his back upon his granddaughter.

Lily tried to find sympathy for Saghani, but she found that it was more difficult now than at other times. Nimiuq knew Saghani well and it was obvious that he stepped in before Saghani drew the matter out any further. His interruption also allowed Lily time to gather her thoughts.

"He would not really give me away as a prize would he?"

Lily expected to see outrage in her friend's eyes, but as she turned toward Saghani she saw instead that her face was alight with interest. A groan of dismay threatened to escape as Lily shook her head and ran to catch up with the men, leaving Saghani to gape at her retreating form. A warning from Gisik caused Saghani to shriek and pick up her pace or risk being left behind. Up ahead, Lily's laughter filled the air, tickling the ears of her band.

The mountains loomed ahead, rising above the ground in majestic splendor as Cahil and Anuk walked side by side. The heavy clouds overhead were tinged with dark gray and they seemed close enough to touch as Cahil watched the sky while an uneasy feeling lodged deep inside.

"I didn't know that you planned to return to the sacred mounds." Anuk's voice was pitched low as if he feared that they would be overheard, but he and Cahil walked alone.

Cahil glanced over at the young man and shrugged. "I have no place else to go except to the mountains that have been here far longer than man."

Anuk contemplated this for a moment before responding. "I hope that we see the woman again, the one that wrapped her arms around me."

Cahil's dark mood lifted slightly as he remembered Anuk's reaction to the young woman named Saghani. The girl's effervescent personality probably led to mischief, but her appeal was not lost upon Anuk. For a fleeting moment, he remembered Lily, the young woman that watched him with a direct gaze that caused him to feel deeply unsettled and yet comforted at the same time. Cahil knew that there was a yawning chasm deep inside where his heart should have been and if not for Delak's disloyal actions he would have at least walked away from his village with his pride intact.

"You are thinking about Delak again." Anuk sighed as he glanced at Cahil's dark expression. "I do not know why you bother to pine after a woman that chose your brother over you."

"Anuk." Cahil spoke in warning as Anuk threatened to continue.

"I would not speak of it, except that you tend to glower when you think that I am not watching."

"You are always watching." Cahil frowned at the meddlesome youngster before gathering more wood.

The evenings often carried a brisk wind and they were delayed by a storm that brought rain and flooding. Even now, he could only hope that the wood they carried would be dry enough to burn throughout the night.

"I will no longer pester you if you leave off thinking about Delak. She was a faithless woman."

"You speak of her as if she is dead." Cahil noticed that Anuk shrugged off all thoughts of returning to their village and he was surprised at the ease with which the young man cast his thoughts toward their future.

"She might as well be dead, Cahil. Tell me, would you want her if she came begging for your forgiveness even now."

"No." His answer surprised him, but he realized that it was true.

"Good. I feared that you lost your wits, but I see that you still have hold of common sense." Anuk's quip went unanswered as Cahil set a fast pace toward an icy overhang that would provide adequate shelter. Cahil lengthened his stride, forcing the youth to run until he was breathless.

"What is this place?" Anuk asked as Cahil removed his carrying pack and set the pile of wood aside. "Is it safe?"

Anuk peered into the icy cavern that Cahil entered without fear. Overhead, wet ice dripped from the high ceiling and he saw that ice melded with stone to form a deep cavern. The beauty around them did not escape his notice as he took in their surroundings. The blue sky overhead and the azure colors swirling through the cavern gave testament to the vibrant land that surprised him at every turn.

Cahil tested the thickness of the ice wall and he surmised that the ice would not melt while they slept. He was glad to find a place of shelter so that they could rest and regain their strength. As it was he found nothing to hunt throughout the day and they could not use the wood that he gathered to make a fire. The ice walls around them would cave in if they were not careful.

"We cannot remain on our own, Cahil." Anuk spoke once they were settled upon dry ground with their sleeping furs wrapped around them for warmth.

"I know." Cahil vacillated between making his own way and returning to Simoi's band. He was concerned that they were already too late, but he and Anuk were not thriving on their own.

Tonight, they would go to sleep hungry and it galled him that he could not promise Anuk that they would find food tomorrow, either. He was a skilled hunter and he needed only to find a herd of bison, caribou or even a lone deer. As yet, they were not fortunate in their travels. He was constantly distracted by the yawning void that existed where his heart and soul used to be.

Yet, hunger was a strong motivator and the past few days showed him that he valued his life, even if he was forever changed.

"Tomorrow will bring better things." Cahil offered into the silence of the cavern.

"Yes, like fire." Anuk responded before he turned his back and covered his head with his sleeping fur.

Cahil remained awake long after the sound of Anuk's snores touched his ears. He watched the night sky from the entrance of the cavern and he considered all that awaited him in the future.

Simoi remained silent, he did not have to ask Gisik to make Lily's death swift. Gisik nodded once in painful acceptance and then he turned to Nimiuq and placed one strong hand upon the older man's narrow shoulder. "I can."

Cahil entered the passage that led to Simoi's dwelling and his chest tightened as he scanned the land below and saw no sign of the familiar skin lodges. He refused to allow his disappointment to show as Anuk trailed behind him, eager to reach their destination. He didn't have the heart to tell Anuk that Simoi and his band were gone.

He reached the place where Simoi first greeted him and he saw in his mind's eye a fleeting image of Lily's dark eyes and warm smile.

"They have already left." Anuk's eyes widened as he recognized their surroundings.

"We knew that it was a possibility that they already left. Simoi said that they begin their journey at the end of each warm season and the warm season has reached its end."

"I can tell that the weather has changed for the worst." Anuk shivered as he unrolled his sleeping fur and wrapped it around his thin shoulders.

Cahil awakened before first light and even though it was dangerous, he and Anuk started walking. He knew the way and he felt a strong urge to reach Simoi early enough in the day to help with the hunt or any other preparations for their departure. Disappointment surged through him as he realized that they were too late.

"Look, Cahil!" Anuk pointed to a strange object that protruded from the ground.

Cahil walked closer and saw that a thick piece of wood had been driven into the ground and a thin red string was stretched out and held down by a heavy stone. Beside it was a green plant that had been pulled from the ground by its roots and hung upside down. The plant was not yet dry.

"What does this mean?" Anuk studied the signs left by Simoi's band with a quizzical eye as Cahil did the same.

Cahil closed his eyes and remembered sitting in this very place as Lily pointed to the seeking star that led them on their journey. When he opened his eyes, he saw that the piece of braided sinew pointed in the direction of the seeking star. "They traveled in the direction of the seeking star."

"But why did Simoi leave this plant to dry?"

"Because it would give us an idea of how far ahead of us they are." Cahil marveled over Simoi's forethought. He never gave the man any indication that he would join him on his journey, but somehow Simoi must have sensed the yearning within him, the bold desire to join him, even if the thought was only momentary.

"I can't understand how a plant can tell us how far ahead of us they are."

"*Aupilaktunnguaq.*" Cahil knelt beside the wooden marker as he spoke the name of the familiar plant.

"If you have bubbles in your stomach, then you should not eat so much dried meat." Anuk's eyes glimmered with mirth as Cahil ignored him.

"See here, the roots are dry, but the flower itself has not started to fade." When Cahil repeated the name of the flower, Anuk's blank expression almost caused him to grin.

"I cannot say that word, but you should tell me what this means? Tell me especially that it means we will have a warm belly full of food before the day ends."

"You ate most of the ground squirrel that I caught, Anuk." Cahil shook his head as Anuk's belly growled at the mere mention of food. "They are a few days ahead of us, but we can catch them if they are delayed or if the women keep the men walking at a much slower pace."

"Good, how do we catch up to them?"

"It is simple, Anuk. We run."

Anuk turned to view their surroundings and when he glanced over his shoulder, he saw that Cahil picked up his belongings and ran full out toward the mountain pass.

"Wait for me, Cahil!"

Anuk grabbed his things and ran to catch up to his companion. He knew that Cahil could quickly outdistance him if he chose to do so, but when he shouted again he was relieved to see that Cahil slowed his pace. Much to Anuk's chagrin, as soon as he caught up, Cahil lengthened his stride, setting a pace that would shorten the distance between them and Simoi's band.

CHAPTER THIRTEEN

Simoi and the other men hurried across a flat barren landscape with sparse brown grass, sedges and small shrubs that slowed their progress. The land was flat for as far as the eye could see, spreading out in all directions before blending into the distant horizon.

"Send the women ahead." Simoi gave the order to Nimiuq as the older man huffed in a deep breath and returned his gaze with a heavy sigh.

Nimiuq struggled to catch up to Lily and Saghani. The young women walked at a measured pace and concern for them urged him on and he considered his creaking knees and labored breathing as something belonging to another man. He could well remember the days of his youth when he ran across the great land with limbs that were full of strength.

They traveled for two days with the men that trailed them biding their time. The tension amongst the men of their band rose until their tempers were short and their features drawn. Simoi decided not to tell his niece about the danger that dogged their heels and Nimiuq agreed to withhold the information from his granddaughter. Yet, the men that followed them finally decided to show themselves and Simoi knew that a confrontation was at hand.

"Saghani, Lily, you must continue on without us for a time." Nimiuq urged the young women to hand over their carrying baskets as he placed one water skin in their hands. They carried their sleeping furs and enough dried meat to last another day.

"Grandfather?" Saghani turned frightened eyes toward Lily.

"Nimiuq, why do you send us ahead of the others, we will keep up with you, do not fear." Lily wanted only to reassure her friend and she thought perhaps Nimiuq was angry or troubled.

"You will do as I say and run ahead of us until we catch up." Nimiuq's weathered features tightened briefly before he gave Lily a fleeting nod of encouragement. "Look after Saghani, she does not know how to watch for melting ice and yellow snow."

The last, was an effort at levity but Lily could not force a smile, not when Nimiuq gazed at his granddaughter as if he might never see her again. Tears filled Saghani's eyes, leaving wet trails on her cheeks as she clung to Lily's hand.

"Grandfather, you must come with us." Saghani openly sobbed as Lily struggled to keep hold of her hand and pull her forward.

Something in Nimiuq's gaze told her that they should not delay, but she searched the distance for any sign of Simoi and Gisik.

"Simoi wants you and Saghani to take the lead, but I must tell you that you should find what strength your youth affords and make haste."

"What is wrong, Nimiuq?" Lily's wide eyes were fearful, but she could not give in to tears. She needed a clear head to confront whatever danger faced their band.

"We have been followed for several days." Nimiuq glanced over his shoulder as he urged both young women forward.

"Are we being followed by another band?" Saghani wiped her face as she turned toward her grandfather. "Perhaps they journey to meet with the other bands for the gathering ceremony, just as we do."

"Perhaps." Nimiuq's watery gaze wavered for a moment as he looked into his granddaughter's face. "But it is more likely that we are being followed by men that have been cast out of their band."

"What could they possibly want from us?" Lily asked as she braced Nimiuq under one arm when his steps faltered.

Nimiuq used his spear as a staff, relieving Lily of the burden caused by his weight. "No more questions! You will both do just as I say. I want you to run as fast as you can toward the meeting place of the various bands. Lily, do you remember the way?"

"Yes." Lily's voice trembled as she clutched Saghani's hand.

"Then go!" Nimiuq made shooing motions with his hands. "We will catch up to you."

He watched as Lily and Saghani clung to one another for a moment before turning away. He stared at his granddaughter as he struggled to memorize the plains of her face.

"Hurry!"

Nimiuq knew that Simoi would have liked to see Lily before falling behind in a deliberate attempt to shield both young women from the men that pressed hard on their heels. He should be thankful that he was given a chance to see Saghani before returning to Simoi and Gisik.

Mustering up strength from the depths of his soul, Nimiuq forced himself to hurry back toward Simoi and Gisik. Already, he could be too late to aid his friends.

"They take power in darkness." Simoi observed as Gisik grunted in agreement.

Simoi watched the men that stalked them for days as they boldly walked forward. He took in every detail of their appearance at a glance as he noticed that their clothing was nothing more than the rancid skins of previous kills, wrapped and folded over their shoulders for warmth. Their foot coverings were well fitted, but likely stolen or taken from amongst the dead. The leader was easily identifiable. He wore a hood with the fur turned in and his eyes shifted from Simoi to Gisik and then back again.

Only a short distance separated them when the leader stopped walking. A slight chill caused Simoi's breath to fog in front of his face as he also waited.

"Where are the women?"

The words were spoken in a guttural tongue that was seldom used, but familiar to Simoi. He could see at a glance that Gisik did not understand the man's words, but he wisely remained silent.

"They are well away from here." Simoi responded as his fingers clenched around his hunting spear. He stared at the leader of the other men and his gut clenched when the man's eyes lit with a menacing glitter.

"No, they are not far. We know this and more."

Simoi did not bother to disagree. If Lily and Saghani ran until the dawn they stood a chance of outdistancing the five men that dogged their trail. However, he knew Saghani well and while Lily was capable of moving quickly for long distances, she would wait on her companion who often lagged behind. Lily would not abandon her friend, no matter the danger to her life.

"If you give us the women, we will spare your lives." The man shrugged his shoulders as if Simoi's response meant nothing to him.

Simoi breathed deeply of the crisp night air. He sensed the lie as spoken by the man with the forked tongue, but he could not determine why the man bothered to do so. A shifting glance of the man's eyes made him recognize that he was stalling for time. Nimiuq walked forward and his breath was labored and halting.

Not enough time, Simoi thought. There was not enough time between Nimiuq's departure and his return. While he refused to give in to defeat, the odds were against them. Pride filled his eyes as he remembered that his niece relied upon him to see to her safety. Lily needed him.

"I am Simoi."

"Your name means nothing to me!" The leader walked ever closer, until he stood face to face with Simoi. Dark hair hung in long braids over his shoulders and in his hand he held a hunting spear with rough markings etched into the weapon.

"My name should matter to you, for it is the name of the man that will end your life, worthless though it might be." Simoi spread his hands wide as Gisik and Nimiuq backed away.

The leader laughed boldly as his men edged forward and Simoi caught his first true look at them. They were not underfed, nor were they weak, the men had the musculature of strong hunters, perhaps even warriors.

"You do not have to tell us where the women have gone. We will simply follow their footsteps until we run them down and then we will take what we want from them." The leader's eyes darkened as he narrowed his eyes in challenge. "You are not the first to try to defend your women from us and you will not be the last."

His four companions circled forward as Simoi met their eyes. "You are men that have been cast out of your band. Unfit to even speak to the people of the great land. Have you also lost the ways that were given to you at birth."

The men sneered as they stepped forward, eager to begin a battle that was slanted in their favor.

"You choose to fight at night, even though you know that if you are killed, your souls will wander the great land forever." Simoi preyed upon the knowledge that he gathered during his time spent with the various bands of the great land. Certain bands would not risk a fight or spear attack at night for they held the belief that if they died without the sun's light, they would wander the dark world forever. He saw one of the men glance fearfully at the others, but when their leader growled in anger and raised his spear, Simoi was ready.

He pivoted so that the leader's spear met only air. Gisik released a war cry that swept over the land as he charged forward, diving into the skirmish.

Two of the younger men encircled Nimiuq as he held his spear in two gnarled hands and bared his teeth.

"A curse upon your souls!" Nimiuq hissed.

First blood was drawn by Simoi, but he did not waste his breath by shouting in triumph. Though it was cold, sweat dampened their faces. Simoi chose to leave his possessions at a distance, along with his warm outer garments. His opponent's bulky cape acted as protection from the sharp point of his spear, but his clothing was also cumbersome, hampering his movements.

When the man suddenly lunged forward, Simoi felt his enemy's spear strike his right arm in a glancing blow. A movement from his left caught his attention, but he could not turn away from the fierce warrior that sought to take his life.

A tortured cry from Nimiuq told him that his longtime friend was injured. With a shout of rage, Simoi spun and plunged his hunting knife into the leader's heart. Gisik ran to help Nimiuq who lay prone upon the ground. With a quick movement, one of the attacking men threw his spear toward Gisik. Unable to block the blow, Gisik spun around placing the man's companion in front of him. The spear caught the man in the stomach and Gisik jerked it free as the man screamed in agony.

Gisik and Simoi stood back to back as they faced the remaining three men. They each held a spear, but there was little hope that they could defeat the three men that walked steadily forward. Yet, Nimiuq's ragged screams only fueled their determination to stand and fight.

Simoi struggled to keep his spear steady as sweat blinded him and Lily's face danced before his eyes. He faced the men that would steal his life and he knew only driving disappointment that he failed to protect his niece from harm.

"Die with honor!"

"Just so." Gisik said as the three men shouted in unison and pressed their attack.

CHAPTER FOURTEEN

In the gathering darkness, Cahil found it difficult to pick up the trail left by Simoi and his band. Anuk did not complain when Cahil set a punishing pace that would sap the strength of most men. They happened upon a lone deer which met the stone point of his spear and while they lost precious time butchering the animal and stowing the meat, they were well fed and their energy renewed.

The people of the great land believed that meat provided nourishment and warmth. The strength in his arms and legs gave credence to this long held belief. The moon hung overhead, lighting the way as their eyes adjusted to the darkness.

"We should have come upon Simoi and the others by now." Cahil spoke to himself as his eyes scanned the landscape ahead. There were dangers inherent with traveling at night and as a hunter and a warrior, he knew them well. Yet, he could not escape the sense of urgency that remained with him, even now. He did not know if he sought only to escape his past, which hung like a burden upon his shoulders or if he hoped to seek a new future as offered to him by Simoi. All he knew was that he wanted to meet up with the small band and join them in their travels.

Anuk kept step with him, pace for pace. In the distance, he could see the shapes of people walking and Cahil smiled in relief. They were close to Simoi and his band, but even as the thought occurred to him, he felt as if something was wrong.

Simoi walked with another hunter, two young women and elderly man. He would have found it necessary to stop at night and build a fire. Yet, the people walking in the distance wore bulky clothing and their steps were firm, although hurried.

Cahil made a quieting motion to Anuk and the youth's eyes bulged as he caught sight of the others in the distance. Anuk's training as a hunter came in handy as the youth remained silent, not giving their presence away.

As Cahil drew closer he saw that he was right. The people that they trailed could not possibly be Simoi and his band. From what he could see, there were five men of various heights walking steadily ahead. There was not enough light to read the signs upon the ground clearly, but the light coating of snow allowed him to count their footprints upon the ground. Small circles broken into the ice at intervals also told him that the men carried spears.

Perhaps they were a lone hunting party, but if so, he could not understand why they chose to hunt game during the night. Something was wrong and Cahil trusted his instincts, which caused his muscles to bunch and tense in expectation of danger.

"Anuk." Cahil spoke in a voice that was pitched low. "Remain here."

Anuk's jaw hardened and his nostrils flared as he shook his head without speaking.

"Anuk." Cahil warned, but the young man would not be swayed.

Instinct drove Cahil forward as he thought about Simoi and the men of their band, they were all that stood between death and the young women that they protected.

An image of Lily's upturned face and smiling eyes flashed into his mind and he grimaced before hurrying forward. He recognized that Simoi's band was vulnerable to the dangers inherent to the land, but he also knew that there was no greater danger than men without honor who sought to do harm.

Cahil ran full out as he struggled to keep up with the men that walked ahead of him. Upon the great land, distances often seemed closer than they actually were. Yet, Cahil was a hunter that often ran at the rear of a herd to make a kill. He did not know fear and he used the strength born of a lifetime spent hunting for every meal to usher him forward.

He outdistanced Anuk as he slid over rock and stone. A great bellow of sound reached his ears along with the sound of fighting. He ran forward with a cry of his own as he caught sight of a figure upon the ground. Three men encircled two others and he saw at once that it was Simoi and Gisik.

He threw his spear with an accuracy that served him well during the midst of a hunt. In this way, his hunting spear became a weapon honed with strength in battle. His spear entered the back of one man, while he pulled his hunting knife free and attacked the man that turned to face him.

With a quick movement, Cahil ducked under the man's spear and drove his knife deep into his opponent's stomach forcing the weapon up, even as he pulled it free. Simoi and Gisik barely registered the death of two men as Cahil swung the back of the fallen man's spear and hit the third man in the head.

The blow stunned the warrior, but he did not fall as he pressed his attack upon the newcomer. The spear swirled in Cahil's hand as he plunged it through the man's chest and Simoi and Gisik did the same with their weapons, sending their spears through the man's back.

Silence reigned as Anuk ran forward and all three men turned upon him with battle rage evident upon their faces. Anuk stumbled to a stop, taking in the scene around him with a bulging glance before his eyes rolled back in his head. The men watched helplessly as Anuk fell in an unconscious heap at their feet.

"How bad is Nimiuq's injury?" Cahil asked as he poured water on Anuk's face. The young man sputtered and coughed as he looked around at the carnage around him.

"He has lost a lot of blood." Simoi knelt beside Nimiuq as he tried to determine how to help his friend.

"He fought bravely." Gisik cut through Nimiuq's parka as he found a spear wound in Nimiuq's side. "It is good that he is not awake or the pain would be unbearable."

Cahil stepped forward to see that the driving force of a spear caused several of Nimiuq's ribs to collapse. Nimiuq's frail body was not able to withstand the blow of a warrior's spear. His breathing was labored and blood trickled from his lips as he struggled for every breath.

Simoi removed his hunting knife as he stared at his old friend. Gisik suffered from a blow to his head and he moaned as pain ricocheted inside of his skull. Simoi closed his eyes as he murmured quiet words before peering at Cahil. They both knew that Nimiuq was gravely injured, but when he regained consciousness he would suffer as no man should suffer.

Cahil knelt beside Simoi as the man held his hunting knife in his hands and stared at the weapon as if he didn't recognize it.

"I must end his life." Simoi's eyes widened as he spoke the fateful words.

Gisik moaned again as he struggled to his knees only to collapse as Anuk rushed to his side.

"Gisik is injured as well and I know he would have taken this burden upon himself if only he could."

Cahil felt Simoi's sadness and he knew that it would forever change Simoi if he was forced to end Nimiuq's life.

"I can end his suffering."

The words came from Cahil as Simoi raised his head with hope shining in his eyes. "Are you a healer?"

"Even a healer's touch would not help your friend." Cahil did not mean to give Simoi false hope and he quickly explained. "I know of a way to take his life that will not add to his suffering."

"No, I will do what I must, as his friend." Simoi struggled with the effort to use his right hand.

"You are wounded." Cahil lifted Simoi's arm as he caught sight of his bleeding arm. "Anuk, bind his arm so that the bleeding stops!"

Anuk hurried forward as he said, "Gisik is injured, but I believe that the dizziness he is experiencing will pass."

Terrible moans came from Nimiuq as he blinked his eyes and clutched at his side. Cahil and Simoi started at each other over Nimiuq's prone form.

Nimiuq struggled against the pain as he screamed in hoarse guttural cries that were made worse by his inability to draw a clear breath of air. Tears filled Simoi's eyes, but he brushed them away as he endured his friend's pain as if it were his own. Cahil waited as Simoi once again stared at his hunting knife.

"I can help you both, if you let me." Cahil saw the inner struggle within Simoi and he understood. He accepted the burden of caring for Anuk, even though the young man made his own decision to join him. If he was forced to take Anuk's life, it would be a burdensome weight that he would always carry, no matter where his footsteps led.

However, no man should suffer the way that Nimiuq suffered. He begged them to help him and yet, they could do nothing for him except to sit vigil while he suffered an agonizing death.

They knew that he would eventually die from his injuries simply because they were untreatable. Yet, Cahil offered Nimiuq a chance to die peacefully, instead of dying slowly while in excruciating pain.

An unnatural sleep claimed Nimiuq, giving them a brief reprieve as his screams ceased.

"Nimiuq, you have been a close companion, since the first day that we started upon our journey until now." Simoi's grief was a living, breathing thing as he spoke quietly to his friend. "I will honor you, my friend. I will watch over Saghani and I will see to her future. Thank you for fighting as a warrior, even though you did not wish to fight. Thank you for your sacrifice."

"If I act now, he will not wake to burning agony again." Cahil saw Anuk turn away as Simoi offered him his hunting knife.

"Do it quickly, before he wakes."

CHAPTER FIFTEEN

The great land spread out before him as Cahil walked ever forward. He followed the running footsteps made by Lily and Saghani until the lack of snow made tracking almost impossible. He continued on by instinct and supposition, backtracking several times as his frustration mounted.

At midday, he spotted an outcropping of rock in the distance that was nothing more than a gray shadow on the horizon. If he was right, the rough stone spire was a possible hiding place and he would find two frightened young women hiding there.

"Lily!" Cahil called out as he approached the large rock mound. "Simoi sent me to find you!"

His heart plummeted as he desperately searched for any sign of the two women. From what he could see one of the women was injured and it slowed their progress considerably. He hoped to find them hiding amongst the rock and stone, taking shelter until Simoi came to find them.

"Saghani!" Cahil called out the other young woman's name, the granddaughter of Nimiuq.

He received no answer and he sighed heavily as he tried to determine what calamity might have befallen them. He edged around the rock mound and found Lily staring at him out of frightened eyes as Saghani quietly wept.

Lily clutched a large rock with both hands as she struggled to her feet. She and Saghani were cold and tired, but she was determined to fight.

"Lily," Cahil held up a hand in caution as the young woman backed away until her friend was pressed into the rock behind them.

"Go away!" Lily shouted as Cahil took another step closer.

"Lily, your uncle sent me to find you." Cahil was relieved to see that the young women were unharmed though he noticed that Saghani favored one foot over the other. He expected Lily to breathe a sigh of relief, but instead as he stepped forward she hurled the rock at him.

"Lily!" Saghani shrieked as Lily grabbed another rock and lifted it overhead even though her arms trembled from the effort.

Cahil barely managed to dodge out of the way as the woman hurled another rock at him. He ducked as a rock sailed past his head. He didn't have time to respond as Lily grabbed another stone and hurled it toward him.

"Stop!" Cahil's voice was angry as he leapt forward and grabbed hold of the stone before she could find the strength to hurl it.

Lily's scream caused him to wince as he lifted her roughly over one shoulder where she beat her fists against his back. "Stop!"

Cahil's voice was less forceful as he noticed the pleasing softness of the young woman's form draped over his shoulder and arm. He once thought that her fragile appearance signified the lack of womanly curves, but as he held her thighs against his chest, he realized that he was wrong. A swift pang of desire filled him as she squirmed to be set free.

Saghani limped forward with wide eyes as Cahil carried Lily toward Simoi's band, leaving her to follow. Last night she relied upon Lily to find a place of shelter and comfort her when she wept throughout the night, but Cahil ignored her tears and he did not offer his help. He simply restrained Lily's flailing limbs as he carried her away.

"Wait for me!" Saghani cried out as she grabbed a stick and used it to aid her footsteps. She almost stumbled and fell as she gathered their belongings and hobbled forward. Pain seared through her ankle, but she pressed her lips together in determination as she hurried to catch up to Cahil and Lily.

Cahil glanced over his shoulder as he swung around and continued walking. Lily kicked him in the chest and he swatted her hard on her backside.

"Put me down!" Lily cried as Cahil walked with measured steps over uneven ground.

"You know that I am a friend to your band, but you threw stones at me as if I am your enemy." Cahil was surprised that the woman thrown over his shoulder could cause him to know any emotion at all.

Since the death of his father, he existed without emotion; he lived without anger or happiness. It was the only way that he was able to survive the void that filled his chest. Now that his father was gone, all that he knew of his past became nothing more than a lie.

"I thought you were here to harm us." Lily replied as Cahil came to a standstill. Loose tendrils of her hair drifted around his calves and ankles as she hung upside down.

"If I set you down, you will cease fighting." Cahil shook Lily for emphasis and he was surprised when she merely nodded against his back.

He set her down slowly, enjoying the feel of her doeskin dress against his bare chest and skin. Her brown eyes spit fire at him, but she remained silent and she did not fight him just as she promised. Saghani hobbled forward and Lily's eyes widened as she moved around Cahil and stood protectively in front of her friend.

"Your uncle sent me to bring you back to him." Cahil repeated as Lily's gaze widened. The concern in her eyes was evident and he felt regret for the grief that would come to her when she learned of Nimiuq's fate. He glanced at Saghani and noticed that she also showed concern for her grandfather and he knew that her grief would weigh heavily upon him.

"What of my grandfather and Gisik?" Saghani clutched Lily's hand as she waited for an answer.

"We must hurry." Cahil refused to answer her question. He turned swiftly as he led the way and the women were forced to follow him or risk being left behind.

As they walked, Lily breathed deeply, unintentionally drawing Cahil's masculine scent into her nostrils. Her heart still pounded and her hands trembled from their heated encounter.

She never expected to see his face again and yet, she should have known that he was not the cause of whatever calamity kept Simoi and the others from finding them. Mindless terror prompted her actions and she was deeply ashamed that she lashed out at the strong man that walked with measured steps ahead of her.

Though she was deeply ashamed, she could not bring herself to apologize for her behavior. She reacted instinctively after having spent a night open and exposed upon the great land without a weapon to keep them from harm and only their sleeping furs to keep them warm.

She should have hesitated to throw a stone at Cahil, knowing that he treated their band with respect in the past. Yet, fear overrode common sense and she reacted first only to reconsider her actions after he plucked her from the ground and threw her over his shoulder.

Perhaps it was the concern in his eyes when he mentioned the men of her band, perhaps it was the way that he looked her and Saghani over for injury before turning his back upon them. Whatever the reason, she realized that she erred in her attack upon him. Despite his fierce appearance and his lack of an explanation for following after them, she trusted him. Completely and without question.

From a distance, Lily heard the sound of Gisik's one-sided sealskin drum beating at a slow pace. Fear seized her heart as she recognized the somber sound as an announcement of death.

Cahil did not call out to the women as they ran forward to greet the men of their band. He knew what they would find when they arrived upon the scene of battle.

Simoi left the bodies of the fallen warriors in place, not bothering to arrange them in death or show honor to men that didn't know the meaning of the word. Nimiuq lay prone upon the ground, but a blanket had been placed under his body and his eyes were closed as if he merely slept. Yet, Cahil knew that Nimiuq had left the world of the living.

Saghani was the first to lift her voice in mourning, but Lily joined her within moments as tears of newfound horror and disbelief spilled from her eyes. Cahil drew himself away from the weeping women as Gisik continued to call sound from his drum with the palms of his hands. Anuk stood at a distance and Cahil found that he could not leave the young man to wallow in brooding silence.

"You think that we should not have come here." Cahil saw that Anuk's shoulders were lowered in defeat and he had his first taste of the evil that men were capable of committing against other men.

"You do not know my thoughts." Anuk's hair stood out at all angles as he turned to face Cahil. "I spent the morning watching Simoi care for Nimiuq's body as if were a brother to the man. I watched Gisik drag himself from the ground and sit and play the drum, announcing Nimiuq's death to anyone close enough to hear."

Cahil remained silent as Anuk struggled to express himself while pain stood at the edges of his vision. There were no blood ties between them, but Anuk remained steadfast, following him like a shadow, while his eyes remained alight with hope. The hope faded from Anuk's eyes and grief marred the dark orbs, casting shadows over his features.

"I saw you. I know that you killed Nimiuq." The words were not said in accusation and Cahil lifted his head and stared hard at Anuk. "You ended his suffering and it was the bravest thing that I have ever seen. Simoi could not perform the task and Gisik was unwell, but you took it upon yourself to ease Nimiuq's suffering."

"I am not proud of taking the life of any man." Cahil's jaw clenched tight as Anuk turned tear brightened eyes upon him.

"This land is harsh and unforgiving. It does not make allowances for weakness or for the faint of heart." Anuk's gaze hardened as he glanced back at those that mourned Nimiuq. The women held one another as Simoi sang in a low voice. Gisik never stopped beating the drum, he swayed in place as the undulating drumbeat lifted to the heavens, echoing across the land. "If death comes for me, I would rather it be at your hand, where there is the hope of dying with honor."

With that, Anuk turned from Cahil to join the others while Cahil remained standing, staring into the distance as Simoi's band mourned. When the beating of the drum ceased, Cahil took halting steps toward an outcropping of stones. They would use the stones to cover Nimiuq's body exactly where he fell. The stone mound would honor his remains and prevent animals from reaching his body. Simoi placed Nimiuq's spear alongside his body as well as several beaded necklaces that he carried with his belongings. Gisik reverently placed Nimiuq's bone hunting knife in his right hand, where it would rest forever.

Cahil returned with one stone after another until the others took up the effort and together they covered Nimiuq, until the land itself wrapped its arms around him, holding him close and in secret. As the last rock was set in place, they were left with only their memories of the proud man that died defending those that rested in his heart.

CHAPTER SIXTEEN

Several days passed as they walked in Simoi's footsteps. Simoi mourned deeply, offering little input, except to direct them over the ever changing ground. Cahil and Anuk followed along, they were silent out of respect for the grief that weighed like a low hanging cloud over the others. Gisik kept to the rear, watching their trail while the women took their place between them.

Lily could not find a reason to speak to Cahil, but the heavy burden of grief that hung over their band did not allow for quiet conversation or meaningless chatter. She knew that everyone suffered their own sadness over Nimiuq's death. Saghani remained quiet and withdrawn. Her grandfather was all that was left of her former band and she mourned his loss deeply.

Oddly, it was Anuk that brought about a change, though he did not set out to do so. If Simoi was not mired in grief, he would have noticed Anuk walking ahead and slightly to the right of their band. The young man's lanky form was a source of amusement as Anuk's arms and legs seemed almost too long for his body. His unruly hair made his head appear larger than it was even from a distance.

Cahil walked forward, but he was plagued by thoughts about his past and the questions that he would have liked to ask Kusug. He glanced up sharply as he heard a loud crack, a sound very similar to thunder. Simoi's loud shout caused everyone to stop walking.

"Stay still!" Simoi yelled out as they all looked at Anuk who froze in place, except for his head which swiveled to stare back at them.

Cahil immediately saw that Anuk strayed farther than the others and he cursed as he noticed that the young man walked on what must have been an underground river. Snow remained under their feet, but deep beneath the snow was a fragile layer of melting ice.

Simoi edged toward Anuk as the ground began to tremble. A long crack appeared between Anuk's splayed feet and the sound of breaking ice could be heard by all.

"Anuk, lay flat." Cahil was at Simoi's side as both men reached out their hands to Anuk, but the youth remained frozen with fear.

"I can feel the ice shifting. It moves beneath me."

"Anuk, you must rest on your belly and move toward us." Simoi spoke over the swell of fear that froze everyone in place. "Now!"

Cahil would have stepped onto the sheet of ice if not for Simoi's painful grasp upon his arm. "No more weight needs to be placed on the ice."

"Cahil!" Anuk's voice was shrill as he called out for help.

"He will die if I do not reach him!" Cahil's voice was panicked as he considered shrugging free of Simoi's hold. The other man was still healing from the injury to his arm and he knew that he could break free of his grasp.

"You will not be able to help him at all if you both fall through the ice." Simoi spoke in a calm, measured voice as he once again urged Anuk to rest on his belly and crawl toward them.

Anuk's eyes widened as his entire body began to tremble, but he did as he was told. He eased onto his belly as he struggled to edge toward them.

"Gisik, tell the women to start a fire." Simoi gave clipped instructions even as he and Cahil urged Anuk to come closer.

Water rose to the surface, melting away the very ground that Anuk crawled over. "Slither like a snake on your belly, Anuk."

"Yes, you are almost there, come closer." Simoi extended his spear to Anuk with the sharp end held in his grasp. Just as Anuk reached out with one hand a distinctive crack caused a groan to fall from Anuk's lips as the frozen river crumbled, taking Anuk with it.

"No!" Cahil would have launched himself into the water, even as shards of ice broke the surface, but Simoi moved with lightening speed as he grabbed hold of the young man's hand.

"Anuk!" Cahil helped Simoi haul Anuk out of the water as Anuk clung to the end of the spear with one hand and Simoi's hand with the other.

Anuk shuddered and gasped as icy water sluiced off of his clothing onto the ground. Cahil lifted the young man as he dragged him away from the edge of the free flowing river. Gisik was there in an instant, stripping away Anuk's rapidly freezing clothing. Cahil's fingers cramped with cold as they all worked to tear the frozen garments from Anuk's thin frame, exposing his body to the cold, but also freeing him from almost certain death.

Simoi struggled to break pieces of wood with Gisik's crude hatchet, which he added to the small fire started by the women. He worked feverishly over the low burning flames until it blazed. Lily and Saghani brought blankets forward to cover Anuk who stood with his eyes squeezed shut as Cahil dragged him closer to the growing flames.

Anuk's teeth chattered and his lips were tinged blue as he swayed, almost falling into the fire. Cahil held him steady, despite the shudders that racked his body.

"Anuk, you must dance." Gisik pushed Cahil and Anuk until they moved around the fire as Anuk shuddered and groaned.

"Dance, Anuk!" Lily and Saghani were terrified that Anuk would succumb to the cold as his entire frame trembled from head to toe. Without his clothing, they saw that the boy was thinner than expected. Lily frantically searched for more firewood, eager to help Simoi build the fire as Cahil urged Anuk to remain on his feet.

They came to a jarring stop as Gisik pressed a piece of dried meat into Anuk's mouth as he scrubbed his body from head to toe with the fur side of the blanket. When Gisik finished, Cahil dragged him around the fire.

"Dance, Anuk!" The women urged Anuk when he faltered and Cahil worked the young man's limbs so that he moved despite the shudders that continued to wrack his frame. Anuk mumbled something incomprehensible and Cahil pressed his ear close to Anuk's mouth as the boy tried to speak. He mumbled again and Cahil growled in frustration as he tried to hear what he said.

"Anuk, you must keep moving, let the fire warm you." Cahil pleaded and cajoled until Anuk took up the motions for himself.

By the time Anuk was able to move on his own, Cahil was drenched in sweat and Simoi and Gisik were in the same condition. Lily wiped tears from her eyes as Anuk finally ceased dancing and fell in an exhausted heap beside the fire.

Once more, Anuk spoke in a quiet voice as Cahil leaned close to listen.

"Did the women see me naked?"

Anuk's gaze was unfocused as he shuddered, but his lips were no longer blue and his eyes were alight with mischief.

Simoi and Gisik were the first to laugh as Anuk struggled to keep his eyes open. With a shout of encouragement they lifted the youth to his feet and moved him around the fire as Cahil merely stared. Simoi clutched his belly in laughter as Anuk tossed an anxious glance toward Saghani, before tucking the blanket closer around his lean hips.

Both young women averted their eyes, but not before Simoi ripped the blanket from Anuk's hands and urged him to dance until warmth returned to his limbs. Gisik howled with amusement as Anuk used his hands to cover his manhood and hide his flat backside from view.

For the first time in as long as he could remember, Cahil openly laughed.

"I must thank you for what you did to ease my friend's suffering." Simoi spoke quietly to Cahil as they stood overlooking the land that spread out before them. It was the first time that he broached the subject of Nimiuq's death.

"I did only what was necessary." Cahil did not mention Nimiuq by name. He was not familiar with the traditions of Simoi's band, but within his own village the names of the dead were not uttered.

"He should have lived out his days beside a fire, being tended to by his granddaughter." Simoi responded as they made their way across a water bogged meadow. "I will miss his never-ending complaints and there is no replacement for the seasons of wisdom that he gained over a lifetime."

"Tell me about the Krahnan band." Cahil touched his necklace as he walked beside Simoi. He was eager to learn about the people that once dwelled in the high places, those that were related to him by shared blood.

The older man walked with an easy stride that spoke of the ease with which he traversed the great land. Simoi carried his pack as well as his hunting spear and his eyes were constantly in motion, moving from left to right as he scouted the way ahead.

"The people of the Krahnan band were once prosperous, but no more. They no longer have the unity that existed in the past. However, the band remains in one place, season after season, weathering the cold in lodges that provide shelter and safety. They have adapted to the ways of the land. Whether they face driving snow, freezing rain or a fair season of warmth, they survive."

An edge of respect entered Simoi's voice as he spoke and Cahil noticed that he increased his pace as if he longed to reach their destination.

"What about the other bands that have chosen to travel to the gathering place? Why do they risk life and limb to join the others?" More than anything Cahil wanted to understand the reason that Simoi chose to undertake such a perilous journey.

He saw that Simoi and Gisik grieved deeply over the loss of Nimiuq and their inability to save the older man's life. He sensed that Simoi held a deep conviction about their journey and he needed to understand what drove him to risk the wellbeing of his band.

"It has always been the way of things that men provide for those under their care." Simoi glanced back at the young women who walked with Anuk, while Gisik remained at the rear of their group, ever watchful, ever cautious. "But what happens when we do not honor the old ways, tell me what happens when we walk forward heedless of what has taken place in the past?"

"I do not understand." Cahil was a hunter, he was a man that effortlessly led other men, but he was not a man that sought the spirit world for guidance or direction.

There were men that sought out the spirit world in his first village and he thought they were often foolish, searching the heavens for omens and looking for signs in everyday occurrences. If Simoi was similar to those men, then he had been wrong about him and he was not the man that he appeared to be.

Cahil's concern must have shown upon his face because Simoi stopped walking and turned to regard him with a measured gaze.

"You turn your eyes away from men that seek guidance from the spirit world." It was a statement simply made as an expression of fact.

Cahil remained silent as Simoi studied his features before narrowing his eyes and turning his face away. Cahil could not say why he felt that he was tested and found lacking, but he knew that it was so.

"I have not seen anything that would tell me otherwise."

"Yet, you decided to leave your village behind and set out on a journey to reach a place unknown to you."

"Yes."

"Then you have learned that regret lives in the one that has yet to try." With a deep sigh, Simoi said, "Tell me, how is it that you knew to journey after us and hurry your footsteps until you walked in the shadow of danger?"

Cahil thought about the five men that lost their lives when they attacked Simoi's band. He failed to give his timely arrival any thought, but he knew that the men of Simoi's band faced death with bravery. "I saw the marker that you left behind and I remembered that your niece described the seeking star that you follow on your journey. It was not difficult to find your trail once I knew which direction you traveled, nor was it difficult to catch up to you, since I was only concerned with Anuk and myself."

"Yes, but how was it that you came to be at our mountain encampment in enough time to reach us here upon the great land when we faced mortal danger?"

"It was merely chance." Cahil's brow furrowed as Simoi shook his head back and forth in denial.

"No, it was a blessing from the Great One of All Things, the one who decides the fate of all men." Simoi would not believe otherwise, no matter that Cahil explained that he ran most of the way with Anuk at his heels.

"I saw that you were in danger." Cahil admitted as he remembered seeing the five bulky shadows that followed Simoi's trail. He did not speak of it, but his fear for the young women of Simoi's band drove him to run like the wind and Lily's wellbeing in particular urged him to take risks that he would have otherwise avoided.

"The young women in my band are only as safe as the men that stand as a protective force between them and the dangers of the land." Simoi sighed heavily as Cahil recognized the burden of responsibility that he carried. "I cannot convince you that your actions were a blessing to my band, but then you cannot convince me that you have not known a moment when something spins loose in your soul, deep below the ribs and you know without question that the thing you have experienced is right and true. Sometimes a person will find themselves walking along a path that has been laid out for them, even before their first breath of life."

Cahil could not find any words with which to respond and so in the way of a cautious hunter, he remained silent. But as a man, he considered Simoi's wise words while the sounds of the land filled the silence between them.

CHAPTER SEVENTEEN

The morning swept over the land, bringing a brisk breeze that pressed against their backs. Brown tinged grass reached weakly toward the sunlight as Cahil kept pace with the others. As he watched a spruced grouse fly overhead, his thoughts drifted to Simoi's niece, Lily. She was fragile, just like the small bird fluttering overhead.

Despite her delicate appearance, he was impressed that she could walk seemingly without cease, never causing the others to slow their progress. She was as unlike her female companion as daylight was from night. As far as he was aware, Lily never complained about the constant walking or the monotony that was common over long distances.

At the end of each day, they sought their sleeping furs with exhausted bodies and new aches and pains. The nights sped by quickly and they began each day before sunlight filled the world around them as they moved at a steady pace.

Fresh water was not a hardship, but by the end of the day the water skins, carrying packs and handheld baskets became a burden, draining away any last reserves of strength. They worked to replenish their supply of food, repaired clothing, sharpened their weapons and replaced broken tools along the way.

The dried meat that the women carried dwindled rapidly, despite their efforts to eat small portions. Cahil offered what was left of the deer meat that he and Anuk carried and as they reached the end of their food supply, they began to discuss the need to hunt.

"We must hunt as we travel." Simoi's eyes clouded with concern as his gaze landed upon Lily. "We have already delayed far longer than we should have and I cannot risk the wellbeing of my small band for the chance at finding game."

Cahil considered setting off by himself to hunt, but he knew that Anuk would simply follow him and there were the dangers of the unknown to consider. He was a skilled hunter, but he didn't see any sign of deer or any of the herds that were common to the land. At midday, he used his sling to bring down a rabbit, but there was not much hope of filling the bellies of six people with one rabbit to share between them.

During the evening, Lily prepared a stew that was tasty, but the meal was quickly devoured. Anuk inhaled his portion of the meal as he drank from a buffalo horn which the women used as a vessel for stews and liquids warmed by the fire. Exhausted and worn, they took to their sleeping places without the comfort of a fire as they shivered their way toward daylight.

Cahil often overheard Saghani complain about her injured ankle, which Lily bound with a strip of animal hide. Simoi paid little heed to Saghani's attempts to delay their progress, though he made a walking staff that would aid her until her ankle healed. Throughout the hardships that they faced, he noticed that Lily remained steadfast and helpful. She was often the last to fall asleep and the first to rise and it seemed to him that she never stopped moving, working until each task was finished.

He tried not to watch the feminine sway of her hips as she moved around their evening fire. He told himself that she was a girl on the cusp of womanhood and he refused to discuss his thoughts with anyone, including Anuk. Yet, Lily constantly drew his eye and he found himself watching over her as they traveled, sensing almost instinctively where she was within their band and where her footsteps landed. He was surprised to learn that Simoi planned to find a mate for his niece and he found that his eyes strayed toward Lily whenever she was near.

In the sunlight, her blue-black hair stood out in striking contrast to the landscape around them. He noticed that she had lost weight from the constant walking and meals eaten while in motion. Her cheekbones were more pronounced than they had been and her oval face was highlighted by the burnished golden hue of her skin. When he met her gaze, he saw that her amber flecked eyes were wide open and watchful.

Gisik carried a rough stone hatchet that he used to cut firewood whenever they found a fallen tree or young sapling. Yet, he could only take what he could quickly gather in his arms, due to the need to press forward. Without hesitation or direction, Anuk helped him gather as much dry wood as he could carry.

There were several nights when they went without fire to conserve their precious wood supply and if the men were not successful in finding game, Lily simply made a meal from the leafy greens and lush foliage that clung to the last vestiges of the warm season. As they walked, a tremulous cry from one of the women drew their attention and Cahil turned along with Simoi as they tried to discern what was wrong.

"I cannot continue at this pace." Saghani made certain that Simoi heard her voice and when he pressed forward despite her protests, she shrieked in anger, brushed off Lily's comforting hands as she tossed her walking stick upon the ground. "No! If we continue at such a brisk pace, I will only cause further injury to my ankle."

Cahil saw a fleeting expression of annoyance flicker over Simoi's face and he wondered how the man would handle the fickle young woman. Over the past few days, he felt only sympathy for Saghani, especially when she wept bitterly over the death of her grandfather. But as time went on, he realized that she used her grief to play upon the kindness and compassion of the others. Cahil kept his distance as he watched Simoi pivot in place and stalk toward the young woman.

A small squeak of dismay escaped her lips as Simoi stood close to her, until they were nose to nose. "I will hear no further complaint from you, Saghani!

"My grandfather died and I have not known happiness since." Tears filled Saghani's eyes as Simoi's sharp gaze pierced her like a spear.

"Your grandfather died fighting for your life. Is it a life that you value so little that you would throw it away because you cannot find the will to continue? You seek to delay our band, but know this, if it comes down to a choice of continuing or leaving you behind, we will leave you behind."

Saghani inhaled sharply as she saw the anger in Simoi's eyes. "Lily would not leave me."

Simoi glanced at his niece and saw that her face was lifted in concern for her friend. "Lily will do as I tell her, because she is a dutiful young woman and she cares for the welfare of our band, our entire band."

Simoi did not wait for a response. He grabbed the walking staff from the ground and wrapped her hands around it. "Life is often a choice over whether to lie down and die or to take the next step."

"Simoi?" Saghani's voice was small and pitiful as Simoi turned his back upon her. With a quick glance at her surroundings, Saghani's breath shuddered from her lips. Anuk gulped as he slowed his pace and offered to carry her belongings if it would ease her burden.

"Walk!" Simoi called out as everyone fell into place behind him, leaving Saghani to stare after them with her mouth open in shock. Cahil walked beside Lily and Simoi's silence regarding their time spent together told him that the man was not opposed to his interest in his niece.

Cahil saw a fleeting smile pass over Lily's face and he wondered if she knew all along that Saghani needed Simoi's threats to quiet her wearisome complaints. She met his eyes as amusement lingered in her gaze and they shared a silent moment of lightheartedness.

"Will your uncle seek a mate for you at the gathering ceremony?" Cahil asked as he glanced at Lily. She blinked at him in startled surprise before answering.

"It appears so." Her words held a world of hope and his heart sped up in return.

"How old are you, Lily?"

He saw innocence in her eyes when she answered, but there was also a hint of determination in her voice that intrigued him.

"I am seventeen seasons of age."

"You are a child."

"I am a woman fully grown." Lily replied with a toss of her chin which unintentionally reminded Cahil that he saw her as a woman in every way. "Many of the young women that walk the great land join with a man and give birth to several children before they are my age."

Cahil knew this to be true.

Even in the Ula'tuk village, it was not uncommon for girls of thirteen or fourteen seasons to be given in marriage. Yet, to him, Lily seemed far different from those other young women. There was a rare mixture of courage and bravery that was a part of her spirit, inherent within her very nature.

"You are very brave."

Somehow her eyes seemed larger as she inclined her head toward him. Cahil was the first to look away, though his thoughts lingered upon her direct gaze and the strength that she showed each day. He glanced up as Simoi beckoned to him and he hurried to catch up with the man.

"It will serve you well to know what lies ahead." Simoi's voice cut into his thoughts as Cahil grunted in response. "We are approaching a tributary of the Krahnan River, once we are across, it is only a matter of three days' walk and we will join the other bands that gather at the ceremonial grounds."

"What happens if we are unable to cross the river?"

Simoi's eyes narrowed until they were mere slits across his face and he pressed his lips together into a grim line. "There is no other choice but to cross or we will be left out in the open with nothing standing between us and the ways of the land."

Cahil understood the ways of the land, like all men. The great land was brutal, harsh and punishing to those that were not cunning, fortunate and wise. "Then let us hurry."

CHAPTER EIGHTEEN

The frozen river was far wider than Cahil expected and mild trepidation filled his heart as he considered walking across the frozen ice to reach the other side. The distance around the river was vast and he could not see where the river began or where it ended. Trees dotted the frozen landscape, cottonwoods interspersed with spruce made their presence known by bursting forth with lush, green foliage, despite the cold that gripped the endless land.

The water that flowed underneath the river was most likely a raging torrent when the ice above melted. For now it raced underneath them like a tortured beast held in bonds that threatened to break at any moment.

"Is your journey to reach the Krahnan village so important that you are willing to risk everything to get there?" Cahil speared Simoi with the question that threatened to burst forth throughout their journey. Despite the turmoil that lived inside of him, he found that he still clung to the need to live, to wake and see another day. He did not relish the thought of an icy death, but their journey itself reinvigorated him, lending him strength and the desire to go on despite all that had befallen him.

He rarely thought of his brother or Delak and now that they crossed his mind, he found that the pain in his chest no longer felt like a crushing, brutal wind intent on destroying him. Somehow, the great land felt familiar and welcoming, despite the dangers. The nameless mountains and trees, the frozen rivers and streams, tethered him to the land as nothing else could.

"If we remain on this side of the river, I cannot say for a certainty that we will find enough game to survive even the onset of the cold season." Simoi raised his hand to shield his eyes as he looked into the distance. "Lengths of cord made from animal hide will create snares, but what use are snares when animals do not seek them out? We know for a certainty that the caribou herds will cross near the Krahnan River and we must strive to reach the other hunters before time runs out."

Cahil might have protested if his belly did not gnaw at his backbone with constant hunger. If there were any herds of bison or caribou they never crossed their path. He and Anuk kept their eyes open for any sign of game and over the past three days they failed to spot animal tracks or even well used trails.

The shifting landscape might account for their inability to find game, but Cahil felt as if there was something hidden, something just beneath the surface that he lacked the knowledge to understand. The odd feeling overcame him at the oddest times and until now, he blamed it on hunger.

"It was good of you to share the spoils of your last kill with us, especially because you included my niece and Saghani." Simoi inclined his head to the tired young women that waited silently while the men discussed crossing the river. Gisik and Anuk stood nearby, both figures standing in complete contrast to one another.

Anuk's hair stood out at all angles and to make matters worse, he ran one hand through his hair in an attempt to tame it. Anuk's lanky form was displayed despite the warm, badly stitched parka that he wore. His knee high moccasins were beginning to fray and the skin over his face was drawn tight from lack of nourishment. Gisik held the appearance of a battle scarred warrior and his lack of speech balanced out Anuk's natural exuberance. Whenever Gisik grew weary of Anuk's constant questions, he merely growled deep in his chest, sending the youth scampering toward Cahil, though Anuk slowed his pace to a walk whenever he outdistanced Gisik.

"Some men would not think to share their provisions with anyone else, let alone two young women." Simoi used his hunting spear to balance his weight as he stared out at the river.

"You shared your provisions with us and I returned the same gesture." Cahil saw the determination in Simoi's gaze and his thoughts went back to Nimiuq's curious expression when he first heard his name. "Do you have any idea why my name was familiar to Saghani's grandfather?"

An odd expression filled Simoi's eyes before he merely shook his head. "Perhaps the answers that you seek can be found in the Krahnan village."

As always, the name of the village sent a pang of unfamiliar emotion through Cahil's mind along with a shadowy feeling of grief. This time he could almost grasp the gossamer threads of fleeting thought before they were snatched away. He ran his hands over his face in frustration as he returned his attention to Simoi.

"If I falter, I will need to know that you or Gisik will see that Lily and Saghani reach the Krahnan band." Simoi raised his head to meet Cahil's eyes.

Cahil thought of Anuk, he accepted the youth as a burden and responsibility, but he knew nothing of the care necessary for young women.

"If anything should happen to you, it appears that Saghani will care for your niece, but I will see to it that they are protected until we reach our destination." Cahil placed one fist over his heart as Simoi nodded his thanks, though his expression turned oddly curious.

"Why would you imagine that Saghani would take care of Lily?"

"Because she is the older of the two." Cahil explained. "Your niece is a strong girl, but she is still young and needs the care of a woman."

A bark of laughter startled them all as Simoi chuckled and then lowered his voice so that the others would not overhear. "Lily is of the same age as Saghani and you do not have eyes if you cannot see that it is Lily that often cares for Saghani's wellbeing and not the other way around."

Without another word, Simoi took the first cautious step onto the ice, leaving Cahil to stand with his mouth open as the others trailed past him.

"You take the rear." Gisik muttered as he brushed past Cahil and walked with surprisingly light steps over the frozen ground.

Lily walked behind Saghani as they eased their way over the frozen ice. She took her courage into her hands and held it close as Saghani's footsteps faltered. Each time Saghani's walking stick touched the ground, Lily sucked in her breath in fear. She sensed the flowing water under the ice, surging underfoot like a living, breathing entity.

A shiver swept over her, even though she was warmly clothed and a feeling of foreboding caused her to hesitate. They were halfway across the river and she could see that Simoi's footsteps did not hesitate. They spread out so that their weight would not overburden any weak places upon the ice, but Lily's hands trembled in fear.

She could feel Cahil's gaze upon her. He looked at her oddly as she passed him while they were still on firm land. She could not say why she was drawn to him and she would probably deny it if anyone mentioned the way that she watched him throughout the day, often stumbling over a rock or patch of dried grass because she did not keep her eyes upon the ground where she could watch the placement of her footsteps.

"His eyes are cold and vacant." Saghani whispered, but Lily would never describe Cahil's gaze as cold or vacant. She sensed a deep, abiding spirit within him and though his eyes were often filled with shadows, he was vibrant and alive. Despite the dangers of their journey, her gaze was drawn to him constantly and unaccustomed warmth filled her whenever their eyes met. She wondered if it was normal to yearn for his touch or the brush of his fingertips, especially when she knew that he did not see her in the same way. Her eyes were drawn to the strength in his shoulders and the proud stance that he took when he spoke in low tones to her uncle. Like the mountains that they called home during the cold season, his arms and shoulders appeared to be capable of offering protection and strength.

"I do not know fear." Lily murmured as Saghani took a halting step and then flailed her arms for balance. Her walking stick landed hard by the heel of her right foot and water pooled beneath the heavy piece of wood before she was able to right herself and move forward.

Lily stared at the small pool of water as it grew before her eyes. Saghani turned frightened eyes toward her as Simoi shouted in triumph when he reached solid ground. In a moment of knowledge that seemed impossible, Lily saw what would happen now that the ice beneath her feet started to break. Time slowed to a standstill as Saghani slipped backward and Lily shoved her friend forward, sending her colliding into Anuk who turned at the first sound of breaking ice.

The ground beneath Lily churned as she tried to regain her balance, but the ice was breaking and her response was sluggish and slow. No matter how she tried to back away from the spreading fractures beneath her feet she knew that it was too late. She felt a vise close around her waist as the ice beneath her shifted and water rose to take its place.

Cahil jerked Lily out of harm's way as the frozen river began to crack and break open, spewing ice and freezing water into the air. Saghani slid out of the way as Gisik grabbed hold of her and ran the last few footsteps to the river's edge. Lily's mouth was open wide in horror as a chasm opened between them, cutting her and Cahil off from the rest of the band.

"Simoi!" Lily screamed as the water began to melt the thin ice with loud clashing sounds and froth.

"Go back, Lily!" Simoi shouted to be heard over the screams of Saghani and the shouts from Gisik and Anuk. He saw Cahil drag Lily up the embankment until they were safe from harm and his stomach settled back into place.

"Where can we cross?" Cahil shouted to Simoi as Lily sat down on the ground, hugging her knees to her chest. Simoi pointed downriver as he made wide sweeping gestures for them to hurry. He was too far away for them to hear the sound of his voice.

CHAPTER NINETEEN

"We must keep moving." Cahil spoke to Lily as her teeth chattered and she struggled to keep step with him. Between the two of them, they carried two water skins and one sleeping fur. Cahil still carried his spear and hunting knife, but the last of the dried meat remained with Anuk, in his carrying pouch. As they ran along the riverbank they quickly lost sight of Simoi and the others.

"There is nowhere else to cross." Lily's voice was filled with despair.

"We will find a way across, Lily." Cahil reached out his hand to her and she shivered as his fingers closed around hers. "You should cover your head."

Lily shrugged into her fur covered hood as Cahil assessed their surroundings. If he was a man that hunted in this area all of his life, he would have known the best place to find shelter or cross the fast flowing river without threat of falling in. As it was, he was responsible for Lily and though she was a woman of the great land, she was now open and exposed to danger.

"Simoi and the others will travel along the river and try to find an area where we might cross." Lily did not know if her input was welcome. Cahil stood as still as stone as he took stock of their belongings and the lengthening shadows which promised to usher in the night.

"We will find shelter now." Cahil started off toward a distant line of trees and Lily glanced back at the river, though she did not protest. She knew that he was right. They were wet and cold and she shivered violently with every footstep. Walking briskly helped, but her heart trembled at the thought of the night to come.

Cahil found a spruce tree and he quickly gathered the dying branches from the bottom of the tree and put them in a pile. He noticed that Lily's lips were almost colorless and he saw that she struggled and failed to suppress the chills that racked her body.

"Are you wet through and through?" Cahil asked as Lily looked at her clothing. Her knee high moccasins were wet on the outside, but inside, her feet were dry. The doeskin dress that she wore was fine for warmer weather, but she would have preferred the heavier caribou dress and leggings that were with Saghani in her carrying pack. Her buffalo skin cape was wet, but the hood was warm and dry. She could not remember touching the river and she tried to imagine how she managed to become half dry and half wet.

"Lily." Cahil stopped working on the fire that he was trying to build and he moved to stand in front of Lily. "I need you to focus."

"The water touched the outside of my moccasins and somehow my clothing became wet, but I am not certain how that came to pass."

"You fell. You fell on your back and I pulled you over the ice." Cahil helped Lily remove the cape, though he would have preferred to see that she kept her head covered. He ran his hands over shoulders, arms and hips and he grimaced as he realized that she was wet through and through. "You will have to remove your wet clothes."

Cahil turned his back upon Lily as he unwrapped his sleeping blanket and sighed with relief to find that it was dry. "You can wrap this around you until your clothing dries."

Lily's eyes widened as she looked down at her wet clothes. "Cahil?"

He lifted his eyes from her feet at the sound of his name upon her lips and he realized that she felt the searing heat of his gaze. "We need to start a fire and finish building a shelter that will see us through the night."

Lily nodded, though she felt as if she stared into his eyes for long moments before he stepped away from her and resumed his attempts to build a fire. Cahil turned his back on her so that she could remove her clothing.

"You have to keep moving. It would be good if you can help gather more tinder for the fire. Look for fallen branches that are easy to carry and preferably dry." Cahil glanced at Lily as she walked in a half circle around their temporary shelter in search of dry tinder. His sleeping blanket cloaked her form, but he knew that she was impossibly cold.

He managed to suppress a groan as he considered the night ahead of them. Simoi and the others were left on one side of the river and he and Lily were alone. He almost gave in to the urge to press his lips against hers, despite the dire circumstances that confronted them. She looked at him in such a way that he knew she would not turn away from him if he claimed her mouth. Instead, he set her away from him, though it took all of his effort to do so. He wondered how he would manage to survive the night ahead without taking the warmth that she offered with complete trust and innocence.

Lily returned to the shelter that Cahil constructed with branches of spruce and leaves. The shelter itself was almost hidden from view by two fallen trees. He selected the perfect location for them to sleep overnight.

She tried to keep her mind focused on the need for firewood and tinder that would burn throughout the darkest part of the night, but it was difficult. Now that the immediate danger was behind them, Lily's shivers increased and she trembled with cold. Earlier, Cahil warmed her with the merest brush of his hands over her body, though she knew that he only sought to assure himself of her wellbeing.

"I found a few armfuls of dry wood." Lily announced her presence, though her voice was uncommonly raspy and she was forced to clear her throat and try again.

"Good." Cahil's voice was clipped and she noticed that he did not look at her.

"I also found a few green plants that are good to eat." Lily gestured to the small pouch that she carried. "It will help fill the empty places in our bellies, at least for tonight."

Cahil nodded as he watched Lily set her burden down and return to the sparse outcropping of trees to gather more wood. He watched her every movement though he told himself to look away. His eyes lit upon her when she returned and he saw that the firelight flickered over her lovely features, lighting her burnished skin and the ebony sheen of her hair.

"I have set your clothing to dry beside the fire." Cahil indicated a place by the fire where he stacked pine boughs, so that she would not be forced to sit upon the cold ground. The temperature fell rapidly once the sun began to take its rest.

"Thank you." Lily murmured as she considered offering to share the sleeping fur with Cahil. He did not appear to be cold, though she knew that he must feel at least some of the brisk chill that encroached upon them.

"I will return shortly." Cahil glanced at Lily, before rising. She appeared fragile and small, sitting in the flickering light from the fire.

He wanted to comfort her, but he told himself that she would not welcome his attempt to do so. He reminded himself that Lily was young and untouched. He firmed his jaw as he chided himself for even considering pressing his attentions upon her, but there was a primal part of him that looked at her and claimed her as his.

From the moment that he first looked into her wide brown eyes, something within their liquid depths called to him. With a deep breath, Cahil forced himself to walk away.

Lily did not raise her head as she heard Cahil's retreating footsteps. Suddenly alone, fear for Simoi and the others caused her to gasp as she pressed a hand against her mouth. Now that she was seated by the warmth of the fire, the enormity of their situation caused her to recoil. Silent tears trickled down her face as she tried to contain her sobs. She hid her face in her hands, but a small sound escaped her lips as she struggled to stifle her sobs.

Wiping her face with both hands, she glanced up, determined to lift her chin bravely and remain strong. A shadow fell over her and she suddenly found Cahil standing above her, panting slightly as he watched her out of dark stormy eyes.

CHAPTER TWENTY

As he walked away, Cahil told himself that Lily would appreciate the quiet and warmth of the fire better if he didn't hover over her. He took a few steps away when he heard her gasp and though he continued to walk, he felt as if the pressure in his chest would crush him if he did not at least glance back.

The sight of Lily trying to quiet her sobs caused the air in his lungs to escape his lips with a hiss. He was surprised that she didn't hear him, but he also saw that she struggled valiantly to stem her flow of tears. She was brave and strong when the need arose and he could not have asked for anything more. Even though she was exhausted and hungry, she gathered dry wood and tinder, even going so far as to bring back edible plants so that they would not go to sleep hungry.

Without thinking, without giving himself time for doubts to arise, Cahil strode back to the fire and stood over Lily. When she looked up at him as if he hung the moon itself, he was lost.

Lily wasn't aware of moving, but she must have done so because suddenly Cahil was beside her and drew her onto his lap, where he held her in his arms, securing the fur around her.

"Cahil." Lily welcomed his touch and the warmth of his arms as he pressed light kisses against the side of her face and hair.

"Lily." Cahil murmured as she tilted her chin to look at him and he saw that her eyelashes were still wet from crying.

She bit her lower lip and he could see that she was at a loss as to how to respond, but he saw the passion in her eyes and he responded to it by pressing her closer to him and brushing her lips with his mouth.

A slight moan escaped her and he repeated the action, this time dragging his fingers through her hair as he loosened her braid. The feminine sounds that she made in the back of her throat as he wound her long hair around his fist and tilted her head so that he could sip from her lips caused him to groan.

Lily was suddenly aware of the width of his shoulders and the warmth of his bare chest. She kept her eyes closed as he pressed her against his chest where she listened to the throbbing drumbeat of his heart.

"I should not have touched you, but I will never regret it." Cahil spoke in a low murmur once he was able to find his voice.

"I would welcome your touch, were you to see me as I see you." Lily swallowed as her mouth went suddenly dry, she could not turn her face away as Cahil nudged her chin so that she was forced to look into the burning intensity of his eyes.

"How do you see me?" Cahil could not tell Lily that doubts assailed him. Ever since Delak spurned him for his brother, he doubted himself in a way that he would have never thought possible.

"I see you exactly as you are and I am drawn to the fire in your soul." Lily murmured, though she barely finished speaking when Cahil's lips claimed hers again and he lightly swept his tongue over the crease her lips.

"Open." He urged and Lily acquiesced though she did not know what to expect. Cahil ran his hands over her shoulders and arms, rubbing his fingertips over the sensitive flesh on the inside of her elbows. Lily gasped and he gently plundered her mouth, circling her tongue before reclaiming her lips. She was caught up in a swirling storm of wonder as tendrils of newfound passion stirred within her, settling deep inside like a smoldering fire.

Cahil kissed Lily with tenderness formerly unknown to him. Yet, he knew that she gave him a gift as she responded to him with an openness that stole his breath.

"I would not dishonor you, Lily." Cahil gasped as he lifted his head and stared into her eyes.

"Never." Lily agreed as Cahil moved his lips over the round surface of her cheeks.

"I have nothing to offer you." Cahil ground the words through clenched teeth as he struggled against the male hunger that raged inside of him. With Lily, there was a primal hunger that called to the wildness that lived inside of him. The mere thought of her being touched by any other man caused a physical ache to settle in his chest. "My brother now leads the Ula'tuk village and his wife is the same woman that I once sought to take as my lifemate."

Lily's eyes widened. "Your brother betrayed you by taking your mate?"

Cahil was silent as he watched Lily closely. "She never became my mate, nor was she the woman for me. I chose her for the wrong reasons entirely."

"Was she beautiful?" Lily bit her lip as she considered Cahil's past.

Cahil nodded. "I found out that she was bitter and rotten on the inside and I do not mourn the loss of her."

He came to realize that it was Lily that consumed his thoughts and his eyes must have betrayed him because Lily's gaze met his as he struggled to share his past with her.

He did not know if he could fully grasp the enormity of the changes in his life, but he knew that losing Lily would be more than he could endure. Despite the turmoil that swirled around him, he knew that if he hesitated, if he waited, he might be too late.

"I am a man without a village or a band. I was not certain that you could ever give your heart to me."

"I already have." Lily answered.

Cahil moaned deep in his throat as Lily lifted her tear brightened eyes to search his face.

"If I had one wish, it would be to claim you as my wife."

"Then you must follow your heart."

Cahil stood and wrapped Lily in his arms as he pressed kisses against her face. Lily's sighs of pleasure filled him with warmth as he gathered her close and inhaled her feminine scent. The need to touch her skin and feel her body pressed against his was overwhelming. Honor demanded that he speak and Cahil ground the words between his lips as he inhaled her warm breath.

"You are my wife, if you say so now." Cahil's entire body trembled as Lily raised wide, luminous eyes to meet his gaze. "I am your husband and lifemate, for the rest of my life."

"I am your wife and lifemate, for the rest of my life." Lily swallowed past the lump in her throat as Cahil kissed her, running his hands over her body, sending surging warmth through her like an unending river. She kept her eyes closed as he spread the sleeping fur over the spruce boughs and gently kissed her eyelids. His warm arms shielded her from the cold as they drifted together again.

He honored her with the tenderness of his touch and the reverent kiss of his lips until she no longer knew where he began and she ended. They clung to one another as they came together for the first time as husband and wife.

Cahil's heart thundered like the pounding of ancient drums. He couldn't find it within his heart to regret the way that he and Lily came together. Nor had he ever imagined that he would know such overriding passion along with the urge to protect her from harm.

Lily shivered in his embrace as he gently shifted her in his arms.

"Did I hurt you?"

She nuzzled his neck as she shook her head in denial.

Cahil groaned as her fingers traveled over his chest and shoulders. She wrapped her arms around his neck as she tentatively moved her mouth over his lips. He felt the hunger inside of him grow as Lily once again welcomed him into her arms.

My wife. He thought to himself as he growled low in his throat, giving in to the urge to possess her, to claim her again in the most elemental way.

She clung to him as he was in turns passionate and tender. They learned the mating dance together and when the dance ended, they fell into each other's arms sated and exhausted.

Cahil remained silent as he gathered Lily close until she settled comfortably in his arms. He was lost in thought as he felt her drift off to sleep, finally giving in to the battle against exhaustion. He was filled with pride that he made her feel safe and protected and he bowed his head over her slight form as he held her like a cherished gift in his arms while the stars shone overhead. An unaccustomed emotion swelled within his chest and he knew as he held Lily close that she was the woman of his heart. His woman, his wife.

Cahil barely slept and when Lily opened her eyes she was nestled in his arms, hidden from the wind by the shelter that protected them from the cold. He offered her a sip of water as she rinsed her mouth and avoided his direct gaze.

"Lily?" Cahil needed to hear that she didn't regret the vow that they made to each other in the dark of night.

"Yes, my husband?"

Cahil's heart clenched when she referred to him as her husband and he saw that her eyes twinkled with happiness. "How do you feel?"

Lily stretched as she considered his question. There was a slight discomfort, but she was not in any pain and she quickly shook her head. "Cahil, you make me feel as I have never felt before."

"I want you again." Lily's eyes widened as Cahil grabbed her by the hips and spanned her waist with his hands. "You are so small and delicate that I thought I might have harmed you."

"I think that I was made for you and you were made for me." Lily saw Cahil's eyes darken and she realized that he bared his soul to her. "I have given you my heart."

Cahil lifted her hand and pressed it against his chest. "I feel you in my heart, you reside here."

Lily felt the drumming beat beneath her palm and she lifted her face for her husband's kiss. They delighted in their newfound passion as early morning light began to filter through the clouds overhead. Cahil stood and checked Lily's clothing. They would have to leave immediately and search for a way across the river.

"Your clothing is dry. We should go now, before the sun fully rises, so that we can find a place to cross the river."

Lily was afraid to speak, she didn't want to let go of the remnants of the night.

"I will speak to your uncle as soon as we are safely on the other side of the river." Cahil's words reminded Lily that she would need to face her uncle. She lowered her gaze in shame, but he forced her chin up with light pressure from his fingers.

"Never do that." Cahil admonished as he gave Lily more water. "Never hide your thoughts from me."

"I am merely ashamed of my behavior." Lily answered, giving him the honest response that he demanded.

"You have no reason to feel shame, Lily." Cahil helped her rise. "I am honored that you have consented to become my wife and I will find a way to reason with Simoi."

Lily sighed in relief as Cahil's eyes swept over her and she found that she was accustomed to his assessing gaze. She straightened her backbone and lifted her head as a possessive gleam entered his eyes.

She quickly helped him bank the fire and remove all traces of their presence as was the way of the people of the great land. Cahil dismantled their shelter and bundled several dead branches with a length of vine before slinging the load over his back. He offered her the fur cape that kept her warm on their journey and she quickly donned the warm garment, raising the hood to cover her hair. The newness of their union caused her hands to tremble slightly, but Cahil kissed her palms and tucked her hands into the crook of his arm, so that he could warm them.

"We must hurry." Cahil extended his hand to Lily and he was content to walk beside her as they quickly moved toward the river.

They were both ravenous and they ate the leafy greens that Lily gathered the night before as they walked.

He searched the ground before finding the place where they managed to land after the ice began to break. In the distance, the sun broke over the horizon, spilling rich crimson shards of deepest red over the land.

Cahil and Lily walked along the river, scurrying over boulders, rocks and outcroppings of stone as they tried to find a likely place to cross. He could see the distant riverbank and he sighed heavily as he considered the dangers of moving out over the ice with Lily. If the ice gave way they would plunge into the freezing water with no hope of escape.

Lily was precious in his sight and he could not risk her life. They walked until the sun was high in the sky and then Cahil suddenly stopped and stared at a large mass of ice that rose up from the partially frozen river. To his relief, Lily did not trail behind him when he admonished her to wait. Cahil caught sight of a fallen tree that hung over the river below and he edged out onto the limb as he tested its sturdiness.

Satisfied, he hurried back to Lily and urged her to follow him, just as they heard a familiar shout.

"Simoi!" Lily's heart sped up as she caught sight of Simoi and the others. They were at a narrow place in the river and if she understood Cahil's intentions they would try to cross by way of the fallen tree.

"Steady and slow." Cahil lifted Lily until her feet rested securely against the tree and he climbed up behind her. He kept an eye on her shuffling footsteps as he considered the brisk pace that they set by walking until they were both near exhaustion.

Lily's legs trembled with the strain of the day and she was not unaware of the danger that they faced as the looming mound of ice drifted ever closer. She felt Cahil's presence behind her like a steady hand, though he did not touch her, nor did they speak.

"Jump, Lily!" Cahil clasped her hand and urged her to jump as they landed on the mound of ice below.

CHAPTER TWENTY-ONE

Simoi's heart leapt into his throat as he watched Lily and Cahil take the only chance left to them. He and the others walked along the river as far as their legs could carry them and they could not find an easier place to cross. He saw that Cahil took the brunt of the fall, turning so that Lily landed at an angle on top of him.

They managed to stop their slide across the ice mass by sheer will power. Cahil grabbed hold of Lily's fur parka as she slid toward the edge of the ice, his hold upon her clothing was the only thing that stopped her from tumbling into the icy torrent.

"Hurry!" Anuk's shout broke the stunned silence that fell over their band.

Simoi and Gisik reached out toward Cahil and Lily as they gained their feet and judged the distance between the moving ice mass and the river's edge.

Cahil felt time slow as he stared hard at the fast moving water which separated them from the river's edge and safety. He saw the anguish on Simoi's face as the man watched Lily, his niece. Simoi kept his eyes upon Lily as she moved toward the edge of the ice mass.

"Cahil." Lily spoke his name in a low moan of terror which swept through him, bringing out his protective instincts, though they were at the mercy of the river.

"Together, Lily." Cahil turned to face Lily, pressing her against the warmth of his chest where she could hear his heartbeat. "You have to be brave. Take courage!"

Cahil did not give her time to wallow in doubt or fear. He urged her back a few steps and then swept her forward, with him, over the edge of the ice and toward the safety of land.

Water swept beneath them as they flew through the air. Cahil swung his arm forward sending Lily skidding across the ice toward Gisik and Anuk. He hit the ground hard, clinging to the snow covered riverbank as he lost his handhold and slid toward the fast moving water below.

Suddenly, Simoi was there, grabbing hold of Cahil's fur parka and hauling him up from the open maw of the icy river. Cahil kicked with his legs, propelling himself up and forward as Simoi pulled with all of his strength.

"Is she safe?" Cahil's entire body trembled from the strain of the last few moments, but he could not rest until he saw for himself that Lily was unharmed.

"Lily is safe." Simoi responded as gratitude filled his gaze. "I must thank you for saving my niece's life."

"Simoi, there is something that I need to tell you." Cahil felt the eyes of the entire band travel over them as Simoi watched him. "I have taken Lily as my lifemate, my wife."

Simoi gaped at Cahil as Lily stood next to him. He took a deep breath as he considered the matter. "Lily, is this true?"

"Yes, Uncle. I consented to become Cahil's wife." Lily raised her gaze to meet Simoi's and she saw that he was shocked and displeased.

"You could have waited until you gained my approval!" Simoi's eyes narrowed in anger, but Cahil shifted forward as if to block Lily from his outburst.

"The fault is mine." Cahil offered. "I will shoulder the blame for ignoring your wishes."

"What about offering a gift to my hearth for the right to join with my niece?" Simoi asked. "Lily has always been a dutiful niece and I would have made certain that you honored her before taking her as your mate."

"Then you will have my help with the caribou hunt and any animal that I strike with my spear will be given to you as a gift for the right to be Lily's lifemate." Cahil was aware of Anuk watching him out of wide eyes. Gisik glared at him angrily while Saghani merely stood by with her head lowered so that he could not see her face.

"I have no choice but to accept your offer." Simoi glanced between Lily and Cahil. "I would like to hear Lily tell me that she became your wife of her own free will."

Cahil looked at Lily and he breathed deeply as she found the courage to meet her uncle's penetrating gaze. "I chose him of my own free will. He is my husband."

"She is my wife." Cahil announced as Simoi nodded and the others wore mixed expressions of surprise.

"Did you see the fast flowing river and the way that Lily pushed Saghani across so that she would not fall in?" Anuk continued to repeat the story of their daring river crossing as evening fell. He spoke to anyone that would listen, despite their having firsthand knowledge of the events that took place.

"Yes, we saw." Simoi indulged Anuk's natural exuberance even as the rest of the band dragged themselves forward by sheer force of will.

"I knew that Lily would be well because Cahil was by her side throughout the night. He is a hunter and knows the land, even though we are in an unknown area, it is much the same as the land surrounding the Ula'tuk village."

"Just so." Simoi could not help but notice that there was a newfound peace within his niece and if he was not mistaken, Cahil rarely took his eyes away from Lily's slender form.

Much to the relief of the others, Gisik managed to find two ptarmigan which he brought down with the use of his bola. He plucked the birds clean of feathers and handed them to Saghani without a word spoken between them. The young woman meekly accepted the offering as she hurried to dress the birds and prepare their evening meal. The tension between Saghani and Lily was palpable, but the two women had yet to speak to each other and the men were grateful for the quiet and Simoi was loath to intervene.

Gisik shuffled over to Lily and extended an offering to her. "A new scraping stone, a good gift for a new wife."

Cahil's jaw clenched as Lily politely accepted the sharp stone.

"Did you see Gisik give Lily a gift for becoming a wife?" Anuk called out to Cahil as he came to sit beside him. Cahil added more wood to the fire, ignoring Anuk's question. Undeterred, Anuk nudged him in the side and pointed at the display of feathers. "Cahil, did you see?"

"Yes, Anuk, I saw." Cahil growled as Simoi glanced up with a question in his eyes.

"It is a good gift." Anuk proclaimed as Gisik drifted away from the fire circle to walk the perimeter during the night. "I have nothing to offer your wife, but perhaps I will find something along the way."

Simoi gathered his sleeping furs close as he wrapped the garment around him and closed his eyes. Cahil watched him for a moment as he tried to determine if Simoi was actually sleeping or merely resting.

"He sleeps." Anuk pronounced decisively as Cahil glared at him.

"Anuk, perhaps you can see if Saghani needs help with the evening meal." Cahil gestured toward the fire where Saghani worked to turn the birds upon a hastily constructed spit. He thought that he saw Anuk's mouth water at the mere mention of food. The young man clamped his lips together and nodded eagerly as he scrambled closer to Saghani.

Cahil glanced again at Simoi before turning his gaze to Lily. She stroked her hands over the stone as he watched. For some reason, it bothered him that Gisik offered her such a personal gift. The scraping stone would be well used, but what mattered most was that Lily would use the stone often and think of Gisik. He realized that he wanted to provide her with small gifts, as well as colorful adornments and decorative trappings that women often cherished.

"I would offer you a trade for the scraping stone." Cahil did not know where the words came from and he was surprised that Simoi managed to keep his eyes closed as he feigned sleep. Lily glanced up in startled concern as she met Cahil's eyes. "A trade?"

"Yes. I have a use for such a sharp stone and you might have a use for this." Cahil held out his clasped hand as Lily waited.

She gasped in delight as he opened his hand to display the bone bracelet that graced his palm. The moonlight made the bracelet glow like freshly fallen snow as Cahil held the trinket up for her inspection.

"Where did you find such a wondrous thing?" Lily asked as she moved closer to him.

He was distracted by the fall of her hair as it shifted about her shoulders and he remembered the weight and gossamer soft feel of it in his hands, wrapped around his wrist like a tether holding them together. Raw male hunger flared inside, sending a tremor down the length of his body. Up close, he saw once again that Lily's brown eyes were flecked with amber shards, highlighted by the fire.

"I traded for the bracelet many seasons ago." Cahil answered as Lily's lips parted on a sigh.

"Are you certain that you have need of a sharp stone? I would not wish to hurt Gisik's feelings."

Cahil saw that she was sincere and he almost laughed as he thought of the large, battle-scarred warrior that often grunted or growled in response to a question. He was uncertain whether or not Gisik's feelings could actually be in danger of injury, but he saw that Lily spoke in earnest.

"I am certain." Cahil waited impatiently as Lily reached out to touch the bracelet.

Small bits of bone were pierced through and linked with strands of sinew. The bracelet was just the right size to fit over a young woman's hand. He could not say for certain why it was so important that he take Gisik's gift from Lily, but when she nodded in acceptance, he quickly handed the bracelet to her.

"It is a good trade." Simoi remarked as his eyes opened and he was once again watchful and alert.

Cahil and Lily jerked apart as they turned toward him. Lily's eyes were wide and innocent, whereas Cahil's face was devoid of expression. He knew all along that Simoi was not truly sleeping, from what he learned during their journey, Simoi never went to sleep hungry if it could be avoided.

Simoi accepted a portion of the ptarmigan from Saghani and as he ate, his eyes gleamed with hidden amusement.

CHAPTER TWENTY-TWO

The next day brought a swell of excitement and a feeling of promise that was contagious. The streaks of crimson and burnished coral that spanned the sky were slowly devoured by billowing clouds. Simoi's steps were firm as he led the way to the Krahnan band, with the others following along in a single line.

In the distance, a dark cloud appeared to hover over the land, but as they drew closer, Cahil identified a massive herd of caribou. The herd moved at an easy pace, eating their fill as they searched the ground for fallen leaves, sedges and mushrooms.

"The hunters from the gathered bands will not hunt the caribou until they observe the first hunting ceremony." Simoi spoke by way of explanation as he observed the caribou herd which moved without fear.

Cahil did not know why Simoi appeared absolutely convinced that the gathering ceremony would not take place without them.

"I would have searched for a husband for my niece from amongst the bands that gather here to observe the sacred ceremonies." Simoi walked ahead of the others as Cahil kept step with him.

Cahil lifted his head as he met Simoi's gaze. "Is it important to you that I observe the sacred ceremonies that you adhere to?"

"Now that you are Lily's husband it is of vital importance." Simoi answered immediately as Cahil digested his response. "The ceremonies that are observed are not only for the benefit of the various bands, but a repayment for a good season of hunting, fishing and good fortune. Everything in existence has been given a life force and it is no small thing to take the life of an animal, eat of its flesh and live another day. The gathering ceremonies also mark the passage of time. In effect, the ceremonies honor the great land and the blessings given to those that seek a means to ensure their survival."

Simoi painted a vivid picture that Cahil was able to see in his mind's eye. He respected the ways of the hunt and often uttered a few words of thanksgiving over a successful kill, but he didn't feel the reverence that he sensed within Simoi.

A spark of interest lit his eyes as he considered the lack of something vital that he sensed, but didn't understand. The certainty in Simoi's voice was a lure that captured his interest as curiosity won out and he decided that he would attend the gathering ceremonies, if only to assure himself that he lacked nothing in return.

"It is good that you have decided to seek answers to your questions about the sacred mounds. There is an elder here, a man of many seasons that might be able to answer some of your questions." Simoi's expression changed as he stared into the distance.

"I will seek him out."

"You should know that there is a man that has marked himself as my enemy. The Krahnan band has established a boundary that marks the land as theirs, even though this is not the way of the people that walk the great land."

Cahil knew that many bands roved about, though if they chose a living place or an encampment they did so out of necessity or because of an abundance of food and game. He was surprised to hear that Simoi was capable of calling any man his enemy and in a sense, he felt as if he also inherited the man's foes.

"Umak and the men that walk with him violated three women and then took their lives." Simoi's eyes darkened as he turned to face Cahil. "Lily and Saghani were gathering berries nearby when Umak and his men attacked."

Cahil's gaze sought Lily as if to assure himself that she was unharmed. Her blue-black hair drew his attention as she flicked her long braid over her shoulder and inclined her head toward Anuk. Lily's natural grace drew the eye and he found himself captivated by her before he was able to drag his gaze away.

"Were they harmed?"

"They were not touched by Umak and his men, but there are some scars that are hidden from the eyes. Lily and Saghani were young girls at the time. However, Umak would have dishonored them just as he did the young women of the Krahnan band and I have no doubt that they would not have been allowed to live." Simoi's mouth twisted bitterly. "When I found them, the girls were huddled together with Umak standing over their hiding place."

Cahil's gut twisted as Simoi spoke bitterly. "I would have killed Umak where he stood, but my mistake was in bringing him before the council of elders."

"How is it that he still lives?" Cahil could not understand how the man was allowed to continue breathing.

"Only Lily and Saghani saw the faces of the men that attacked and killed the Krahnan women." Simoi's eyes were devoid of expression as he turned to face Cahil. "The elders and other men of the Krahnan band were not willing to accept the firsthand account given by two frightened children and they were unwilling to end Umak's life without due cause."

"Who is Umak, that he should strike fear into the hearts of men?"

"He is the son of the leader of his band and the son of a man that I once called brother and friend." Simoi clutched his throwing spear in his right hand. During their journey, he worked to strengthen the arm that was injured in battle and his diligent efforts showed as he raised the spear like an extension of his limb. "Umak deserves to die for his treachery and I will see him brought to his end."

"If killing Umak will bring dishonor upon your name, you should have avoided the hunters' gathering at all costs." Cahil's brow furrowed in concern, as Simoi's eyes clouded with an unreadable expression before he shook his head in answer. He raised his palms to the sky and spread his hands in a sweeping gesture that encompassed the wide domain around them.

"I have every reason to return. If the bands that gather together observe the gathering ceremony, they will receive a sign in the form of radiant dancing lights that appear in the heavens. It is like nothing you have ever seen before. The heavens spread like lightening dancing over water, but lifted high into the sky and with more color than anything in the world. It is a rare occurrence, but far more beautiful because of the good fortune that is sure to follow."

Cahil considered Simoi's words as he stared into the distance. Anger burned in his chest like a physical pain when he considered the threat that Umak posed to Simoi and his band along with the thought of any harm befalling his wife. Yet, he realized that the quelling numbness that had been with him since his father's death no longer blurred the world around him into indistinct shapes and images. Ever since he took Lily as his wife, he felt settled deep in his spirit.

"We will reach the Krahnan band before sunset and then you will have to ask the questions that you have withheld until now. Perhaps you will remember that I have been a friend to you, just as you have been a friend to me during this journey."

Cahil was surprised that Simoi felt the need to issue such a reminder. He nodded his acceptance even as Simoi inclined his head and said, "Welcome home."

A lone figure was hidden by a copse of trees overlooking the great land. From his vantage point, he could see far into the distance. Over the past several days, various bands arrived at the encampment claimed by the Krahnan band, but they did not arouse his interest. He watched for one band in particular and he waited patiently for their arrival.

His chiseled features hardened as he caught sight of a small group that slowly drifted forward. He waited impatiently for their features to become easily identifiable.

He lived amongst men that were known simply as hunters, yet he was something more, something different. By nature he was a killer of men, taking what he could from those weaker than himself. Others feared him and he relished the widening of their eyes and the distance that they gave him whenever he walked across their path.

Long black hair graced his shoulders and his tawny skin was coated with bear grease, giving his face a sheen that matched the glittering hardness of his eyes. He stood tall, though he was not overly muscular, instead he was lean, powerful and strong. His eyes narrowed and his nostrils flared as he scented the wind, giving his features a hawkish expression that defined who he was at heart. He was a winged predator walking in the skin of a man.

The people of Simoi's band were too far away to notice the lone man that watched their approach. They did not see him blend into the shadows of the nearby copse of trees, nor did they see his eyes light with remembered rage when he caught sight of Simoi, the man that hounded his footsteps in the past.

"I see that you have returned, though you would have done well to remain far away where you would be safe from the reach of my spear." His mouth twisted ironically as he noticed that Nimiuq was missing. "Has the old man finally died?"

The smaller figures of the women caught his attention and his mouth flattened as he remembered the faces of two frightened girls. "But they are no longer children. Nimiuq's granddaughter is a woman fully grown and the other girl, Simoi's niece, is ripe for the taking."

A larger man walked at the rear of Simoi's band and he snorted in disdain as Gisik's battle-scarred features came into focus. Gisik's eyes were constantly in motion, but he looked in the wrong direction. Gisik expected to see his enemy waiting with the rest of the gathered bands, but he would be disappointed to learn that he was outmatched and outsmarted.

The man started to turn away, but then his attention was captured by a gangly youth that ran to catch up with Gisik. He almost missed the last man that walked behind the others. The newcomer was completely unknown to him, but there was something in his bearing and posture that was familiar.

He saw that the man did not carry himself in the way of a hunter. Instead, he walked as a warrior, with his head up, feet carefully planted with each footstep and eyes that were alert and watchful. On his back, he hauled a carrying pack while his water skin and hunting knife rested near his waist. There was nothing about the man to mark him as different, yet he sensed a threat in the way that that the newcomer held himself and the noticeable lack of expression upon his face.

He stood to his full height as he recognized an adversary that was both formidable and strong. His nostrils flared. One wild animal scenting another. He froze as the man turned his head to peer directly at him.

A low growl rumbled in his chest and he almost stepped forward in challenge, but the wind whispered through the trees and he heard a message given to him by the land. The man could not see him watching and he was unaware of his presence.

"I am Umak, son of the great land. You do not know me, but you will."

Without another glance, Umak disappeared into the copse of trees that shivered in the chill wind. He was welcomed by cold dark shadows and gloom. They accepted him as a kindred spirit, recognizing him for what he was. One of their own.

Cahil lifted his head and stared into the distance as the others hurried forward. He saw Anuk run to catch up with Gisik, who finally relaxed his guard long enough to walk with the others. He could not say why he decided to fall behind Simoi's band, but he was overwhelmed by the sights and sounds of the encampment.

There were more people than he expected gathered together in one place to observe sacred ceremonies and take part in the hunt. Skin lodges dotted the land from one side of the encampment to the other, but he saw at a glance that they were organized, possibly by band or family unit. The colorful adornment on the outside of each lodge fascinated him. Some of the people painted the hide covering of their lodge and a few decorated the entrance with shells, feathers and beading. Cahil recognized the hides of many animals used for the construction of the temporary lodges, amongst which were sealskin, bison and caribou. The scent of many fires drifted on the breeze, as well as the delicious aromas that came from the preparation of food.

The wind caressed his face and he lifted his head as he stared hard at a large copse of trees nearby. The fine hairs on the back of his neck stood up and he felt certain that he was being watched.

All eyes turned toward them as Simoi called out to the men and women that were in the midst of various tasks. Children ran unhampered through the milling crowd and Cahil forgot his earlier wariness as he watched the men, women and children of the great land.

He saw Lily's face light up with happiness as she was embraced by several women. Saghani was also welcomed, though less enthusiastically. Anuk's posture told him that the youth was uncertain of himself and his surroundings, but that did not stop him from approaching a group of young men close to his age. As with many young men, they stared at one another silently before comparing weapons and gesturing widely as they boasted of their success in the hunt.

Simoi spread out his arm toward him and Cahil knew that he was being discussed, though he was not surprised. It appeared that most of the people were either related or close to the others that gathered together.

"Cahil, I need to speak with you." Anuk broke off from the group of youths as he moved quickly to Cahil's side.

"It can wait, Anuk."

Cahil tore his gaze away from Lily. He was close enough to see the faces of the two elders that approached Simoi. Silence descended upon the crowd as the others backed away while Simoi spoke quietly with the two older men.

Despite the onset of the cold season, the exertion from walking caused sweat to dampen his chest and torso. Cahil removed his warm weather parka and set it down upon the ground with his carrying pack and water skin. He left his spear behind, though his hunting knife rode on his hip. It was not uncommon to see other men bare-chested with only their leggings and foot coverings. Most of the hunters knew that it was best not to sweat if it could be avoided.

The two older men lowered their heads and Cahil thought that Simoi must have told them about Nimiuq's death. An unfamiliar well of sadness opened deep inside as he remembered Nimiuq.

"I do not believe that it can wait, have you noticed anything odd about some of the people, especially the men?" Anuk's voice wavered with nervousness and Cahil absently brushed his hand away as he continued forward.

"Anuk, it is only normal to be nervous upon first meeting a new band, yet, as you grow older you must learn to control your response." Cahil dismissed Anuk as the youth stared at him with wide eyes.

Satisfied that he gave Anuk sound advice, Cahil returned his attention to the matter at hand.

It appeared that Simoi and Gisik never disclosed to Saghani or Lily that he was responsible for ending Nimiuq's suffering. Cahil did not know why that was important to him, but he didn't want Lily to look at him in fear. The women hadn't heard Nimiuq's agonizing pleas to die with honor and they would never understand why he chose to end Nimiuq's horrific suffering.

As Cahil met Lily's compassionate gaze, he thought perhaps he was wrong to dismiss her ability to understand his actions. She smiled with encouragement when he stepped forward and Simoi and the other two men turned toward him.

Once again, Simoi's hand swept toward him in entreaty. "You are welcome amongst the various bands of the great land. Come forward and meet Suntar and Ashish, two honorable elders of the Krahnan band."

"Wait! I must speak with you." Anuk shook Cahil's arm and he glared at the youth as he stepped forward.

"Do not interrupt." Cahil saw Anuk's eyes dim as he was duly chastised. The youth would have to learn that there was a time for such things and that time was not now.

He noticed that Suntar stood at least a head taller than Simoi and his face was creased with time and age. His eyes crinkled at the corners as he smiled in greeting. Ashish stood closer to Simoi's height, though his face was round and his body was a close match. Both men were of a similar age to Nimiuq and as such, they were to be shown honor and respect. Cahil strode forward to stand at Simoi's side.

"I greet you, honored elders."

He bowed his head and included both men in his greeting as they nodded, though he noticed that the man called Ashish looked at him in open astonishment. He stared at the necklace that adorned his bare chest and his mouth opened and closed without sound.

Cahil's hand automatically reached for the ivory pendant that hung at the end of a length of braided hide. He managed to avoid the unnecessary gesture by relaxing his arms so that his hands remained at his sides.

"I need to speak with you, right now." Anuk once again chose the wrong moment to interrupt, despite the quelling glare that Cahil sent his way. He shook his head once in a request for silence before returning his attention to the older men.

"What is your name?" Ashish spoke in a sharp voice and the men and women nearby stopped what they were doing to watch the proceedings with renewed interest.

Cahil looked at the older man and he noticed that his face drained of color. "Are you unwell?"

Anuk jostled his arm, but Cahil's full attention was on the elder when he spoke as if the sound was torn from his chest.

"Your name!" Ashish responded in a tone that demanded an immediate response.

"Cahil."

"No! It is impossible." Suntar clasped his hands over his heart as he turned wide eyes upon Simoi. "Did you know?"

"I suspected, but I did not know until now. He has recently become the lifemate of my niece." Simoi stared at Ashish who blinked rapidly as he struggled to speak. "I believe that Saghani's grandfather knew all along."

"Knew what? Simoi, what has happened?"

Cahil was not certain if he erred in some way, but he was aware of the odd reactions from the honored Krahnan elders and at the edge of his gaze. Lily came to stand at side and he took her hand, while Saghani and Gisik stood to his left. Anuk widened his eyes as he looked around and then returned his gaze pointedly toward Cahil. If there was a message in his expression, Cahil could not fathom what it could be.

"Simoi?" Cahil could not take his eyes away from the faces of Suntar and Ashish, both men stared at him as if he was an apparition.

"He is the image of our leader reborn." Ashish spoke in a voice filled with wonder. "He even wears the same pendant that has only been worn by our former leaders since times long lasting until now!"

"The time of despair has ended, many of the ones that strayed from our band will now return!" Suntar's voice rose as he raised his palms to the sky and spoke an incantation that caused the skin on Cahil's arms to prickle with unease.

He remembered that Simoi took a similar stance when he asked for a blessing from the heavens during their journey and it troubled him that he was the object of their focus.

Without turning his eyes away from the older men, he spoke in a low, sharp tone to Simoi. "What is it that you failed to tell me?"

CHAPTER TWENTY-THREE

Word quickly spread through the encampment that something of importance was taking place. Men and women whispered and murmured as each one tried to search out Suntar and Ashish, the elders of the Krahnan band. Those that were close enough to overhear, remained carefully silent as expectation and interest washed over the onlookers.

Simoi stepped closer to Cahil and Lily as Suntar finished speaking in a language unknown to him. "You have not noticed the faces of the other men."

Cahil felt as if his mind was clouded with one thought after another. Their entrance drew a crowd, but he was caught off guard by the greeting of the Krahnan elders and he failed to look closely at the other men.

He noticed their weapons first, tools of the hunt, made of bone, sinew and stone. He saw well made spears and hunting knives, along with bolas, snares and traps that were either in the process of being made or resting at their waists.

Their clothing was unlike his, but very similar to what was worn by Simoi and Gisik. Warm weather parka's turned fur side out exposed their chests and torsos, along with their arms. Several of the men wore leggings that fit close to the skin and all or most wore similar foot coverings, moccasins that came to mid calf or as high as the knee. Some of the men wore decorated moccasins or preferably mukluks, displaying an array of colorful stitches, shell beading, small feathers and sharp teeth from past kills.

Still, it was difficult to meet the eyes of the men that belonged to the various bands of the great land. With a deep breath, Cahil raised his eyes even as Lily squeezed his hand in silent support.

He could not say which man caught his attention first, but his eyes widened as he took in their features. Some of the men were completely unfamiliar in appearance, but as he continued to look closely, he saw that several of their faces were eerily similar to the reflection that he saw in clear pools. Their eyes were his eyes, their noses and lips, his alone. He noticed sloped noses and oval nostrils along with the familiar line of his own jaw and chin.

"I look similar to many of the men."

Cahil touched his face as he turned his attention back to Ashish and Suntar. Their wizened faces hid their features from him upon first meeting, but now he saw definable similarities and he realized that they were older versions of himself.

"No." Simoi said as he raised his eyebrows and met Cahil's eyes. "They look like you."

"Now do you wish to hear what I have to say?" Anuk grumbled as Cahil stared at the elders in fascination, confusion and wonder.

"How can this be?" Cahil questioned as Ashish and Suntar ushered them through the milling crowd.

"Cahil has returned to the Krahnan band! The days of darkness are behind us!" The pronouncement of the elders rippled through the crowd and Cahil stood still as the men and women moved forward as one, whispering his name and reaching out to touch him with hands that were almost worshipful. Lily clung to his hand, apparently as shocked by the turn of events as he was.

Simoi and those of his band trailed along, while Anuk ran in starts and fits, only to slow to a walk when he outdistanced the others.

"There is one that you must meet, though you do not appear to remember him." Ashish refused to answer Cahil's questions and the older man's flashing eyes were obstinate. "There is little time to delay."

"Simoi." Cahil turned his head toward the man that he considered to be his friend as he tried to elude the clinging hands of the people, some of the women wept and the older men looked at him with shining eyes. He noticed that the men that were near his own age listened to the wise, older ones that whispered in their ears and he wished that he was privy to the secrets that were shared. "What does this mean?"

"Saghani's grandfather." Simoi swallowed as he spoke of Nimiuq and Cahil recognized the spark of grief that caused his voice to thicken. "He knew that your name was familiar, but I never questioned him on the matter and he also recognized the pendant that you wear around your neck."

"My name? What does that have to do with the strange greeting that I have received?" Cahil glanced at Lily before releasing her hand. He clasped the pendant that swayed with every step and he held it up and inspected it with a critical eye as the people around them gasped as one. The design was foreign to him, but he realized that it meant something to Ashish and Suntar. He stared at the three interlocking ivory spheres that had been painstakingly crafted by a skilled hand.

"Cahil, you have the same appearance as the man that once led the Krahnan band."

"Is my appearance the reason that the elders are angry?" Cahil knew that there were many things that were forbidden within individual bands, not to mention various offenses that he might have unknowingly committed. It was for this reason that he had been very careful in his greeting of the Krahnan elders. However, he could no more change his face than he could take wings and fly. He glanced at Lily's frightened face and he willed himself to remain calm. She smiled tremulously as he returned his attention to Simoi.

"They are not angry." Simoi responded.

Cahil noticed that Lily's eyes were filled with an emotion that he could not name. His attention returned to Simoi and the older men as they approached a dwelling which had been made from large bones and the stretched skins of caribou hides, held fast by long poles that were firmly set in place by rocks anchored into the soil.

"Long ago we were a strong band, but most of our people have been scattered across the land." Ashish stared at him as if he expected a specific response, but Cahil remained silent. "This is the lodge of one our most revered elders, his daughter's husband was the former leader of the Krahnan band."

"Simoi." Cahil ground the words through his clenched jaw as Ashish and Suntar watched him without speaking. "Explain."

"All will be well." Simoi said with a nod that was unconvincing. "Go inside and speak to the most honored elder of the Krahnan band. I will stay with your wife until you are finished."

Cahil glanced again at Lily as she nodded and pressed her lips together.

"Keep her safe." He speared Simoi with a glare that would have felled a weaker man and then he scratched upon the lodge entrance flap made of animal hide, as he entered in one fluid motion.

The scent of sickness was carefully cloaked by sage, which burned in the center of the lodge. The smoke escaped out of a hole at the top of the dwelling and as Cahil looked around he saw that it was far more spacious inside than he expected.

A figure lay upon sleeping furs at the back of the lodge and Cahil cleared his throat as he tried to see into the shadows. His heart pounded, causing the sound of drums to fill his ears.

The figure shifted and Cahil saw an elderly man with long hair as white as newly fallen snow and features that were weathered with age. The man moved as he drew closer and Cahil wondered if he should announce his presence. The polite clearing of one's throat was usually enough to draw attention. He knelt upon one knee and breathed in deeply as he tried to slow the furious beating of his heart.

"Come closer."

Cahil was surprised to see that the elderly man was not only aware of his presence, but alert and watchful. The elder stared at him with a piercing gaze that appeared to see through him, down to the place of spirit. When the older man motioned for him to sit close to his side, Cahil bowed his head in acknowledgement though he would have preferred to sit across the small fire that burned low.

"Honored elder." Cahil thought of the men of the Krahnan band, they were hunters all, but they also held their spears in the way of warriors.

If erred, though unknowingly, his transgression might have placed Simoi's entire band in danger. Lily's face flashed through his mind as he was finally able to discern the veiled expression etched upon her face and echoed by her eyes. Concern.

She was concerned for him and he was moved to speak in a respectful tone as he asked for forgiveness. "If I have erred in some way, please accept my humble apology. I am not aware of the ways of your band and I did not seek to offend those that dwell here."

Cahil silently cursed Simoi for leaving him unprepared.

He was also angry with himself for not asking more questions during their journey, but he was distracted with the everyday struggle for survival.

A fit of derisive laughter almost escaped him, but the older man struggled to lift himself into a sitting position and his feeble appearance caused Cahil to inhale sharply. He respectfully turned his eyes away as the man adjusted his position so that he sat against the lodge wall. Every instinct told him that the honorable elder would not welcome his assistance and when he turned his eyes back to the older man he saw that he was correct.

Pride surrounded the man like a cloak. A harsh cough escaped the man's lips as he wiped his mouth with a clean strip of hide. He extended his hand and Cahil was at a loss, until his fingers curled in a beckoning gesture and he saw that the elder's eyes were riveted on his necklace.

Though reluctant to do so, Cahil removed the necklace and handed it to the elder. He could only hope that the man would not mistake his intentions. Often a gift was offered when a newcomer came to a band or village, but the necklace was not something that he would ever willingly give away.

He watched as the older man traced his finger over the pendant with reverence before handing it back. Once again, the man studied his face with an enigmatic gaze that was both compelling and wise.

"I never thought that I would live to see this day. If only my daughter and her husband could have seen your return."

The man's voice was soothing and somehow familiar, like the sound of many rivers rushing toward the great water. Cahil blinked as he realized that he had been momentarily lost in a memory that was not quite formed and then his eyes focused as the elder reached out a feeble hand to him.

"Cahil." A sheen of tears filled the older man's eyes before another racking cough seized him.

Cahil tried not to notice the man's frailty, but in the warmth of the lodge the elder was clothed only in a loincloth which displayed his chest and legs without the bulk of clothing. He saw that the man's flesh, while clean, barely clung to his bones and his chest was thin, though his flat stomach and muscle tone spoke of a life lived upon the great land as a strong hunter.

"How is it that you know my name?"

"I know your name because it was once well known to me and our entire band." The feeble elder struggled for breath as he speared Cahil with a glare that held the strength of youth.

"I see." Cahil remarked as he realized how rare that must be for the Krahnan band. Like many of the people of the great land, a name was not shared. Many thought that if a child shared the same name as an adult, then the spirit itself would be lost and confused. Likewise, the names of the dead were not spoken, yet the elderly man said that his daughter and her husband no longer lived.

"You have the look of my daughter's husband and the son that was born to their hearth." The elder wiped his eyes as he peered at him.

Cahil saw the resemblance between himself and several of the other men. He could understand why the elder was moved to tears to see a man that reminded him of his lost daughter and her husband.

"Perhaps your grandson and I will become friends." Cahil said in a tone that he hoped would comfort the elder and ease the way for Simoi's band.

The elder's laughter surprised him, for it sounded both bitter and joyous. Cahil found himself staring at the man in confusion. The elder extended a small wooden bowl and Cahil accepted the offering as he waited for any indication of how he should proceed. The man motioned for him to drink and Cahil knew that to refuse was to offend. He drank the contents in one long swallow and found that the taste of the drink was vaguely familiar.

"That would be impossible." The elder coughed harshly as he struggled for breath in response to Cahil's earlier statement.

"I see." The aftertaste of the drink and the scent itself spoke to him, though he could not bring the memories to the fore. Suddenly feeling vaguely nauseous, Cahil considered how he could take his leave without causing offense.

"No." The elder spoke sharply. "You do not see, but I see clearly and my heart knows only joy. You are Cahil, the son of my daughter and her husband who was once the former leader of our band. Your father was a man of great strength and might. You have finally returned, though we thought that you were lost forever, taken from us in your childhood by a vengeful enemy."

Cahil would have spoken, he would have found something to say that would pacify the pain that he saw lance through the elder's gaze, but there was a humming sound in his mind that grew until it was a dull throb. The pain merged into a vicious pounding and he pressed his hands against his eyes as he struggled against a void that threatened to steal his soul.

CHAPTER TWENTY-FOUR

When Cahil opened his eyes, he saw the toothless smile of the elder peering down at him. He scrambled to a sitting position as dizziness swept over him and he took in his surroundings. The lodge walls were familiar and he remembered that he was in the dwelling of a Krahnan elder, but his mind felt as if it drifted in fog.

"I will not tell the others that you, a strong warrior and a brave hunter, lost consciousness at the feet of one old man." The elder laughed for a moment before his face sobered. "Do you remember what happened?"

"You gave me something to drink, something that caused me to see double and stop breathing." Cahil could not hide the accusation in his voice.

"I gave you bitter berry juice. The same brew that our children drink in the warm season." The man's eyes were clear and devoid of any deceit. "You learned that you were my grandson, Cahil, the son of my daughter and her husband, the former leader of the Krahnan band and then you slid to the ground, like a tree falling."

Cahil blinked to clear his vision so that he could glare at the older man. He tried to remind himself that he was speaking to an honored elder.

"You are mistaken."

"I do not lie." The response was immediate and once again he caught a glimpse of the man that the elder had been in his youth.

"I am simply a man like any other. I journeyed here from the Ula'tuk village and I traveled with Simoi's band at their invitation."

"Just so, but that does not change the truth of the matter. You are my grandson." The elder's eyes dared him to challenge his statement and Cahil sighed.

"I do not even know your name."

Cahil knew that his words could be taken as an insult. In his village, it was considered rude to ask the name of a person before it was offered freely. Names were meant to be shared only as a sign of trust and friendship. Yet, Cahil's patience was at an end. His head ached with lingering shadows that would not abate and he was concerned about Lily and the others.

"You do not remember my name, but then, you were only four seasons when you were taken from us and you did not often call me anything other than Grandfather." The elder's eyes twinkled as he cast his thoughts back to the distant past. "You are thirty seasons of age. A man fully grown and no longer burdened by the ways of an untried youth. Have you taken a wife? Do you have children?"

Thirty seasons. Cahil was stunned that the elder correctly guessed his age. Time spent upon the great land aged his features, but he told himself that the elder was wise and easily guessed correctly.

"I have taken a wife, but we do not have any children."

"Ah, but I sense deep emotion in your voice when you mention a wife. She must be the woman of your heart."

Cahil's thoughts centered upon Lily and he turned his gaze away. He did not wish to share everything that he felt for his wife with the man sitting next to him.

"What is your name?" Cahil asked again.

"I am called Takotna." The wise elder's eyes crinkled at the corners. "But in the past, you called me Grandfather."

Lily watched Cahil stalk from Takotna's lodge and she caught a glimpse of the tumultuous storm brimming in his eyes as he stared accusingly at Simoi.

"Lily, come with me, when you are ready." Cahil did not speak to the others. Instead, he grabbed his hunting spear and parka from Anuk and walked away without another word.

"Simoi." Lily could not look away from Cahil's retreating form. "Did you know about this?"

"We knew only that Cahil favored the men of the Krahnan band. How were we to know that he was the lost grandson of Takotna?" Simoi was aware of Ashish and Suntar standing nearby and he kept his voice pitched low.

"I must go to him."

"He will need you now more than ever. You must learn that all marriages are tested, but together you will find your way." Simoi's gaze was piercing as Lily turned to face him. He turned away from her to join Ashish and Suntar.

Lily took a hesitant step forward and then before she could doubt herself, she ran to catch up with her husband.

She did not speak for long moments as she kept pace with him. Out of the corner of her eye, she noticed his height and the width of his shoulders. His features appeared to be cut from stone, but as he stopped walking and turned her way, she saw that his eyes were full of swirling thoughts and deep emotion.

"It cannot possibly be true." Cahil stared at Lily as if she could give him the answers that he sought.

"Do you remember nothing of your early childhood?" Lily asked as she clasped her hands together to keep from reaching out and brushing a lock of hair away from his forehead.

"My first memories are of the Ula'tuk village. I remember learning how to hold a spear and I remember the birth of my younger brother, Makiye."

"What are your memories from before that time?"

Cahil's gaze was piercing as he struggled to remember. "There is nothing there but empty space, no memories or thoughts, just shadows and fog."

"Do you remember anything from that time?" Lily hoped to spark a memory with her question. She reached up to brush a lock of hair from the side of Cahil's face. Her touch was whisper soft as she allowed her fingers to linger upon his cheek.

Cahil's eyes flashed as he grabbed hold of her delicate hand and stared at it before responding. "It is as if my memories begin in the Ula'tuk village."

"When we first met, you told me that your father was not your father and that your brother was not truly your brother." Lily reminded him as he stared at her palm as if searching for his memories in the light markings centered in her hand. "Perhaps it is possible that you were taken from the Krahnan band as a young child."

"It is not possible." Cahil responded, even as his brow furrowed in confusion. "My father never traveled here. The people of my village remain in the same place, season after season."

"Perhaps if you heard the story from Takotna, you would remember something of great importance. Takotna will take part in the first gathering ceremony when the moon rises. Perhaps if you simply listen to what he has to say, you will learn more about his reasons for believing that you are his grandson."

"I cannot remember what is not there and never has been. Thank you for your concern, little one, but I need to be alone with my thoughts. Go to your uncle and I will find you before the sun rests."

Lily nodded hesitantly as Cahil turned and walked away. She could still feel the warmth of his hand, so large and strong as it cupped hers. She could still smell the fresh, clean scent of his skin and the pent up strength that existed within him. Lily watched Cahil until he disappeared from sight as she considered how she would help her husband, the man that owned her heart.

Cahil turned his warm parka fur side in as he walked a distance away from the sounds and sights of the encampment. With his hood covering most of his face, he received a few curious stares from some of the people, but the rest merely accepted his presence. Daylight was fading, giving way to the early evening and very soon darkness would fall over the great land. He promised his wife that he would return to her before the sun sank from the sky and he meant to keep his promise.

He was angry in a way that he could not fully describe. By withholding the truth from him, Kusug left him with more questions than answers. "I cannot rage at a dead man."

Cahil bent to one knee and rested his head upon his hands. Grief over his father's death still weighed upon him and it showed itself in spurts of anger and thoughts of disbelief. In his prime, Kusug had been a strong man and the sickness that came along with old age should not have won the fight over life and death.

Cahil was beset with feelings of guilt for having been away from the Ula'tuk village when his father breathed his last breath. However, despite the odd circumstances that confronted him now, he could not say that he regretted his decision to leave his village behind and strike out into the unknown.

His thoughts returned to Lily. She was utterly feminine, delicate and fragile in appearance, but when the occasion called for it, she was fully capable of calling forth strength.

He found it difficult to focus on their conversation when she stood close to him and touched his cheek. Her hair smelled like the warm season, newly opened flowers and lush fragrant greenery. The black fringe of her lashes were the perfect frame for dark brown eyes which were flecked with amber shards. Everything that he knew about her called out to him and he was entranced by the upward swell of her lips, which were full and inviting.

The sound of drums beating in the distance announced the beginning of the gathering ceremony. Cahil's shoulders remained tight with tension and confusion. He knew that Anuk would come looking for him if he did not return soon, but he remained kneeling upon one knee as he breathed in and out, gathering his thoughts as he sought balance.

When he closed his eyes the land called to him and the feeling was unmatched even by the mountains that hid the sacred mounds. He wanted to know why he felt such a strong kinship to the land that the people of the Krahnan band claimed as their own and he was reminded of Simoi's words about knowing deep within that something was right and true.

Yet, he would not believe, not even for a moment, that he shared the same blood as Takotna.

CHAPTER TWENTY-FIVE

"Tell me what you have learned." Umak spoke to the young woman that drifted closer as he beckoned her forward.

She lowered her eyes demurely as he reached out and touched her chin, causing her to flinch. She was thirteen seasons of age and her body was close to maturity. He liked the inkling of awareness and fear that reached her eyes. "Tell me now and you can return to your mother."

"The people in the village have said that a man has come with Simoi's band." The girl swallowed as Umak ran a hand over her bare shoulder. She inhaled sharply when his hand moved lower, before drifting away as she rushed to tell him all that she knew. "His name is Cahil and he is said to be the grandson of Takotna, returned to the Krahnan band when all hope was lost."

"Good." Umak remarked as the girl quickly fastened her dress and he slowly handed her enough meat to share with her widowed mother. "Is there anything else that you have not told me?"

"It is said that Cahil has not accepted Takotna as his grandfather, though he resembles Takotna's son greatly."

"The last leader of the Krahnan band." Umak remembered hearing rumors of a lost son. He pounded his fist into his hand as he considered what Takotna sought to accomplish by claiming the man as his grandson when all hope was lost.

"He has also claimed Simoi's niece as his wife."

Umak narrowed his eyes as the girl flinched. "Return to the village and listen closely to all that is said, when you learn more, you will come tell me."

"Yes, Umak." The girl's eyes misted with tears as he held her wrist in a punishing grip.

"Good." Umak dismissed her with a flick of his wrist and she scrambled out of his lodge. He did not take her body, though she would have been powerless to stop him. He preferred the raw torment that he read in her eyes when he told her to remove her dress. She stood before him naked and trembling, awaiting her fate and he felt powerful as her wide eyes swept over him.

Days went by and he did not speak to her or seek her out, but she knew that he was watching and her terror excited him. The flower that once adorned her hair remained in his hand and he was certain that it was a gift from her mother. She was called Ashlu, Little Flower. He preyed upon her attempts to help her mother and even though she was revolted by his touch, she remained at his mercy.

He crushed the flower in his hand, grinding the petals between forefinger and thumb until nothing of its former beauty remained. Very soon, he would crush Ashlu in the same way, but for now he delighted in drawing out her terror.

"Takotna." Umak spoke to the empty lodge as he cast his thoughts toward his old mentor. "You should not try to restore the Krahnan band to its former glory by claiming the newcomer as a man of your shared blood. You had your turn and now the Mirotuk band will have theirs."

Umak made a sound of irritation with his mouth as he reached for his knives and spear. The weapons were made of whalebone and they were sharper and more accurate than the tools made of stone or caribou bone.

He was superior in every way. In time, the various bands of the great land would come to understand that he walked as a leader of men. Nothing would stand in his way.

Cahil found Lily waiting for him near Simoi's lodge. He was surprised to see that the men constructed the skin lodges in the short time that he was away.

They were drawn toward the sphere of light that marked the place where the gathering ceremony would be held. The sound of the beating drums stirred his blood, calling to the people of the great land. As a lengthening darkness settled over the land, the scent of many fires drifted on the light breeze.

He moved through the crowd with Lily at his side as the people chanted together, embracing their history. He became accustomed to the wide gazes that he received from the men and women, along with the occasional brush of a hand or a palm against his shoulders and back. It seemed that the people were certain that he was the beginning of a change for the scattered remains of the Krahnan band and those that would return to them, simply because he existed.

"Three fires." Cahil said as they drew closer.

Lily's eyes sparkled in the firelight as he admired her dress made of caribou skin and trimmed with fur. Her hair was free of the long braid that she usually wore and it was parted in the middle and slicked down where it hung almost to her waist in sleek swaths. Abalone shells graced her ears and she wore several beaded necklaces as adornment. Her shoulders were bare and the dress clung to her lithe form as the firelight caressed her body. Cahil was never more aware of her as a woman than he was in that moment as a smile played upon her lips and she lifted her eyes to search the crowd.

"How did you know that there would be three fires?" Lily asked as Cahil looked at her and then followed her gaze toward the three fires.

"I don't know."

As they drew closer Cahil saw clearly that three fires were spread in an interlocking circle and a lone figure stood nearby. The people sat in ever widening circles around the fires and though he was not familiar with the gathering ceremony, he was immediately intrigued.

A cloaked figure raised his hands for silence and Cahil caught his breath as the man removed his fur hood and showed his face.

"Simoi." Cahil should have known that Simoi was certain that the gathering ceremony would not begin without him simply because he led the ceremony.

In the flickering firelight, Cahil caught sight of Anuk standing next to Saghani and Gisik. He noticed that they were dressed for the ceremony and he glanced down at his own travel worn appearance. Simoi shifted in place, drawing all eyes toward him.

"Caribou, muskoxen, and bison, these are the large game animals that keep us well fed and warm during the cold season." The drum sounded, punctuating each word for emphasis as Simoi's voice rose and fell and a hush settled over the crowd. "We seek a blessing so that we can feed our children and they can grow strong on what the great land provides."

"Yi!" The people chanted as Simoi began to move around the fire, shedding his long fur cape and parka. He moved into the steps of a hunter's dance as he began to chant in an undulating voice that reached the edge of the crowd. He lifted his hunting spear and made powerful slashing motions as the people called out. "Aya-ay!"

A rattle made of shells accompanied the sealskin drums, but there was no other sound other than the pounding of Simoi's footsteps as he danced around each fire pit. He moved seven times around the three fires and the people swayed in rhythm to the beat of the drum as he danced feverishly, moving in time with the drumbeat.

Simoi spun in place as his hands lifted an object from the ground. When he raised his head, he wore a mask with the face of a bear and he roared as the crowd reared back in surprise.

A weathered voice called out, loud enough for all to hear, "He has become an apex predator! Who is stronger than the white bear which walks the land searching for seals that are caught unaware?"

Cahil watched Takotna separate himself from the crowd and he was surprised at the strength in the elder's voice as he took his place beside Simoi. Takotna was adorned in full raiment, from his multi-feathered cape to the beaded parka and colorful leggings that he wore. Cahil knew from the way that the others settled upon the ground that Takotna took the position of a storyteller, raising his walking stick high overhead. Following the example of the others,

Cahil settled onto his haunches as Takotna's voice washed over the crowd.

"There is not a hunter among us that does not revere the great white bear. He stalks the land seeking prey that is almost invisible when the white snow covers the ground. Who has seen the white bear in search of a seal? He enjoys the flesh of the youngest walrus that makes its home upon the ice. From times long lasting until now we have not raised our spears against the white bear and they do not harm the men that walk the great land."

"There is balance between such a great predator and men who are weak in comparison. In this way, we gather the various bands of the great land and we ask for a small portion of the game that runs unfettered."

"In times past, the leader of the Krahnan band would follow the seeking star on a journey to seek out the dancing lights in the sky. You remember the days when the seals came to our spears as easily as air filled our lungs. Those days have passed. The men of this village no longer find the seal, nor do we hear their cries when the ice gathers near the great water."

"We have lost balance, we lost it long ago and it has not been restored until now." Takotna stared into the crowd as his eyes landed upon Cahil. "I tell you now that balance has been returned to the Krahnan band and this will bring good fortune to all who gather to mark the hunting ceremony."

Cahil saw that several men lifted their sons high above their heads as they accepted Takotna's promise. Children were highly valued amongst the people of the great land and he did not have to know them intimately to understand why this was so. It was the same within his own village simply because children were the lifeblood of any band, any village.

He saw a promise in Takotna's eyes and he knew that he would have to seek out the wizened elder and speak to him if he hoped to settle the matter between them. For now, Cahil enjoyed his time with Lily as they took part in the singing and dancing that swelled over the crowd, continuing deep into the night.

CHAPTER TWENTY-SIX

"You stand as a man of the Krahnan band, but you do not belong to any of the bands that have gathered here."

Cahil spun around as a shadowed form stepped forward. He saw a man cloaked in darkness except for the flashing whites of his eyes and he was immediately glad that he left Lily with her uncle and the others. He was surprised that the man managed to walk up behind him without giving away his presence.

"I am no concern of yours." Cahil sized up the shadowed figure. There was not enough moonlight to see by and he admitted to himself that light would have been more than welcome.

"You are my concern if you seek to become the leader of the Krahnan band."

"The Krahnan band has no leader." Cahil knew that Takotna, Ashish and Suntar worked as a council of elders to make decisions for the band.

"I remember the leader of the Krahnan band and you look nothing like him."

Cahil grimaced with distaste, he would like to agree, but doubts assailed him even as he made his way to Takotna's dwelling. "Whether I look like him or not, the matter does not concern you."

"Ah, but you are wrong."

Cahil was unprepared when the man lunged toward him, striking out with a knife that was serrated at the edge. He caught sight of the knife's gleaming white edge as he struck out, acting instinctively to knock the weapon away.

In their struggle, the man's hood dropped away and Cahil saw his features clearly just as he grabbed hold of the knife as it narrowly missed his face. He twisted the weapon in his hand despite the searing cut that graced his right palm and he thrust his attacker away from him as the sound of footsteps reached his ears.

Cahil spun to face the man that attacked him without cause only to find that there was no one nearby. He diligently searched the darkness as a family hurried past, offering him a brief greeting which he was not certain that he returned. Blood pooled in his hand as Cahil walked with long strides toward the dwellings of the Krahnan band.

Takotna stood outside of his lodge and it was as if he had been waiting for Cahil to come to him. Cahil glanced down at the cut that graced the palm of his right hand. The wound was deep and it would need binding, but his desire to hear what Takotna would say overrode everything else.

"Cahil, it is good that you have returned." Takotna's eyes moved over him in a possessive manner and he was reminded of the way that Kusug once looked at him, as if he was an extension of himself. Cahil sighed heavily as Takotna ushered him inside.

"Tell me why you believe that I am your grandson."

Pain flared in Takotna's eyes before he nodded in acceptance and motioned toward the low burning fire. Cahil waited for Takotna to take his place and then he sat across from the older man.

"The Krahnan band once roved the great land, we followed the various herds that are good for hunting, seeking out caribou, bison and muskoxen. My daughter's husband, Nanuq, followed in the footsteps of his father and he became a capable hunter and a natural leader of men. As a hunter, he learned that the knowledge of the land was the salvation of our people. Our band grew in size and strength as families blended and their children married. In our village if a man takes a wife, his wife and often her family are made welcome amongst us. You must understand that Nanuq's bloodline was impossibly old, it is said that his blood was sacred simply because he walked as a man that was especially blessed. Under Nanuq's leadership the people saw a great and prosperous future."

Takotna inhaled the steam from the wooden bowl that he held and then he sipped and swallowed audibly. He handed Cahil a clean strip of softened animal hide as he gestured toward his clenched hand. Cahil silently wrapped his palm as Takotna continued speaking and he was relieved that the man did not ask him about the injury.

"At that time, Nanuq joined with a young woman from a small, roving band. She was a rare woman with a quiet spirit, though she matched him in intensity and she was a fitting mate for the leader of a growing village. Her name was Surak."

At the mention of his daughter's name, Takotna took a deep breath as if suffering from a deeper pain than the cough that rattled his chest. A pain that struck the spirit.

"You must realize that things were not always peaceful, our hunters determined that the caribou followed various trails, season over season and many decided to remain in one settlement instead of traveling the great land in search of food, shelter and warmth. Nanuq was the first to step away from the old ways and encourage the others to remain in one place; it was his hope that we would establish a village. Many of the bands that came to hunt during the mating season and before the beginning of the cold season became angry. There was fighting and much bitterness that grew between the men. I urged Nanuk to welcome the other bands to gather with us and hunt together."

"However, Nanuq was brash and filled with youthful vigor. He was powerful, standing as a man that led other men and he refused to bend. He did not listen to the older men, nor did he welcome the various bands into our midst. He grew to see those that were not related to us by blood ties as a threat. My daughter, Surak, gave birth to a son and he remained by my side from his first step until the last time that I set my eyes upon him."

Cahil saw that the events of the past were still fresh within Takotna's mind and he waited patiently for him to continue. Finally, when he saw that Takotna would not speak without prodding, he voiced his question. "What happened?"

"A band came to us and asked that they be allowed to hunt upon the great land. It was a time of starvation for many during the beginning of the warm season when the caribou delayed their return and the food caches from the cold season were empty. You must understand that Nanuq thought only to protect our band from starvation. He told the leader that if he saw that their hunters took food from the Krahnan band, he would find them and strike them down."

"The leader of the Ula'tuk band was incensed that the prosperous Krahnan band would deny his people the right to hunt upon the great land." Takotna made a wide sweeping gesture as Cahil envisioned the wide domain around them.

"He denied their right to hunt?" Cahil was enthralled with the story as told by Takotna. His heart sped up at the mention of his people, the Ula'tuk band.

"I pled with Nanuq to soften his heart toward their plight. The great land does not belong to any one man, no matter that a man should stand in one place and build a permanent lodge held up by spruce poles and gathered by caribou hides. Nanuq's heart was obstinate and he would not turn aside from the path that he chose to follow. My daughter pled with him to relent and she reminded him of the old ways, those followed by his father. As his wife, she sat silently in their lodge when he spoke to the leader of the Ula'tuk band, a man in his prime, fierce in appearance and capable of becoming a true ally. Surak saw the leader's own son, a boy of four seasons and she recognized the signs of hunger that were etched upon his young face."

"Nanuq would not relent." Takotna's eyes glistened in the firelight as he held Cahil's gaze. "Much to our grief and despair, he chose to attack the Ula'tuk band after he learned that they butchered and killed two caribou. The warriors of our village went against the Ula'tuk band and they were caught unaware and unprepared."

The walls of Takotna's lodge reflected the firelight as Cahil leaned forward and peered at the wizened elder. "Often two caribou are enough to feed an entire band."

Cahil envisioned Nanuq, the leader of the Krahnan village, striking a much smaller band and he was reminded of the fighting and skirmishes that were often caused by disagreements over hunting rights.

"I believe that he meant only to scare them and make a name for himself throughout the territory marked by our band. He would have allowed them to leave with whatever they could carry, but one of his warriors threw his spear at the leader of the Ula'tuk."

"Kusug roared with fury as he threw his body over his son. The warrior missed Kusug by a hair's breadth, but he unintentionally struck Kusug's son, killing the child instantly."

Cahil lowered his head as he imagined the grievous turn of events.

"Nanuq cried out in agony, but his cries were overshadowed by the grief that rose up from Kusug as he lifted his child's lifeless body to the heavens and cursed Nanuq for his actions." Takotna's voice drifted away as Cahil was drawn back in time. He could envision the grief upon Kusug's face as he held his son's lifeless body in his arms and cursed the man that unintentionally brought about his son's death.

"I will take what is yours and you will see what it is to be left with despair and the cold hand of grief!" Kusug vowed as he stared at Nanuq, the leader of the Krahnan band.

"My warrior acted without thinking." Nanuq was speechless, he intended only to scare the Ula'tuk band so that they would not remain nearby and he thought to make a name for himself throughout the territory marked by the Krahnan band.

"Your thoughtless actions have taken the life of my son." Kusug's face contorted with rage as Nanuq stared at him without speaking, while horror over his unthinking actions was reflected in his gaze. "Listen to the cries of my wife!"

The child's mother screamed and wailed as she cuddled his lifeless body against her breasts. Kusug stood over the pair and his eyes were terrible to behold. "Leave us!"

His voice was a strident demand and Nanuq could only stare as the entire band grieved the loss of their leader's son. Nanuq's men dragged him away amidst the agonizing sounds of the woman's heart wrenching grief echoed across the great land.

When Nanuq returned to the Krahnan band, he gathered Surak into his arms and held her close. She listened as he related the disastrous events of the day and his wife was the only one that knew that he bowed low during the moonrise, removing his head covering in grief over his actions. No hunter ever removed the hood of his parka during the night, yet Nanuq bared his head and bent low to the ground. Though the spear that took the child's life was thrown by one of his men, he took full responsibility for the calamity that had befallen Kusug, a strong hunter that sought only to feed his band.

"If Kusug was a part of our band, he would have been a man that I would have readily called friend and brother." Nanuq spoke quietly to his wife as she held their son in her arms. The child slept peacefully and his features were those of his father. Nanuq pressed his lips against his son's head tenderly as his wife laid the boy upon their sleeping pallet. His heart knew only pain that his son was alive and well, while Kusug's son was covered by stone and rock upon the cold surface of the great land. It was at that time that Nanuq passed the necklace that marked him as the leader of the Krahnan band over to his son. He hoped that the emblem would protect the boy from harm and shield him from his enemies.

Surak and Nanuq watched their son sleep and they did not take their rest, nor did they find comfort throughout the night. Nanuq knew that Kusug would sit beside his son's burial cairn until he was forced to move on for the wellbeing of his band. It grieved him to no end that he had been the reason that a child died and he was haunted by terrible dreams from which he could not wake. As time passed, guilt lodged in his heart and he came to realize that he was a man that would take the life of a child for the value of two caribou.

CHAPTER TWENTY-SEVEN

Takotna's voice was dry and grievous as he drew Cahil back to the present. They were once again surrounded by his lodge walls with the small fire crackling between them.

"Nanuq gave you the name Cahil, as a living reminder to himself and all future generations. The name is interpreted to mean a man that will kill only in battle."

Takotna's eyes were dark, fathomless orbs that prodded at Cahil, seeking entry to his most private thoughts.

"Throughout my life, I was led to believe that I was born into the Ula'tuk band." Cahil's throat began to close with anger and grief. "How did this happen?"

Takotna grimaced, causing his mouth to turn down as he considered his response. "Many days passed and Nanuq thought that all was well. He left with the other men to fish and hunt while your mother kept you by her side so that she could begin preparations for new garments that you would wear during the cold season. She laughed with happiness that she would have you in her arms without interruption while your father was away. Surak took you to the river to wash and when she returned there was blood on her hands and you were gone…"

Cahil was drawn into the distant past as Takotna's voice merged with long forgotten memories that broke free, flooding his senses and sending him back to the fateful day when his life changed irrevocably.

Cahil was a young boy, only four seasons, and his father was away on a hunt. His mother smiled at him proudly as she told him that he would grow to be powerful and strong, just like his father.

Surak's black hair hung in two braids and a light sheen of oil coated her face, hands and arms. Her smile was wide and happy as she rubbed the water from his body, careful not to dislodge the necklace that his father gave him. He remembered glancing across the stream as his eyes landed upon a pair of mukluks, warm foot coverings worn by many of the men of his band.

However, the man standing across the stream was not a man of the Krahnan band.

"Run, Cahil!" Surak gasped as Cahil remained standing in place, transfixed by the large warrior that stared at them.

She held her hands against her chest, clasped together in silent supplication and then fearfully stood. "Please."

Cahil felt his mother's fear as she held out a staying hand as if to hold back a violent gust of wind. The man walked forward and his eyes were hard and cold as he spoke.

"Your husband deserved to die for taking the life of my son." Kusug ignored the woman's startled cry as he shoved her to the ground and she struggled against him with her son clasped in her arms. "I would have taken his life, but he must suffer as I have suffered."

"Please!" Surak pled as the man overpowered her and tore her son from her arms. "No!"

Kusug felt the warm weight of the boy and he knew that his decision was right and just. The child stared at his mother as tears seeped from her eyes. "Take my life! Kill me if you must, but do not harm the boy."

Kusug was almost moved by the woman's offer of her life, but he had been inside of her husband's lodge and he knew that the man looked at his wife with warmth, but he looked at his son with fatherly pride. The boy was tall and sturdy for his age and he would quiet the grief that plagued him constantly. He and his wife suffered in agony night and day since the death of their son.

"Your husband must suffer." Kusug did not blame the man's wife and he was sorry for her grief, though he thought that her grief would dim when she welcomed more children to her lodge. His wife's womb remained barren and there was little hope of any other children. "He will suffer the knowledge that my son is dead and your son lives, but he will never see him again, just as I will never again see my son."

The woman screamed in denial as he hurried away, carrying the warm, living burden in his arms. The boy's eyes were large, fringed with black eyelashes and shadowed with terror as he reached out his arms toward his mother. She screamed and fell, fighting terror and pain to reach him as she scrambled over the stream.

Blood graced her palms when she held up her hands in supplication, but the man did not stop running, nor did he look back.

"He asked me my name." Cahil searched Takotna's lodge walls as he struggled to remember the past, but the memories were shadowed and vague. "I was young, but I knew that my name was Cahil."

Takotna's eyes were shadowed with remembered grief. "Your father was truly grieved by his actions, but never more than when he returned to find that you were taken away by Kusug."

"Your mother wept bitterly for you. She never had any other children." Takotna sighed heavily as he closed his eyes and struggled to continue. "Your father never stopped looking for you. Before he left on the hunt he gave you the necklace that you wear as a talisman, an offer of protection."

Cahil jerked his head up as he considered Takotna's words. "Was their no end to their grief?"

Takotna stared at him and then he said, "A father should never outlive his child. Nanuq journeyed across the great land, season over season. He looked for you everywhere. We could not predict where the Ula'tuk band would be at any given time. They were known to walk the land in search of the animal herds, but your father was relentless in his pursuit of Kusug. He was relentless in his efforts to find you."

"What happened to my mother?" Cahil asked as he thought of the woman's shining hair and dark eyes. She had been young and beautiful and he could only imagine how grief shaped her life.

"My daughter could not live with her grief. She existed as a shell for several seasons after you were taken. Your father gave her into my care and he returned at times, but his eyes were haunted and he carried his heart was laid bare. He was gone when Surak's overwhelming grief crushed her spirit. One day, she removed her clothing and wandered into a blowing snowstorm. We found her, but it was too late, the wind spirit of the cold season stole her from us, just as surely as you were taken."

"Your father lived on for a time after her death. During that time we lived in the mountains and our band suffered through sickness and various ailments that brought many low and killed others. Many of our people are buried far from here, protected forever by the high places and their bodies were covered long ago by sacred mounds."

Cahil bowed his head as he was swept along by Takotna's words. He remembered the strong spirit of his people in the high places that were protected by the mountains.

Takotna continued, "Your father died while seeking a blessing from the heavens during the sacred time when the lights dance in the sky. He was a formidable warrior and a strong leader, but the loss of his son and later the death of his wife, crushed him as nothing else could. He would be proud to know that you are alive. At the time, there was very little hope that Kusug spared your life."

Cahil could not remember his first father, no matter how hard he tried, but he understood now why he was drawn to the sacred mounds and why his necklace held the same image as the rocks that marked the ground. He closed his eyes and breathed deeply, but the memory of his father's face would not come to him. As if sensing his effort to remember, Takotna pointed at him with one gnarled finger.

"You have only to look into a still pool to remember your father. You are the very image of him and now perhaps you can understand why I rejoice that in my old age, I have seen the face of my grandson, though my daughter is lost to me. I am overjoyed to welcome my grandson back into the band of his birth."

Cahil stared into the fire as Takotna silently watched him. A cold wind blew over the great land and Cahil thought of his mother, driven to take her own life by the burden of grief that was too enormous to bear and he thought of his father, a man that regretted his actions and lost his only son to the very man that he once wronged.

He lifted his head as he sought answers, but Takotna breathed deeply, having long since taken his place upon his sleeping furs. Cahil remained silent for a time as he watched over Takotna, the father of his mother. His grandfather.

Simoi rose early, before most of the people encamped at the outskirts of the Krahnan band. He walked a distance away from Saghani who slept inside a skin lodge that was erected before the first part of the gathering ceremony. Gisik and Anuk decided to sleep outside while the weather was tolerable.

With his spear in hand, he searched the distance for any sign of danger. The air was clear and crisp, though he could sense that the changing of seasons was underway. The dark green spruce trees in the distance rustled in song as the wind moved their weighty bows.

He sensed danger, but there was no sign of an enemy stalking the land. Simoi was a man that trusted his instincts and he read omens in the coming of the dawn and the calamities or blessings that befell his band.

Nimiuq's death was a bad omen and did not see the danger until it was too late. He knew that his old friend would not hold him responsible, but he carried the burden of anger and guilt as if Nimiuq hounded him day and night. A raven landed at a distance and Simoi froze.

"Good day to you, my winged brother."

The raven turned cold eyes upon him and lifted its beak in disdain. Simoi removed a piece of dried meat from his carrying pouch and set it reverently upon the ground. The raven called out sharply and leapt into the air with a flurry of wings, only to land in a nearby tree where it could keep watch.

Simoi backed away from the place where he welcomed the dawn. He did not take his eyes away as the raven swooped down to the earth and tore into the dried meat with relish.

My gift has been accepted, he thought to himself. Though he knew that the raven was often a messenger and could also play the role of a trickster.

"Better to have left an offering than to suffer for an unintentional offense." Simoi's mouth moved, but very little sound escaped. He was a man that knew the ways of nature. He did not disturb the natural world around him, not with the offensive tone of his voice, so unlike the incessant chatter of the crawling insects or flying birds. As he returned to his lodge, he saw Cahil walking with his niece in the distance and he thought that he understood the raven's message. "There are many changes yet to come and I must be prepared."

With Lily walking at his side, Cahil moved toward the tree line that surrounding the Krahnan band on one side. With a grimace, he realized that he did not know where to begin, but the flare of concern that he saw in his wife's eyes drew him like a moth to a flame.

"Walk with me?" Cahil asked as he glanced around for any sign of the others. He and Lily spent the darkest part of the night wrapped in each other's arms, taking comfort in their passion for one another. "Where are the others?"

"They are still sleeping, though Simoi has most likely gone to welcome the morning." Lily could see the direction of Cahil's thoughts, though she wished that she understood the deep roiling emotions that clouded his dark brown eyes. Black winged eyebrows drew down in deep thought as he studied the ground.

"You have injured your hand." Lily's eyes widened in concern as Cahil held up his hand and inspected it as if for the first time. He was glad that she hadn't noticed the wound until now. "You should wash and bind the wound."

"I will." Cahil was reminded of the fight and his unknown attacker.

"I can help you." Lily offered and before he could refuse, she used fresh water from her water skin to cleanse the wound. The cold water numbed the injury and Cahil was able to admire Lily's features and delicate hands as she used the clean strip of hide at the end of her braid to bind his injury.

He was transfixed by the sight of her hair, loosened from the braid and the tenderness of her touch as she tied the binding and placed his hand over his chest.

Lily was not uncomfortable in the measured silence that lingered between them. She knew that Cahil studied her, but she did not find his intense gaze displeasing. Instead, her heart lurched when he gently clasped her elbow to help her step over a rocky area.

Inhaling deeply, she returned her attention to the land around them as she found enjoyment in the brown grass which blanketed the land and crunched softly underfoot. She inhaled the fresh scents of spruce, birch and alder as they neared a copse of trees.

"Tell me about the land." Cahil's eyes were wary and watchful as Lily's chest rose and fell. He needed a distraction from the heavy thoughts that settled like boulders in his mind until he could barely concentrate. He listened closely as she spoke about the wide open spaces and the land that went on forever in all directions.

"In the warm season there will be wild berries, blueberries and more. Many of the older women no longer search for such delicacies, but the younger women are eager to do so and they extract a promise from their aunts, mothers and grandmothers."

Lily's eyes sparkled with excitement as she stopped walking and turned to face Cahil.

"What promise is that?" Cahil liked the way the light danced over Lily's blue-black hair and he saw that her cheeks held a hint of color.

He enjoyed the clean, fresh scent of her skin though she did not seem to realize that her very nearness caused his nostrils to flare and male hunger to dance at the edges of his senses.

"The younger women suffer the sting of thorns and tired limbs in an effort to bring back baskets of sweet berries. But they extract the promise that the older women will make a special treat from their efforts." Lily smiled as Cahil gave her his full attention. She forgot to breathe for a moment as she looked into his eyes. "The women mix whipped tallow from the caribou to produce agutak. It is a rare treat and there are not many that know how to make it properly."

"I have never tasted agutak before." His eyes washed over her and her heartbeat thundered as she met his gaze.

"It is worth the effort to sort out the rotten fruit from the rest so that the entire batch isn't soured. You would enjoy it immensely."

"I am certain that I would."

Cahil lapsed into silence as he was once again reminded that his father was not his father and Takotna was far more than a revered elder of the Krahnan band. He was also his grandfather.

"The morning feels different." Cahil said as Lily walked a few steps ahead.

"Just so." Lily turned to face him, with the sun at her back she seemed to be lit from within. "You have undergone an awakening. The morning is different because you are different."

Cahil was surprised by Lily's insight. She easily explained the chaos that swirled inside of him like a powerful storm.

Instead of speaking, Lily took a step toward him and then as he matched her forward progress they found themselves in each other's arms. He held her reverently while she leaned her head against his chest.

His senses swirled with the enticing scent of her hair and a feminine essence that belonged solely to her. He stood before her as a strong man, a hunter and a warrior. She knew that he fought the rogue band of men that followed them on their journey. She understood that he was capable of taking a life without undo remorse and yet, she did not fear him.

He held her gently and though she was small and fragile in his arms, he felt as if she braced him like a bulwark in a storm. When she accepted his embrace by welcoming the searing touch of his lips, he found that he was humbled down to his very soul.

CHAPTER TWENTY-EIGHT

Cahil knew that Simoi often went to welcome the morning and he searched for him briefly as the sun rose overhead. He found him standing on a swell of land that overlooked the encampment of the various bands. He approached by making enough noise that Simoi was well aware of his presence long before he came into sight.

"A man fought with me yesterday, after darkness fell." Cahil raised his hand to show Simoi the injury. "He struck my right hand with his knife and then disappeared."

Simoi's cautious eyes missed nothing as he noticed Cahil's injured hand as well as his impassive expression. "Did you learn his name?"

"No," Cahil replied. "But I would know him anywhere."

"Good, then you can point him out during the evening ceremony when the hunters gather to share stories with the various bands that have journeyed from afar."

"I am more than capable of fighting my own battles." Cahil answered as his eyes narrowed suspiciously.

"You are fully capable, but if the man that attacked you is the same man that I have marked as my enemy, then I would prefer that it was my weapon that ended his life."

"If it is the same man, and he comes against me again, I will strike him down." Cahil's voice was filled with certainty and Simoi lifted his head and narrowed his eyes.

"I believe that you would try, but from what I have seen, you fight fairly. If you ever face this man in battle, you must remember that he is a predator. He preys upon the weak and he will strike you only when you are most vulnerable, only when you are open and exposed."

"Then I will heed your warning." Cahil nodded firmly.

With a glance, Simoi sought out Lily and saw that his niece knelt beside Saghani and Anuk.

"There is something that you wish to say to me, is there not?"

Cahil followed the direction of Simoi's gaze to see Lily stand tall, like a willow as their eyes met across the distance. "I must determine where we will live. Your niece has been a part of your band since childhood and I wish to hear your thoughts on the matter."

Simoi grimaced, "Naturally you will join my band. You are a man without a band of your own."

"I was once the son of the leader of the Ula'tuk village."

"Once, but no more." Simoi lessened the effect of his harsh statement by pressing his lips together in understanding.

"It would make sense to join your band even though it is the custom of my people that a wife should join the band or village of her husband."

Simoi nodded in relief. "I knew that you would see reason."

Cahil recognized that Simoi did not wish to lose Lily, his beloved niece, but he was not willing to sway from the course that he set for himself and his wife. "However, I have learned that I am the grandson of Takotna and my father once led the Krahnan band."

"The Krahnan band is not what it once was and perhaps it never will be again."

"Why?" Cahil noticed that the band held a spirit of quiet despair and he could not understand why it should be so. From what he could see, the encampment rested in a well planned location. They were near a water source and protected by a copse of trees that trailed the Krahnan River. There were creeks and tributaries that broke off and snaked across the verdant landscape. Tall grass grew near the water and there were ptarmigan, geese, ducks, rabbits and an abundance of wildlife everywhere that he looked. A true center of abundance.

"Many of the smaller bands that have journeyed to reach this place for the gathering ceremony are not a part of the Krahnan band."

"I thought that this place would hold a prosperous village." Cahil remembered their previous discussions about the land and he also recognized the building blocks needed to establish a growing settlement.

"When their leader died, the people lost hope and many drifted away, taking their women and children with them." Simoi gestured toward the horizon. "The people were once glad to settle into a permanent location where there was good hunting and a source of clean, fresh flowing water. Yet, after the death of their leader, the village was thrown into despair."

"Again, I ask why?"

"Simply because your father was the last of his kind and it was said that he was especially blessed, capable of leading this village as a hunter and a warrior when the occasion arose." Simoi stroked one hand over his upper lip and then he narrowed his eyes as he studied Cahil. "Your father kept the old ways, it is said that each season, before the gathering ceremony, he followed the seeking star until he reached the place where the dancing lights are revealed."

"This is not the first time that I have heard about the dancing lights." Cahil sighed deeply as Simoi merely shrugged in an indifferent gesture that only stoked his irritation. "Lily and I will remain here, though you are welcome to join us. Takotna has suffered tremendous loss in his lifetime. I wish to remain by his side, if he approves."

"He will welcome you with open arms." Simoi placed his hand over his face and drew his features down as he considered Cahil's offer. "Lily has been my reason for joy, season over season. I do not look forward to parting ways with her."

"I know." Cahil responded. "You will find it very difficult to leave the Krahnan band behind."

"You are her husband, though it will take more than a well made bone bracelet to show that you honor Lily."

"I have only the things that I was able to carry upon my back along with my water skin, spear and hunting knife."

"It is a fine hunting knife." Simoi gestured toward the bone knife etched with markings against stone, skillfully sharpened to a fine point. "But you would do well to use it with the other hunters on the caribou hunt."

They glanced toward the gathering circle where the men gathered in preparation for the hunt. Simoi's words stood as a reminder between them that Cahil promised to hunt the caribou.

Cahil was a man that would take down as many of the stampeding beasts as he could, knowing that there were many mouths to feed and the time of the cold season was already upon them. Simoi knew him well enough to anticipate a successful hunt and he walked away whistling a pleasant tune as Cahil watched him with growing appreciation.

Simoi and Gisik worked together to make new spear tips in preparation for the upcoming caribou hunt. Simoi left the more detailed work to Gisik, though he could successfully make a spear point, Gisik perfected the task. Simoi chipped small parallel flakes off of one side of a stone blade and then another.

"You never said that we would remain here, amongst a dying band." Gisik growled low in his throat as he glanced up at Simoi, turning his attention away from the spear point that he skillfully worked.

"I never intended to do so, but the path of this band has been irrevocably changed and we must consider what is best for our band." Simoi took it upon himself to speak to Gisik before talking to the others.

"You do not know what the future holds."

He knew that Gisik was always alert to danger, just as he was. "I cannot see into the future, but even I can sense the changing tide that has swept over the people that belong to the Krahnan band. Even the leaders of the roving bands have been affected. They are questioning their decision to leave the Krahnan band. The people recognize that the one with the blood of their former leader stands among them."

"He is not ready to lead." Gisik said as he turned the spear point in his hand and blew over the stone before beginning to work on the opposite side.

"Not yet, but he was born to lead others, you saw for yourself the way that he took charge when we journeyed here. We were injured, our friend was dying and Cahil took the lead."

"You should not blame yourself. You were injured and unable to help Saghani's grandfather."

"Even if I was not injured, I am not certain that I could have ended his suffering." Simoi spoke of Nimiuq and his voice dipped low in grief over the loss of his friend.

"You would have done what was necessary." Gisik replied, though he knew that he would have been forced to make an impossible choice if Simoi faltered. He felt a depth of gratitude toward Cahil, but it did not override his independence. Simoi led them for many seasons and they survived by keeping to the rituals of the past. He did not understand why that should change.

"You risk your life and your future by remaining in a place where you have sworn to kill a man that others hold harmless." Gisik's reminder to Simoi about Umak caused the other man's eyes to harden with remembered anger.

"I have not forgotten Umak and his band, nor will I release my vow until he has breathed his last."

"The council of elders will order your death if you take Umak's life without just cause." Gisik warned. "You would do well to leave him in peace."

"There is no peace for the families of the young women that were violated and killed," Simoi replied. "Umak must die for the wrongs that he has committed and I will make certain that my actions will never be called into question."

"Does she still live in your heart?" Gisik saw that his question brought Simoi unintended pain and Simoi did not have to answer after all. His silence was answer enough.

Long ago, Simoi planned to take one of the young women killed by Umak as his wife. He would not speak of that day, but

Gisik recognized that the pain was as recent as if it occurred only yesterday. He also knew that the young women had been badly used before Umak and his men slit their throats and left their bodies lying naked and exposed on the open ground.

He remembered standing beside Simoi as he mourned the death of the young woman that knew the song in his heart and he held Simoi back when Umak taunted him over the senseless killings.

"Does Lily know to remain close?" Gisik asked, in an effort to shift Simoi's focus.

Simoi's dark glowering visage smoothed out at the sound of Lily's name. "I will see that she does, but I do not have to watch her as I have done in the past."

Gisik would have asked Simoi what changed, but he already knew the answer. *Cahil.*

Cahil's presence in their lives changed everything and nothing would ever be the same again, of this he was certain.

CHAPTER TWENTY-NINE

"Why have you summoned me?" The question drew Umak out of his reverie as he turned to face the large warrior that stood before him.

"Have you no greeting for an old friend?" Umak asked as he peered at the other man, daring him to reach for his hunting knife while surrounded by the men of his band.

"Your father is man that we once called friend and brother."

"My father has fallen ill and he grows weak and tired." Umak strode forward to stand eye to eye with the other man. "He will breathe his last breath very soon and we will mourn him deeply."

"Again, I ask, why have you summoned me?" The man fairly growled the question, though his dark eyes took in the armed men of Umak's band, a people known by their leader's name, Mirotuk.

"My band has grown in size since the last time that you were here." Umak raised his spear and saw that the other man stood ready to fight if he moved toward him with his weapon. "We are strong men. We know the ways of the land and have discovered the trails that the herds have walked since time beyond memory."

A grunt of disdain was his only response.

"My men will dance the hunters' spirit dance at the evening fire and we will have the necessary strength to bring down many of the caribou that seek to cross the Krahnan River."

"Just so."

"The scattered bands of the great land will have no choice but to accept that the former glory that once belonged to the Krahnan band is gone forever." Umak declared boldly as he waited for the other man to respond. Anger grew inside his chest as the man remained stubbornly silent. "I have been told that there is a man that claims to have the blood of the past Krahnan village leaders running through his veins."

"If you already know about Cahil's existence, then why have you called me forth?"

"Because I wish to know his intentions. Has he any interest in staking a claim upon the position of leadership?"

"You would do well to consider the threat to your life should you face Simoi ever again." The man replied. "As it stands, Cahil does not even know of your existence."

"Is that so?" Umak's smile was bitter and cold. "I would like to think otherwise. I always make myself known to my enemies."

"You are a fool if you think that the scattered bands of the great land will fall into place behind you."

"The last man to call me a fool felt the sharp tip of my spear as I pierced his heart."

"Your threats mean nothing to me."

"Ah, but that is where you are wrong." Umak declared. "My wishes and plans for the future should matter to you, simply because they affect your future and your family."

"I am not related by blood to any of the bands that have gathered here." The man narrowed his eyes as he held Umak's hard stare.

"This is true, but your brother's wife and their daughter were not lost in a snowstorm last season. They are both alive." Umak stepped closer to the large warrior, so that they stood face to face. "You will do whatever I say if you ever want to see your niece or her mother again."

"Ashlu?" The man's eyes widened briefly as he remembered a young girl of twelve seasons with eyes like those of his brother. Her mother, Inu'la, had been ill from the time the girl was a mere child.

"Is that her name? I rarely remember the names of the young women that I take to my sleeping furs, but perhaps you are right." Umak was prepared when the man reached for his hunting knife just as he pressed the tip of his spear against his neck.

He knew that nothing would have stopped his opponent from seeking vengeance for his niece, but the handful of armed warriors surrounding them aided him greatly.

"Where is my niece?" The man ground the words through lips that were pressed flat against his clenched teeth.

"She and her mother remain with a few of my men. At my request, they are being held at a distance." Umak saw the man's eyes light with defiance, but he expected resistance and he was well prepared. "You will never find them."

"You do not know what I am capable of accomplishing."

"Gisik," Umak chided softly. "As I have said, we have much to discuss and if you give your loyalty to me, I will see that Ashlu and her mother are given into your care. If not, they will remain beholden to me. As it stands, I grow weary of feeding two extra mouths. Even if you were to search for them, I have given my men the order to slit their throats if anyone approaches except me."

Gisik's eyes hardened as he breathed deeply to gain control of his rioting thoughts. He could see that Umak would take his anger out on Ashlu and her mother if he was provoked and any thought of trying to find his niece was quashed as he listened to Umak's threat.

"Nod if you agree to my demands." Umak said, only after Gisik removed his hand from the hilt of his hunting knife.

A brief nod of his head was his only answer, but he expected nothing less and though his face remained impassive, deep inside he was certain that success was near at hand.

Umak turned his back on Gisik as he stared at the horizon. Tomorrow, the men of his band would join the others in the great caribou hunt and he would see to it that the threat against him was eliminated, once and for all.

"Gisik has behaved in a strange manner all day." Saghani complained as she and Lily worked on their contribution to the evening meal. There was to be a large feast, attended by all during the evening hunting ceremony. The hum of excitement was almost tangible as the women worked to prepare savory contributions that would be shared by all.

"We should be thankful that Simoi and Anuk were able to find waterfowl this late in the season." Lily murmured as her fingers moved nimbly over the task of plucking the birds. It was apparent that Saghani was more interested in talking than working, but Lily was unable to find fault with her friend. Saghani was in turns petulant and humorous depending on her mood and Lily treasured their friendship.

"Simoi will appreciate it if we save the feathers for his use." Lily remarked.

"You should listen to me when I tell you that Gisik is behaving strangely."

"I am listening." Lily sighed as she raised her head to meet Saghani's gaze. "But perhaps you are simply upset because Gisik pays you very little attention now that we are surrounded by so many people."

"He barely notices me at all." Saghani responded with a heavy sigh. "Lily, I am sorry that I almost caused you and Cahil harm on our journey."

Saghani knew that Lily had been angry with her and she could not endure another day without the bond that they shared as friends.

"I know, Saghani, but you must never again put anyone else in danger." Lily knew that Saghani never intended to break the ice that they walked upon and she was glad to put the past behind them as Saghani leaned over and embraced her. "Perhaps if you stop seeking the attention of the young men from the various bands, Gisik will realize that you have feelings for him."

"No." Saghani sighed and Lily saw that her expression was both vulnerable and earnest. "I ruined my chance to win Gisik long ago. He doesn't see me as a woman that he would take as a wife."

Lily winced as she heard the note of finality in Saghani's voice. Gisik was a quiet man, less apt to talk and more likely to practice fighting with his knife or spear. As the seasons passed, she watched Saghani's interest in him grow, but Gisik made it clear that he was not interested in pursuing Saghani as a wife.

"Now that my grandfather has passed and you have married Cahil, I have become a burden to your uncle."

"Perhaps he has other things on his mind." Ever since Nimiuq's untimely death Simoi was often distracted and Lily admitted to herself that her attention had been fully captured by her husband and their growing feelings for one another. Lily ducked her head as she remembered the intimate touch of Cahil's lips and the way that she welcomed his embrace each night.

"I am a burden to Simoi and I know that he would see me joined to a young man from one of the many bands, but I cannot simply go to a man that he picks for me and accept my place as his wife." Saghani placed both birds upon a spit where they would roast slowly over the small cooking fire. "I cannot, Lily."

"If Simoi chooses a man for you, then you will do as you must." Lily shuddered with relief as she considered what her life would have been like if she had been forced to join with a man that she did not know. She could only hope that her friend would be as fortunate.

She was exceedingly grateful that she and Cahil were now husband and wife. Cahil knew the song in her heart and he was the only man that she would ever willingly choose for herself.

CHAPTER THIRTY

Cahil did not have a chance to speak to Lily as the day waned and darkness began to creep over the land. He spent the day with Takotna and he was forced to admit to himself that he was eager to learn all that he could from his grandfather. Kusug's betrayal had been like a spear to his soul, striking at the heart of everything he believed to be true. To learn that Kusug was the enemy of his father and that Nanuq was partially responsible for the death of an innocent child was both devastating and enlightening.

Throughout his life, he sensed a distance between himself and Kusug, but instead of dwelling on it, he merely pushed himself harder, seeking to be a son that the aging warrior would be proud to call his own. He noticed the light of pride in Kusug's eyes when Makiye became skilled at the same tasks. Yet, he couldn't fault his brother, nor did he grow envious of Makiye's place within Kusug's heart. He held a fondness for Makiye, prior to his brother's betrayal.

At times, Cahil thought that he should have remained in the Ula'tuk village and fought his brother for the position of leadership. However, he would lose his honor if he used strength to steal the position of leadership from the one that his father deemed worthy.

"Makiye was chosen by Kusug and I was not." Cahil spoke to himself as he strode toward the large fire where the other men were gathered.

"Cahil, are you talking to yourself?" Anuk appeared at his side and the young man seemed to have grown by a hand's width since the previous day.

"Anuk, what are you about?"

"Your grandfather asked me to come find you and bring you to the village fire. He has gathered several people there that wish to meet you."

Cahil nodded once as Anuk walked at his side and he was relieved that for once, Anuk chose to remain silent without being admonished to do so. He was surprised to see that the men that he favored in appearance were present and they were standing with his grandfather.

"Cahil, I would like you to meet your relatives." Takotna's hand trembled as he urged Cahil forward and his eyes glittered with excitement and joy which was only enhanced by the caribou hunt to come.

"These men are hunters that roam the great land and they survive by following the caribou herds. They are related to you by blood ties and they would like to make you welcome."

Cahil straightened his spine as he met the eyes of the first man that stepped forward.

"I am Nisku, your father was my uncle." The man's voice was deep and he stood eye to eye with him as they regarded one another.

"You could be brothers, the resemblance is so strong between you." Anuk interrupted the meeting and then quickly lowered his head as two pairs of eyes glowered at him.

"This is Pi'ut." Takotna indicated a man that stood a head shorter than Cahil and Nisku, their eyes were similar, but their resemblance ended there. Pi'ut's body was wide and stout and his protruding belly spoke of many seasons of hearty meals. He wore several beaded necklaces and Cahil noticed that he carried two knives tied to a belt that went over one shoulder and around the waist.

Pi'ut inclined his head as they silently studied one another.

"I am the nephew of your father. Nisku and I are brothers, though we have different mothers."

"Good health to them!" Anuk inserted as all eyes turned toward him and he swallowed audibly.

"Good health to who?" Nisku asked with a narrowing of his eyes.

Anuk responded although Cahil's glowering gaze warned him to remain silent. "Good health to both of your mothers."

"Both of our mothers have breathed their last breaths." Pi'ut replied as Cahil stepped forward to diffuse what could possibly turn into an argument. "But if they were alive, they would thank you."

Cahil was wise enough not to ask the men about their father. He was certain that his uncle would have been present to greet him if he still lived.

"Who is this odd young man with hair that stands on end?" Nisku asked Cahil and he saw at once, that his eyes gleamed with forbearance.

"He is called Anuk." Cahil answered before Anuk could step forward and introduce himself. "It is said that his mother gave birth to him in a shallow stream and he remained underwater too long before taking his first breath. At times, I fear that his wits are addled."

"Cahil!" Anuk raised his eyebrows in surprise as the other men stared at him with interest. "Is that true?"

Cahil answered as his cousins watched his impassive face for the first flicker of expression. "I was not present at your birth. Who is to say?"

He was relieved when Nisku and Pi'ut echoed Takotna's laughter. In his own way, Anuk diffused a potentially volatile encounter. He was invited to sit with his cousins as they spoke of their wives and children. Takotna excused himself after a time and Cahil realized that he sat comfortably with Nisku and Pi'ut for far longer than anticipated.

Both men shared stories of their lives and the ways of the hunt. They offered to join him during the caribou hunt the next day and he readily accepted. Their initial meeting went well, though for a time, they were like wolves scenting one another for dominance.

Yet, they managed to find common ground and there was an air of honesty present in Nisku and Pi'ut's forthright manner that immediately put him at ease. If not for the wound healing on his palm, he would have been able to set aside the sense of calamity that hovered at the edges of his vision.

He silently reminded himself that he should be relieved that neither one of his cousins were responsible for attacking him in the dark of night. He would have been forced to dim the joy in Takotna's eyes by challenging a relative to a fair fight in the broad light of day. Cahil clenched his hand into a fist as Nisku asked him a question, distracting him from such dark thoughts.

Umak approached the village fire and he was pleased to see that the men from the various bands stepped aside so that he could take his place at the front of the fire circle.

"Good day to you, Umak." Several of the men called and Umak acknowledged them with an inclination of his head and a measuring glance.

"Good day." Umak released a pent up sigh as he caught sight of the man that had been foremost in his mind throughout the day. Simoi approached the fire in full raiment, wearing the highly decorated headdress of a hunter of the great land. Shells were strung together at his wrists and ankles, and with each movement, sound echoed. Suntar lifted a rattle into the air and a hush fell over the assembled crowd.

Umak was gratified to see that there were not any women or children present to observe the hunters' ceremony. He believed strongly that women sucked the strength out of strong hunters and their presence would have reduced the chances of success for the caribou hunt.

Savory dishes of stewed rabbit, roasted duck, raw fish sliced thin and placed upon large green leaves were passed from one hand to the other as Simoi walked around the fire. His ceremonial parka was dyed red and yellow, the colors of the fire and his hunting spear was adorned with multicolored feathers. All eyes turned toward him as he called out to the hunters that made the journey from far and wide to hunt the caribou.

"Hayaia!"

The resounding cry from the men filled Umak's chest with a sense of power and pride. "Hayaia!"

It was the cry of a hunter, the shout of success, the supplicating appeal to the heavens that enriched the joined voices of the men.

"From times long lasting until now, we have gathered together as one to hunt the caribou." Simoi's voice rang with feeling as the men listened closely, giving him their full attention.

Umak met Simoi's eyes and lifted his chin in acknowledgement though he was surprised that Simoi kept control over the cold rage that flickered in his eyes as he returned to the ceremony at hand.

"We are men of the great land, hunters all!" Simoi caught sight of Umak sitting proudly with his band of men and he clenched his fists in anger, though he kept his voice steady out of respect for the sacred words that he was honored to relay.

"A man is not a hunter unless he knows the ways of the land. Can a blind man find the caribou trails and lead his band to a successful hunt?" Simoi asked as the men waited in silent expectation.

"He can if he is a hunter of the great land!" Simoi shouted as the men reacted with loud cries of agreement and feet that stomped the ground, causing a resounding sound to clash like thunder from the throng of men.

"What hunter does not know the ways of the land? What hunter has not learned from his father or his father's father where the caribou run and when they will return?" Simoi pounded his chest with a closed fist as his eyes landed first upon Umak before circling the fire until he found Cahil.

"Even a man that is not of this land has learned the ways of a cautious hunter at his father's knee."

CHAPTER THIRTY-ONE

Simoi saw that Cahil sat with Nisku and Pi'ut, men that he called brothers of the hunt. As he turned around, he found Umak's eyes upon him and he wanted nothing more than to take his spear, which was reverently dressed for the evening ceremony, and run it through Umak's dark heart. He used his anger to call strength to his voice as he spoke to the men of the great land.

"The caribou are plentiful and they run across the open land in search of food. Which hunter does not know the ways of the caribou and yet calls himself a man?" Simoi pounded his chest again as the men responded with heedful cries of agreement.

Ashish and Suntar began to chant slowly, until they were joined by Takotna. Simoi moved around the fire as their weathered voices drifted into the bedarkened sky.

Up above, the luminaries hung overhead, lighting the sky just as fire lit the ground below. Simoi gave himself over to the hunter's dance as the drums blended with his pounding heartbeat. His footsteps were the footsteps of his father, brother and uncle who walked the sacred path, long ago.

Lost in the steps of the dance, he was not aware of Umak or the men with him that stood in recognition of the power that stalked the land. He did not see Cahil lean closer so that he could see across the fire circle to the shadowed figure that watched Simoi so closely.

Cahil breathed deeply as the swell of power surrounded the hunters gathered close to the fire circle. He did not need to understand the ancient words chanted by Ashish, Suntar and Takotna to comprehend their meaning.

The revered elders asked for a blessing from the heavens, a successful hunt, with plentiful bounty for all. They begged for the ability to survive the cold season and they asked protection for the women and children that relied upon the strength of their bodies and the accuracy of their spears.

Cahil was swept away by his first hunters' gathering, but he also caught sight of a man that he would recognize anywhere. A dark figure stood watching Simoi dance as the drums thundered and the elders chanted. Suddenly, Cahil realized that the man that attacked him in the dark of night was known to the other men present. He was accepted by all as a hunter, when in truth he walked as an enemy.

Umak caught Cahil's eye and raised his uninjured right hand in silent challenge. He saw the flare of anger in the newcomer's eyes and his lips lifted in satisfaction. It would suit him perfectly if Cahil challenged him before the council of elders and the hunters of the gathered bands. He held a position of strength and he would like nothing more than to see the light in Cahil's eyes dim with death's strong hold.

Simoi's dance came to an end and the drumbeat stopped suddenly so that only the sound of breathing could be heard. Ashish, Suntar and Takotna stood as one and stepped out of the light given by the fire.

Umak stood, casting off his warm cloak as the other men turned their attention toward him. "I wish to offer a dance from the band of my father, Mirotuk. We will perform the spirit dance known to the hunters of our band and it will honor the elders of the Krahnan band as well as each man that calls himself a hunter."

"Umak!" Simoi started to move forward, but Gisik appeared at his side and placed a staying hand upon his shoulder.

"This is not the time to settle your dispute with Umak." Gisik murmured as anger flashed in Simoi's eyes, though he grudgingly relented.

Umak ignored Simoi as he walked forward with strong steps. All eyes turned toward him as the light from the fire lit his features and his eyes glittered with strength of will. "My father is ill, but he asked that I dance in his place and I have promised to do so."

Pride caused Umak to lift his chin as the men of his band stepped forward. They were hunters, but they were also warriors. Each man wore only his loincloth and knee high moccasins. The men of the Mirotuk band wore white paint upon their faces, arms and legs and their spears were decorated with feathers and paint in preparation for the hunt. Umak wore white paint around his throat and in two bold lines down his chest, continuing over his muscular thighs and legs, while white rings of paint circled his arms.

Cahil watched the Mirotuk band as one of the men stood apart with two large drum poles that were used to elicit sound, while another blew through a round gourd, bringing forth the sound of the wind. He immediately saw that Umak took on the dance of the caribou while his men danced as mighty hunters. The red strips of hide that the men wore across their foreheads signified blood and as Umak arched his back and stomped his feet rhythmically, Cahil was drawn into the hunter's spirit dance.

Umak clasped both hands together, with his left hand pointed palm up and his right hand facing down. He spread his legs wide, squatting low as he danced into the center of the hunters. Two men raised their spears against him and Umak did not cower, instead he bravely exposed his chest, thrusting his hands out to his sides as he welcomed the hunter's spears.

An honorable death.

The hunters imitated the act of spearing Umak with sharp slashing movements that blended and melded into the dance as Umak released a blood red cloth from his hands, signifying the blood of the hunt. The hunters grabbed hold of the red cloth and pulled it toward them as Umak continued to dance and one of the men began to sing with a mournful wail that caused a shiver to pass over the assembled crowd.

Umak gestured wildly, bowing backward so that his head hung almost to the ground, a caribou in its death throes, as the hunters danced around him and the undulating cry drew to an end. Umak fell to the ground and rose to stand strong and proud, in imitation of the caribou herd which was massive and never-ending, though one might fall, others were quick to rise in its place.

Cahil was stunned by the reverence shown by Umak, a man that Simoi marked as his enemy, a man that attacked him seemingly without cause. By watching the dance, he realized that Umak honored the caribou and sought to give them an honorable death, just as any warrior would seek for himself.

Umak separated himself from the other men and came to stand before Cahil as they silently watched one another. Like the other men, Cahil was awed by the strength with which Umak and the hunters of his band danced. The men cheered and Umak's words were almost drowned out, but Cahil watched him steadily and he heard him clearly.

"Tomorrow, we will hunt the caribou, but tonight I have won a victory over the men." Umak's dark eyes narrowed as Cahil lifted his head in silent challenge instead of backing away in defeat.

Umak's harsh laughter blended with the sound of cheering and revelry incited by the Mirotuk spirit dance and when the others drew him away, he did not resist the pull of their hands.

"Nisku and Pi'ut told me that the men of the great land know the location where the caribou will cross the river." Anuk's eyes gleamed as he walked at Cahil's side. "The men of the Krahnan band once chose to remain here, simply because the caribou have been known to cross nearby for seasons untold."

Cahil listened as Anuk described the hunting style of Nisku and Pi'ut though both men were within hearing distance. He knew that Anuk was alight with excitement and honored to be included in the caribou hunt.

"We will drive the caribou across a narrow place in the river and each man must seek out the caribou that will come to his spear." Pi'ut explained the way of the hunt to Anuk, but Cahil knew that he spoke for his benefit as well. As a hunter, he was aware of the ways to hunt large game animals, but each village and band carried out the hunt in their own way.

"Each hunter carries two spears, so that we will have more than one chance to bring down one of the caribou."

Cahil could not stop thinking of his wife. She had been awake when he returned to the fire and he managed to talk to her, albeit briefly when she turned to greet him as he strode toward Takotna's lodge.

"I must return to my grandfather." Cahil glanced at Saghani's sleeping form. He was almost certain that she listened to every word. "He is ill and the events of the day will have tired him."

"I understand." Lily whispered, though she too glanced at Saghani before returning her eyes to his face. "Are you well?"

"I am well. Take your rest and I will return as soon as I can." Cahil wanted to tell Lily that he was filled with doubt and confusion, but instead he went to check on his grandfather and returned to hold her in his arms as she slept wrapped in several sleeping furs.

For his part, Cahil could not sleep. His thoughts swirled around the events of the past few days. His very presence caused Umak to name him as an enemy and his grandfather wanted him to follow his father's dreams of the future by leading the Krahnan band and establishing a village. To Cahil's practical eye, Umak held the position of strength, but Takotna felt that everything would change if he announced his claim as their leader. The place of leadership was his by right of blood if he chose to claim it.

"Cahil?" Anuk called, drawing him back to the present. "I will shadow you on the hunt, if that is your wish."

Cahil saw that Anuk would have accepted his place at his back during the hunt and he thought of himself at Anuk's age, a young man eager to prove his manhood. "No. You will stand as a hunter, just like the other men."

He felt Nisku and Pi'ut's eyes upon him and their expressions were full of approval.

Cahil caught sight of Simoi and Gisik as he raised a beckoning hand toward the men.

"I am glad that we were able to find each other." Simoi kept his voice pitched low as he glanced at Gisik.

Cahil watched the other hunters, men of the great land that moved like shadows over the ground, drifting ever forward. The men walked toward the river, honoring the caribou with their reverent silence.

Gisik offered no greeting, though Cahil noticed that he did not growl at Anuk.

"We must speak after the caribou hunt." Cahil's voice was pitched low as Simoi turned brilliant dark eyes upon him.

"What is it?" Simoi asked.

"We will speak later." Cahil murmured, as he moved away from Simoi and walked in the footsteps of the hunter in front of him. He could not know that his eyes were fiercely lit and his stride completely focused on what was to come. Nor did he realize that the men that once belonged to the Krahnan band watched him with eyes full of expectation and hope.

CHAPTER THIRTY-TWO

"The caribou herd is just ahead." Simoi crouched low over sagebrush and sparse grass as he gestured ahead.

The men closest to him followed the direction of his hand and they saw for themselves the milling caribou herd. All eyes looked for the lead bull that would draw the herd over the fast flowing Krahnan River and toward the distant grazing land.

Cahil lay flat upon the ground as he watched Nisku and Pi'ut creep closer to the herd. Each of the hunters slithered forward on their bellies as they tried to edge closer without being seen. His breath was heavy in his lungs as he thought of the task ahead of him. Cahil would have preferred to use the antlers of a large male to form the tip of his spear, but he wasn't given a choice in the matter. He spent most of the previous night making a second throwing spear and he could only hope that he balanced the weapon and sharpened the bone spear tip properly.

He preferred to test out his weapon first, before using it on a hunt, but in this case there was not enough time. Simoi explained that the herd would swim over the Krahnan River and disappear until the warm season. Several bands rested on the opposite side of the riverbank and they would follow the herd, picking off stray members as the cold season loomed.

The Krahnan village and the bands that gathered together to hunt were given one chance to kill the caribou and then butcher and store the meat or they would suffer hunger and deprivation over the cold season to come.

"One of the men will call out and the others will do the same." Simoi advised. "That is how we will know that the hunt has begun."

Each man was aware that lives could be lost in the hunt. The caribou were strong animals, large beasts with antlers that could pierce a man's body and hooves capable of breaking bone. The animals were brown in color with brilliant white fur gracing their necks, rumps and legs.

The search for food drove the caribou to seek the distant forest where they would forage and survive the coming cold season. Cahil grimaced as he considered that the search for food was present in both man and beast. He slithered on his belly as his empty stomach growled. Like the other men, he chose not to eat anything after the evening ceremony of the previous night. Experience taught him that hunger kept his senses alert and active. Hunger also fueled quiet desperation.

"It is quiet desperation that drove the first hunter to seek out the caribou herd." Cahil shared the stories of the hunt with his cousins and Anuk as they listened closely. "A hunter must become more desperate than his prey. It is the only way that a man who cannot run as fast as a four-legged animal, can accurately explain the phenomena that occurs during the hunt. It is the legacy of our ancestors, men that rose up from the land and dominated the moving creatures, choosing them as a source of food."

"Predator and prey." Cahil breathed out with a long exhalation of breath and then the piercing cry from one of the men announced the beginning of the hunt. As one, the men rose to their feet and pounded over the barren landscape, each one seeking to outdistance the other as they ran toward the frightened herd.

The caribou moved like a russet wall as the lead bull broke off and led the herd across in one indistinct mass. Cahil was aware of the men at his right and left, running full out toward the caribou. Each hunter was eager to sink his spear into the yielding flesh of the caribou.

Cahil lost sight of Anuk, Nisku and Pi'ut as the first wave of hunters reached the herd. He was surrounded by men that understood their tenuous hold on prosperity. If the hunt was successful, they would have enough to eat over the time of long cold. If they failed, their food caches would quickly empty and they would become a burden to their band.

He immediately rejected the females, though like the males they were adorned with antlers, however, they were easily identifiable by their smaller size. Cahil raised his spear as he caught sight of a large male. The animal danced wildly toward the river, pushing and prodding the others so that he could cross in their stead.

He came alongside the male as he aimed for the place between the shoulder and throat. He shouted as he felt his spear enter the animal's neck and he used all of his strength to make the kill. The great animal ran for a distance as it fought the inevitable and just as the caribou fell to its knees, Cahil sensed a presence behind him. He spun and caught sight of Umak bearing down upon him with his spear raised.

His heightened senses told him that Umak did not seek to drive his spear through a nearby male caribou and Cahil drew his second spear as Umak leapt over a fallen animal and drove his spear toward his heart. Cahil turned to avoid Umak's spear thrust and then he pivoted just as quickly in the other direction as the man struck again, moving faster than the eye could follow.

Cahil reacted instinctively, scrambling out of the way until a few of the straggling caribou cut him off from Umak's attack. It was clear to him that Umak sought to kill him, whether it was by his hand or the stampeding herd. A large male caribou thundered across the spongy muskeg and snow.

Instead of fleeing, Cahil faced the animal, knowing instinctively that it would take all of his strength and skill to bring the caribou down. Time slowed as Cahil threw his body into the air, driving his spear out and down just as the caribou sped past.

For a moment, he was airborne as the caribou shook its neck and flung him to the side as if he weighed nothing at all. The jarring impact of the ground knocked the breath from his lungs and the pounding cadence of the stampeding herd drowned out all sound.

A resounding slap cracked through the air and Cahil winced as he opened his eyes. Knees pressed into his chest and he found that he could not inhale as the flat of a man's palm connected with the side of his face.

"Umak!" Cahil roared as his vision cleared and Anuk stared back at him.

"No, it is me, Anuk." The youth stared hard at Cahil and then he seemed to realize that Cahil did not take kindly to him sitting on his chest.

"I saw the caribou throw you through the air like a stone thrown by a child's hand and I came to see if you were dead." Anuk replied cheerfully as Cahil struggled to sit up.

"Get off of me." Cahil winced as a stone cut into his back.

Anuk scrambled off of his chest, but not before he was prodded by bony knees and a sharp elbow. He suppressed the desire to grab Anuk by the neck as he took in his surroundings. The caribou herd faded into the distance and everywhere he looked there were downed carcasses. Loud whoops of success filled the air as the men claimed coup over their kills.

"You speared a caribou!" Anuk shouted as Cahil shook his head to clear it.

"I speared two caribou." Cahil frowned as he walked toward the river. Several of the men walked past as they searched the ground for their distinctive spears.

"I only saw you spear the caribou that threw you like a child throws a rock." Anuk repeated as he caught sight of Simoi, Nisku and Pi'ut. "Cahil killed a caribou."

"I killed two caribou." Cahil said as the men approached and began to boast over their kills.

"Cahil, one caribou is enough to feed several people. You should be proud of your accomplishment." Simoi would have said more, but Cahil walked away from him and searched the ground where he made his first kill of the day.

He found Umak standing proudly over the large male that fell under the thrust of his spear and clouds of red filled his vision. Cahil's spear was on the ground beneath the animal, but Umak's spear was driven through the caribou's neck, just above the shoulder.

"Have you come to compare my kill with yours?" Umak asked as the men of his band surrounded him.

Cahil noticed the show of force and he saw that Umak held the loyalty of many armed men, warriors all. Suddenly, Simoi was there and Cahil angrily shook off his hands as he tried to pacify him.

"I killed this caribou!" Cahil asserted as Umak threw back his head and laughed.

"Then how is it that my spear punctured a hole in the animal's neck?"

"Cahil, your spear lies underneath." Anuk was wise enough to back away when he saw the fury in Cahil's eyes.

"I killed this caribou and the one that lies over there." Cahil could barely speak over the rage that built inside. Umak's gleaming eyes were triumphant and he wanted nothing more than to accuse him of removing the spear and replacing it with his own.

"You are mistaken." Umak's eyes lit with interest as Cahil advanced forward. "If you would like to settle this as warriors, instead of hunters, then you need only say the word."

"Caution, Cahil." Simoi murmured as he pressed one finger against Cahil's damaged hand. The wound was deep and slow to heel and it was then that Cahil remembered that Simoi warned him that Umak was skilled with all weapons, including the knife that he wore tied down over his thigh.

Cahil would have ignored the warning, if not for the way that Umak's eyes flashed toward his hand. It was then that he understood something that he had not known before. Umak could have taken his life when they fought in the dark of night, before Cahil was able to rally and defend himself. However, he chose to let him live.

Cahil studied Umak's dark eyes as he tried to determine what drove the man, what motivated him. He inhaled sharply as he realized that the same honor that was intrinsic within him had been bred into Umak, though its interpretation was vastly different. Umak purposely injured Cahil's right hand, damaging his fighting hand and then claimed the caribou so that Cahil would challenge him to a fight in front of the other men. Even though Cahil understood Umak with an uncanny certainty, he still considered giving in to the urge to fight him.

Cahil took one step back as Umak's eyes widened in surprise. "I was mistaken."

Cahil turn his back upon Umak as he saw the man's hand run across his knife, before resting at his side. It was then that he understood that while he marked Umak as his enemy, Umak did the same to him.

CHAPTER THIRTY-THREE

"Cahil, I did not expect to see you until morning." Simoi spoke as Cahil walked toward him until he stood at his side overlooking the encampment below. From this vantage point, they could see the permanent lodges of the Krahnan band, though they were few. The various bands of the land constructed skin lodges that were easy to dismantle and carry when they left the encampment behind until the next gathering ceremony.

"I only brought down one caribou." Cahil said as Simoi turned to face him.

"We both know that is untrue."

Cahil stared hard at Simoi as the man watched him closely.

"I saw you." Simoi answered the question apparent in Cahil's eyes. "I saw you bring down the large male that Umak claimed and I saw you fight Umak, before he drove you into the herd."

"You saw me."

Cahil was at first relieved and then just as quickly he realized that whether or not Simoi knew the truth, he failed to lay claim to both kills. Simoi's band needed the meat that two caribou would have brought to them. Even with snares and traps, they would be fortunate to catch ground squirrels, rabbits and voles, but success was not guaranteed. The meat of two caribou would have been enough to ensure their survival over what threatened to be a long cold season.

"Umak has marked you for death." Simoi warned as Cahil stood without moving.

"He is the man that I fought with on my first night in the Krahnan village."

"I suspected as much." Simoi sighed as he stared hard at Cahil. "I will not accept his death at your hands. I must be the one that ends his life."

"You say this and I must ask you again, what does it matter as long as he dies?" Cahil watched Simoi's features tighten and he saw the need for vengeance in the older man's eyes.

Just as quickly, Simoi returned his gaze to Cahil and said, "Between the two of us, Gisik and I were able to bring down one caribou. I will accept your speared caribou as a gift to my hearth, only if you and Lily share in the spoils of the hunt within our band. This is our gift to you."

Lily raised her head sharply as Cahil moved around the caribou hide that she scraped with a sharp stone and swept her into his arms before she could even begin to form a protest.

"Cahil?" Lily glanced over Cahil's shoulder and saw Simoi and the others watching with smiles upon their faces.

"Your uncle has accepted the caribou that I killed as a gift to his hearth." Cahil's eyes flashed with happiness as Lily laughed. "He has accepted my place as your husband."

Lily she couldn't have formed the words to speak even if her life depended on it. She was completely overwhelmed by Cahil's return and she trembled in his arms as he carried her away from prying eyes and set her down near a shallow pool.

Lily should have felt embarrassed as Cahil removed her fur parka and leggings, striping her mukluks off with fingers that were skilled and firm. Yet, she was enraptured by the intensity of his eyes and the primal way that he touched her as if she was something rare and of immeasurable value. His eyes worshipped her body as he bared her to his gaze and she stood before him naked and exposed, wreathed by moonlight.

With her hands spread over Cahil's bare chest, Lily couldn't form a complete thought as he began to wash the dirt and grime from their bodies. Butchering the caribou and scraping the hides was a difficult task and they were filthy, worn and tired. The icy touch of the water was invigorating and yet as soon as they were clean, Cahil quickly wrapped Lily in her fur cape and lifted her into his arms.

He pressed his mouth against hers and breathed in her scent.

"I will cherish you all the days of my life." Cahil breathed deeply, searing the moment into his memory as he held Lily in his arms, unwilling to let her go.

Lily would have spoken, but Cahil kissed her again as he carried her to Takotna's lodge.

"Your grandfather might return." Lily finally found her voice as Cahil swept under the entrance of the lodge and she placed her feet upon the hard packed floor.

"Takotna will remain with Simoi tonight. He has given us his lodge until the sun rises." Cahil thought of the perfection of Lily's body, he was entranced with the soft flush of her skin and the feminine curves that he bared to his gaze. He was intoxicated by the swell of her breasts and her soft sighs of pleasure which called to him as nothing else ever would.

He saw that she shivered and he immediately stoked the small fire until it emitted warmth that caused Lily to shed the fur cape that hid her body from view.

"I will always be your wife." Lily murmured as Cahil barely refrained from pulling her into his arms and claiming her body.

"Yes and I will always be your husband."

Tears threatened and then fell free as Lily laughed softly and launched herself into Cahil's arms. He caught her fast against the strength of his chest and when he crushed her against the length of his body she responded with a newfound passion that delighted him fully.

His passionate kisses and tender words stole her breath and seared her soul as he laid claim to her body. He memorized her shape with upward sweeping touches of his hands and she realized that he took her to a place that she never knew existed. They matched each other in every way as moonlight whispered over them in secret and the stars drifted overhead.

CHAPTER THIRTY-FOUR

The days passed one after another, as the cold season grabbed hold of the great land with an icy fist. Cahil and Lily came to know each other as husband and wife and they were made welcome by all after Cahil decided to erect a permanent lodge.

"My uncle has decided to remain with us throughout the cold season, but he will not speak of the future." Lily glanced at Cahil as her husband returned from the food catch where he stored the meat that would see them through the cold season.

She noticed that Cahil wore the traditional head covering preferred by the men of the Krahnan band. She crafted the fur hood for him and she knew the texture of the fur that blanketed his head and neck. He caressed the side of her face and Lily looked up from her task of basket weaving to see that he fixed his gaze upon her face without looking away.

"Simoi is welcome to remain with us and I have told him so." Cahil responded as he continued to watch Lily. She was clothed in a bulky parka and leggings that hid her slender form, but he knew her body as well as he knew his own. "There is a lodge for the women where they are welcomed depending on the dance of the moon."

Lily blinked as she tried to hide a smile. "Yes, I know of the women's lodge. It is not often spoken of by men."

Cahil grimaced and nodded. He had come to learn that many of the Krahnan men were superstitious. They believed that a man that mated with a woman during her moon flow would lose his ability to lure fish or call large game to his spear. Cahil was not certain whether such things were true, but he knew that he sated the male hunger that Lily aroused, as often as possible and her woman's flow never crossed his mind until now.

"You have not visited the woman's lodge since the day that you became my wife."

Lily's smile widened. "Just so."

It was Cahil's turn to blink as he tried to determine what would make her face beam like sunlight on a warm day.

"I carry your child, Cahil." Lily rested her hand upon her stomach which was slightly rounded, though hidden beneath layers of warm clothing. "I think that I have carried new life within me from the first night that you took me as your wife so many moons ago."

"A son?" Cahil asked as some of the light in Lily's eyes dimmed and he bent to his knees beside her without noticing. "A son to sing my songs over the fire and continue to teach his sons the same."

"If you want a son, then it is my wish that I carry a male child in my belly." Lily bit her lip as Cahil rested his head upon her stomach and she placed both hands upon his thick black hair. "But it could also be a girl that I carry and I would like a daughter to spend time with and teach."

"A daughter?" Cahil frowned at the thought. "I would prefer a son."

"A healthy child." Lily smiled warmly, though her heart beat in trepidation as Cahil nodded distractedly and reclaimed his position on his knees beside her.

"A strong son to follow in my footsteps." Cahil's eyes lit with happiness and Lily did not care to diminish his joy over the future birth of their child, but she was also concerned that Cahil did not acknowledge that the child might not be a boy.

"I have always wanted a son." Cahil said as he pressed his lips against Lily's round cheek and kissed her gently. She delighted in the feel of his fingers as they spread through her hair, massaging her scalp and the arch of her neck. She wore her hair loose most of the time simply because she knew that her husband enjoyed the touch and feel of her hair.

She welcomed Cahil into her arms, knowing that the unexpected blessing of their child pleased him more than she could have imagined. The new life that she carried was a spark of light that they would always share, together as husband and wife.

Umak and his men returned from a successful hunt and they were weary, though emboldened by the events of the day. One of his trusted men reported that Gisik was spotted trailing their band and Umak's jaw tightened.

"Sinaaq," Umak called the man over to his side. "Go and bring Gisik to me, I grow tired of hearing about his search for his niece."

If the young girl, Ashlu, had been available he might have taken out his growing anger on her, but she and her mother were far away, outside of the reach of Gisik. As long as Ashlu and her mother were under his control, he could keep Gisik in a stranglehold that would not allow him to act.

Already, Umak worked diligently to increase the food stores of the bands that remained nearby. He sought to entice them with the offer of a regular supply of food during the cold season so that they would bend to his will.

After his father's long awaited death, Umak stood as the leader of his band by default. There was no one else with the knowledge or the will to lead so many strong men. Umak held a powerful position, a place of strength that the Krahnan band could not hope to overshadow.

"Umak, is there anything else that I can do for you?" Sinaaq shifted uncertainly as Umak's eyes drifted over the men that were settled inside of skin lodges that would keep them warm.

"Sinaaq, one day our band will know prosperity and honor." Umak responded, though his voice was barely above a whisper. "Our men deserve to have a permanent settlement that offers good hunting, fishing and access to water."

"You have the strength to lead a village, Umak, this is true." Sinaaq was several seasons older than Umak and he was a trusted advisor within his inner circle. It was for this reason that Umak deferred to him when he heard the note of doubt in Sinaaq's voice.

"Forgive me for saying so, but it has become apparent that Cahil has taken a place in the heart of the people of the great land."

"I have fed them, I have hunted for them and yet, Cahil has taken a place in their hearts?" Umak stood suddenly, transforming his appearance from relaxed poise to warrior. His chest gleamed in the firelight and his dark eyes danced with anger. His mouth tightened as Sinaaq lowered his eyes, giving Umak time to gather his thoughts. "Continue!"

"I know that you did not wish to slay Cahil without cause, but if you wait for an opportunity to present itself it might be too late."

"Cahil has brought the bands of the great land together simply because of his existence. If I slay him without cause, I will not gain their favor, nor will I have the same hold on their hearts that Cahil does."

"If you delay, Cahil will become a force that will be impossible to topple. It appears that the people have rallied behind him, knowing that he was born of sacred blood. They remember that his father successfully led the Krahnan band, as did his father before him and the people that have since scattered to the wind have now returned. The elders have reminded everyone of the former glory of the Krahnan band."

Umak pounded his fist against his hand in fury, but Sinaaq bravely continued speaking. "The people hold Takotna, Ashish and Suntar in high esteem. The men hunt for them, the women feed them and even the children lower their heads in difference to the older men. The revered Krahnan elders look to Cahil as the next leader of their band, they have said that he has brought the people together as no other man could."

"Sinaaq, I say to you now that I will let nothing stand in the way of my future. The people of the Krahnan band were once blessed with prosperity and good fortune while we roamed the land in search of food and shelter. I will not return to that way of life ever again. I will destroy any man that stands against me." Umak's dark eyes were cold and his voice was filled with dire certainty. "I will crush Cahil under my heel and that will be the end of the matter!"

"I do not like the taste of fermented seal flipper." Anuk complained as Simoi led the way over the land to reach his cache of food.

"It is a delicacy, Anuk and you would do well to keep quiet because the elders of the Krahnan band enjoy the taste and you do not wish to offend them."

"Why do they only ferment the seal flipper and not the tail or perhaps the ears?"

The question brought Simoi to a standstill as he frowned, "Perhaps the ears are too small and I have heard that the tail is bitter. Long ago, I would often journey with Gisik to hunt both walrus and seal."

"We would have to travel many days to reach the great water and only then would we hope to find anything to hunt."

"This is why the seal flipper is a delicacy and if Takotna wishes to enjoy the treat, then I will find it for him."

"Where did they bury their cache?" Anuk glanced around at the scattered rock mounds which had been painstakingly placed to conceal their food stores.

"We marked Takotna's cache with a piece of skin stained yellow." Simoi located the food cache and began to move rocks out of the way as Anuk scurried over to assist him.

"Some of the people have said that Umak brings food to them and he leads the Mirotuk band with strength." Anuk's brow furrowed as he glanced at Simoi for confirmation.

"Is that what they are saying?" Simoi asked as he deftly lifted stone after stone out of the way until he revealed the flat surface where the seal flipper had been left to ferment.

"Now that Cahil knows that his true father was their leader, as well as his father before him, I thought Cahil would take his rightful place as the leader of the Krahnan band."

"I see." Simoi added, using his hands to cup the soil and move it out of the way. The pungent scent of the fermented meat stung his nostrils as Anuk held his breath and his skin took on a sickly hue.

"Well?" Anuk asked. "Are you planning to speak to Cahil or will I have to sit and watch as he loses his rightful position, yet again?"

"Again?" Simoi asked as he held the wrapped seal flipper at arm's length and studied Anuk. "What do you mean?"

"Has Cahil not told you that the former leader of the Ula'tuk village withheld the position of leadership from him?"

Simoi narrowed his eyes as he considered how he would answer Anuk. It appeared that he would learn more about Cahil and his past by listening to the young man at his side. Thus he shrugged his shoulders as Anuk launched into a one-sided conversation about Cahil's upbringing and the death of Kusug. Simoi listened carefully and he learned much about Cahil from young Anuk.

CHAPTER THIRTY-FIVE

"Cahil!" The sound of Anuk calling his name from outside of his lodge drew his attention. Cahil glanced at his sleeping wife, rolled to his feet and ducked under the lodge entrance. Dawn light filtered across the land and he was already clothed though he enjoyed watching his wife sleep.

"What is it, Anuk?"

"You must come and see, Simoi and Gisik have returned with terrible news."

Cahil hurried toward Simoi's lodge and he saw that Saghani was on her knees by a small fire. His heart lurched when he noticed that her face was streaked with tears. He glanced back at his lodge and assured himself that Lily was safe inside, wrapped in the warmth of their sleeping blankets.

"Cahil." Simoi stepped forward to meet him. "Gisik and I went to collect more meat from our food cache and we found it empty."

"Empty?" Cahil repeated as he tried to understand how so much meat could have disappeared. Between Simoi and Gisik there was enough to feed them all, with food to spare and he kept a separate store of food for himself and Lily.

"There was nothing left, not even a morsel of meat remained behind."

"Was it a scavenger, perhaps a bear or a pack of wolves? Animals such as those are known to scavenge for food." Cahil's eyes swept toward the horizon where the sun began to crest over the snow covered ground. The light would not be enough to melt the snowy barrier that coated the land.

"Our food cache was covered by several layers of rock and heavy stones. We left nothing uncovered and there were not any signs of animal tracks." Simoi responded as Gisik raised his head.

"What hunter of the great land would have stolen from us?"

"We cannot accuse any of the hunters of stealing. Many of the bands are determined to endure the cold season with us." Simoi said, even as Cahil nodded in understanding.

The people of the great land did not lie and they did not steal, such things were foreign to them. To accuse a man unjustly of such an act was to invite him to respond to the charge against his honor. Men lost their lives over less.

"I have enough caribou meat to share with you and the others, if we are careful and ration each portion." Cahil was quick to offer his help to Simoi and Gisik; he never forgot how they welcomed him to their mountain encampment and willingly shared their food.

"Cahil." Simoi's eyes were dark with concern as he captured Cahil's full attention. "Your food cache was also emptied. There is nothing left for any of us."

In that moment, Cahil realized that Simoi and Gisik took it upon themselves to check his food cache as well. He closed his eyes as he thought of his pregnant wife and his heart almost stopped as he tried to imagine how he would care for Lily and their unborn child.

Takotna raised his palms to the heavens as Ashish and Suntar waited nearby. When Takotna finally lowered his arms, his limbs trembled with fatigue and he struggled to suppress the rattling cough that threatened to erupt from his lungs.

"The various bands of the great land have been questioned and no one saw anything that would tell us who would steal your grandson's store of meat, or take meat from the mouths of Simoi and Gisik." Ashish sighed heavily as Takotna acknowledged his words with a gesture of thanks.

"It is troubling, to think that any hunter would steal from another." Suntar lowered his eyes as he considered the calamity that had befallen Takotna's grandson and the others.

"The people that remain with us are more in number than we have seen since your daughter's husband served as our leader."

"Yes," Takotna responded. "I would have expected the people to take as much meat as they could carry on their backs and upon their sleds, but they have remained to endure the cold season as one."

"Your grandson has united the people, by his very presence alone and we cannot express our gratitude with words." Suntar nudged Ashish as Takotna looked between them. "Many of the people laud Cahil's actions since his arrival. He has taken the time to share the ways of the Ula'tuk band with most of the hunters. It is said that he sets snares and traps for those that have not gathered enough for themselves."

"He is much like his father, a strong and powerful young man, capable of leading our people toward a greater destiny." Suntar said.

"Yet it appears that he has no interest in leading our band." Ashish inserted as Takotna's eyes flashed toward him. "He has only to say the word and many of the scattered bands would swear their loyalty and remain here in permanent dwellings. He is capable of returning our dying band to its former glory."

Takotna was silent for a time as he listened to the wise counsel of his friends. They spoke to him as they would anyone else, yet he heard the nuances in their speech and saw the burning intensity of their eyes. Like him, they felt their time upon the great land growing short and they remembered the days of their youth when they had been strong men and capable hunters. Their lives stretched out before them like a winding river, never-ending.

However, he knew that all things came to an end. Yet, the Krahnan band, though nearly destroyed, could be revived if Cahil decided to sit in the place of his father.

Takotna saw that Suntar and Ashish watched him expectantly and when he lifted his head and nodded decisively, they both breathed an audible sigh of relief.

Cahil walked with Lily to the central fire that many of the people gathered around. It was rare that they should gather together during the dark of night and with the cold season pressing down upon them. He helped his wife over the uneven ground as Lily placed both hands upon her belly, and she told him that they would welcome their child very soon.

He managed to hunt during the day and during that time Simoi and Gisik would often accompany him. The snares that he and Anuk set returned good results and they were glad to find the traps full upon occasion.

Yet, it is not enough, Cahil thought. His face was lean, now that he refused to take his morning meal as was their custom. Instead of eating twice a day, he ate only toward the evening, though his stomach rumbled more often than not. Cahil put Anuk and Lily before himself, knowing that his wife needed nourishment for the child that she carried and Anuk was still growing. It seemed that he was finally catching up in height to the length of his limbs. Some of the clumsy ways of his youth were disappearing day by day.

"Takotna has summoned nearly everyone." Lily said as she cast wide eyes around the fire circle.

She noticed the fur covered overcoat and parkas that were worn by most of the men. Each hunter kept his head covered, as was their way and the women's faces shined with bear grease, if it could be found. The unpleasant scent of the grease was better than the bitter taste of the wind and Lily knew that the women were just as warm as she was, despite the chill in the air and the snow underfoot.

With her husband's help, Lily sat next to Saghani as Cahil went to join his grandfather.

"Saghani, what has caused you to smile in such a way?" Lily watched her friend closely as Saghani surveyed the gathered crowd with a joyful expression upon her face.

"I have found a young man that cannot keep his gaze from straying my way." Saghani indicated a young man sitting across the fire.

Lily hid a smile as she saw that the young man was slightly older than Anuk. "He is young."

"I like young men, they do not have the weight of older men and their bellies are flat." Saghani lowered her voice conspiratorially. "He will speak to Simoi in the next few days."

"I am glad for you." Lily responded, though she was confused by Saghani's quick acceptance of the young man. "Are you certain?"

Saghani narrowed her eyes, "Even if Simoi gives his consent, I will wait until the warm season to make my decision. After all, I will not be certain until I have seen him in his loincloth."

Lily covered her mouth with both hands as she struggled to contain her laughter. Saghani barely noticed as she widened her eyes innocently and continued to stare across the fire at the object of her affection.

Cahil glanced over to see his wife whispering with Saghani and he could almost hear their laughter. Returning his attention to the task at hand, he searched for his grandfather amongst the men. Takotna gave them the skins to build a lodge, shortly after he took Lily as his wife. Much to his surprise, Simoi accepted his offering of the caribou that he took down in the hunt, but he kept only the skin and gave Cahil the meat as a gift.

Several of the men greeted him with expressions full of expectation and Cahil took their greetings in stride. Ever since his arrival, the people welcomed him with awe and great rejoicing. As time passed, he came to understand that they revered not only the village elders, but his father and the men of his bloodline.

Nisku and Pi'ut were the first to tell him that his very presence increased their standing within their band. It was a matter of amusement to him, but he knew that Takotna would not be amused. His grandfather recently took him aside and spoke to him about his responsibility and Cahil reflected upon their conversation.

"Your father would have expected you to follow in his footsteps." Takotna watched Cahil as he spoke. "He would have raised you to become a leader of men, honest and fair, honorable and just."

Cahil refrained from speaking of Kusug with his grandfather. Kusug raised him just as Takotna said, but he knew that his grandfather would not wish to hear about such things.

"I am content to be a hunter of the Krahnan band. I am a man with a wife that awaits our first child." Cahil felt pride over the mere thought of holding his son in his arms and his eyes lit with an inner fire as he spoke, though he was not aware of it.

"It is good that you do not hunger for power or thirst for glory. Part of the reason that your father suffered was because he lost sight of who he was for a time and he did not honor the old ways." Takotna went on to tell him that Nanuq failed to seek out the dancing lights by following the seeking star to the barren lands. "If your father honored the old ways, the good fortune and prosperity that our village once knew would have been made certain for another season."

Cahil listened with half of his attention as Takotna spoke. He thought that his grandfather would appreciate his attention and time, but Takotna grew angry.

"You listen, but you do not hear. You look, but you do not see." Takotna threw up his hands in anger, the first sign of a temper that Cahil ever noticed.

"Grandfather." Cahil held up a placating hand, which Takotna brushed away with the blunt end of his spear.

"No!" Takotna's back was rigid with anger as he stared at his grandson. "Your father did not waste the gift that was given to him on the day of his birth. Your blood makes you worthy to carry on the honor of leading our band, a dying band that you can revive simply by taking your rightful place."

Cahil would have spoken, but Takotna began to cough and choke, so that he feared for his grandfather's life. When Takotna regained his breath, his face was red from exertion and anger and Cahil felt duly chastised, though he could not say exactly why he should feel that way.

"I will speak no more of this. You will have to see that you have a responsibility to the very people that seek an assurance of hope."

"An assurance of hope?" Cahil could admit to himself that he was intrigued, though he never considered becoming the leader of the scattered bands that once belonged solely to the Krahnan band. The murderous rage that he once felt for his brother caused him to turn away from any thoughts of leadership. He told himself that he wanted a simple life, he wanted to live only as a hunter, a husband and very soon, a father.

"Are you aware that what our people desire the most is the assurance that they will not suffer disaster and deprivation?" Takotna stood so that he faced Cahil as he ushered him out of his lodge.

When they stepped outside Takotna raised his hands high overhead as Cahil looked into the dark sky. He felt a stirring of something that told him that there was more to life than what he could see, touch or feel.

"The people want to know that they have been granted a blessing, something rare that can only be gained by one that is especially blessed. A man like your father and his father before him. A man like you, Cahil. Though you would reject all that is within your reach, simply because you are unwilling to try."

"Grandfather," Cahil started to deny Takotna's words, but he realized that in part, they were true.

He wanted to lead a quiet life without the burden of providing for an entire village and the daily decisions that could prove to be a matter of life or death.

"Be silent my grandson." Takotna cautioned as Cahil threatened to undermine his words by speaking. "I ask only that you consider what I have said, tomorrow we will have a ceremony near the central fire. Bring your wife and see that she is rested and well."

Takotna dismissed him with a wave of his hand and Cahil left, though he glanced back to see his grandfather standing proud and erect with his face lifted to the night's sky.

"Your grandfather is about to speak." Anuk's voice pulled Cahil back to the present and he lifted his head to see that Takotna took a place beside the fire.

Takotna added a piece of dry wood to the blaze and all eyes turned his way as the fire crackled and burned with new life. "Like a fire burning, the Krahnan band has smoldered and burned since before I was born."

"At times, we were only burning coals, kept warm by the mere memory of a fire and then when our last leader lived, we blazed!" Takotna's weathered voice carried over the assembled crowd and there were murmurs of agreement and nods of understanding.

"Perhaps the time to blaze anew has arrived, who can say?" Takotna raised his hands toward the people with his palms displayed toward all as he turned in a circle.

Takotna stood tall, with his long, white hair pulled into two tails on either side of his head and there was a proud bearing to his posture that spoke to him. His grandfather was revered by the people that gathered together. He remembered the old ways and the people that remained upon the great land were eager to hear what he would say.

Takotna met Cahil's eyes. "There is one of you that sits as a hunter, a warrior, a man of strength and might. I implore that one to consider the future of the Krahnan band, do not allow the simmering coals to die out, not when there is a chance of growing into a strong blaze, capable of holding back the night."

Whether it was the steady beat of the drum or the fermented brew that was passed around, Cahil felt as if his spirit rose outside of his body and he looked down upon the gathering, where he saw himself sitting next to his wife. Lily held one hand upon her belly and her other hand was captured in his grasp. The fire was its own circle of light, uniting the people that gathered together despite the cold and darkness.

He saw what he had been unwilling to see, even though his grandfather nearly begged him to open his eyes.

All things came to an end, but the people around him were living, breathing beings who sought only to protect their children, feed and clothe those that relied upon them and above all, survive.

CHAPTER THIRTY-SIX

Cahil stood before the central fire as the people gathered close in anticipation. He took several days to consider his future and he knew that Takotna would be pleased by his announcement.

The people watched him with rapt attention. He stood tall and proud as he raised his hands for silence. "I know that I was taken from the Krahnan band as a young boy and raised by another. But I have returned to you as a man fully grown and capable of leading, just as my father once led."

Cahil remembered the way that Takotna pled with him to take his rightful position and he looked into his wife's shining eyes as she lifted her chin and clasped her hands against her heart.

"I will take my place as the leader of the Krahnan band. By right of blood and lineage, I will lead this band into the future!"

The people shouted their approval as Simoi, Takotna, Ashish and Suntar stepped forward, surrounding him in a show of solidarity.

Cahil was aware of Umak's dark eyes upon him as the man stood with his arms crossed over his chest and his mouth turned down in a grimace. Simoi and Gisik were ready for a response from Umak and his men did everything they could to stop Cahil from taking his rightful place. Cahil noticed that Simoi shadowed his movements, waiting for Umak to strike out against him, but no one was more vigilant than Cahil himself. The safety of Lily and their unborn child remained foremost in his mind.

What he did now, he did in memory of his father and mother and the people of the Krahnan band. They looked to him for guidance and direction and they were eager to return to the band that they once knew, not only for a time, to reap the benefits of good hunting, but forever. The men and women that gathered close hoped that Cahil's return would signify the return of prosperity and good fortune to the Krahnan band.

In his mind's eye, he saw the flickering fire and his grandfather standing in front of the growing flames. "Never let the fire die out."

Standing up as the leader of the Krahnan band, Cahil felt certain that he made the right decision. Umak and the men that followed him would have to learn to accept him as the leader of the Krahnan band. Cahil was determined to keep a watchful eye upon Umak and the men that were loyal to him.

His relatives and friends stepped forward to welcome him as their leader and he took time with each one, listening to their vows of loyalty and accepting them into the warm embrace of a band that became a village within a single day.

"Cahil," Saghani called as Cahil and the other men returned from the river. "Lily says that her time is upon her."

Cahil's knees went weak as he envisioned his wife's body, slender and supple, with her burgeoning belly extended in front of her. He prepared for the birth of their child by adding to their food stores and watching over his wife.

The days blended one into another as Lily's time of childbirth neared and Cahil was filled with dread that his young wife would have to endure an agonizing birth.

Cahil started to enter his lodge, but Saghani placed a staying hand upon his arm. "You will not enter."

Cahil started to object, but Simoi and Takotna were there to remind him that women preferred to have other women nearby during childbirth. He heard stories form Nisku about the birth of his sons and daughters and Nisku assured him that it was best to remain far from his lodge until the entire ordeal was over. Pi'ut wholeheartedly agreed and yet Cahil yearned to see Lily's face one more time, before their lives were irrevocably changed.

He expressed concern over Lily giving birth to their child without a healer present. Yet, Lily looked at him out of the eyes of a woman that embraced motherhood with the full force of her being.

"I am surrounded by men and women that are related to you. I have my uncle and Saghani, along with your grandfather, Anuk and even Gisik." They both laughed as she mentioned Gisik for he had been uncommonly quiet and stern.

"I would sit by your side as we welcome our son into the world." Cahil was uncertain where he erred but he saw the light in her eyes dim slightly and he turned to her in question.

"We will both look upon our child together, whether we have a son or a daughter, we will whisper in the child's ears as a man and woman that will be called Father and Mother." Lily's eyes lit with excitement as the child within her belly kicked and Cahil saw what could have been a foot or an elbow.

"You are not certain that we will have a son?" Cahil asked, though he knew that he should have kept her from worrying over the gender of their child.

"Cahil, you want a son so that he can imitate your ways and sing your songs into the future as a man that belongs upon the great land. But when I look at you, I see a man that was born to walk this land, a place that is both harsh and beautiful. Your first father a man of great strength and you are the same."

Cahil lifted his head as Lily forced him to meet her gaze. "Your adoptive father, the one that took you from this village, he was also a strong man, was he not?"

"I do not often think of him." Even as he spoke, distant memories surfaced. He remembered Kusug teaching him how to throw his spear or catch fish upon the frozen ice. He saw Kusug patiently showing him how to survive in the snow and cold if he was ever caught outside of the reach of their village by a sudden snowstorm. He heard Kusug praising him for accomplishments that were both large and small.

The memories did not sit well with him, simply because he learned that Kusug took him from his family, stealing his past, just as surely as Nanuq stole the future of Kusug's first son.

"Your grandfather wants you to honor the ways of your father and seek out the dancing lights by following the seeking star. I know that you refused to do as he asked, but have you changed your mind?

"No." Cahil answered immediately. He was the Krahnan village leader, but he would not follow all the ways of the men that came before him.

"Simoi has said that a man of your shared blood would do well to seek out the dancing lights and ask a blessing. I urge you to remember the things that are good and fine that your adoptive father taught you. It is this that you should share with our son or daughter." Lily smiled as Cahil listened closely. "You must also share the stories of your first father with our child, those passed down to you by your grandfather and the people of this village. Honor your Krahnan father, welcome the future and remember the past. How can you ever truly know yourself if you cannot accept the things that have shaped your life?"

"You speak as if you can see into the future." Cahil hoped to lighten the moment and Lily's eyes dimmed again before she rallied and shook her head in denial.

"I do not know what the future holds, but you know the song in my heart. I knew that you were the man that I would be proud to call husband from the first moment that I saw you. Promise me that if our child is born healthy and whole, you will seek out the dancing lights before the cold season. Ask a blessing from the heavens with a humble heart and it will be given to you."

"I promise."

Cahil blinked as Simoi grabbed his arm and slapped him upon the back. Takotna smiled with encouragement gleaming in his eyes though Cahil winced as he heard a low moan issue from the entrance of his lodge.

He hoped that Lily would rely upon the strength that was inherent within her, so that she survived the birth of their first child. He would be lost without her, cast adrift upon the ice with no hope of rescue. She was everything that he ever wanted and he knew it well.

CHAPERT THIRTY-EIGHT

Lily clenched her teeth together as another pain caused her stomach to spasm and a moan of agony to issue from her mouth. Saghani's face showed the strain of the past day. Time passed slowly as Lily labored to deliver her child.

Fresh blood seeped onto the pallet beneath her thighs and Lily held out her hands as Saghani and Nisku's wife, Aniag, helped her rise to her knees. Her belly protruded, riding low across her hips as she pressed her palms against her stomach and spoke to her child.

"Che-no-nura." Lily breathed the name of her child as she envisioned a daughter, born healthy and strong. She could see the child in her mind's eye and she knew that it would be so.

"Lily." Saghani cautioned as Lily closed her eyes and turned her face away from her friend.

She knew well that she should not speak the name of her child until it was born and Cahil had been given a chance to decide if he would name the child immediately or wait until he was certain that the child would live.

Lily groaned as another pain seized her and she felt her womb contract. There was a tearing edge to the pain that frightened her and she screamed despite her efforts to keep the sound of her birth contained.

Tears seeped from Saghani's eyes as Lily sagged against her and once again repeated her daughter's name in a desperate whisper. "Che-no-nura."

Lily stared into Saghani's eyes, silently wringing a promise from her though Saghani wanted to deny it.

Yes, she silently answered, I will tell your daughter what her name means. She read the appreciation in Lily's gaze as her friend found the strength to bear down.

Deep, racking sobs erupted from Lily's throat as her child slipped from her body and Saghani lifted the child, using clean garments to wipe the baby clean. Aniag was a silent witness to the birth as Lily sighed heavily and reached for her child, pressing the infant against the warmth of her breasts.

A daughter. A girl child with dark eyes like her mother and a crop of black hair that stood out on end. The baby released a lusty wail and Lily sighed in exhaustion and overwhelming relief. Che-no-nura.

Cahil entered the lodge with eyes that sought out the face of his wife. Lily was propped against the sleeping furs with their child nestled in her arms. Inside, the lodge was warm, causing Cahil to shed his warm overcoat and parka as he pressed kisses against the side of Lily's face. She was almost asleep as he peeled back the covers that hid the child from his eyes, but she blinked and smiled as he looked at their child for the first time.

"A girl." Cahil felt a moment of disappointment, but he quickly hid it away as Lily looked into his eyes seeking warmth and approval.

"She will be a good older sister to the sons that will be born to your hearth."

"You have just given me a gift, a girl child with the beauty of her mother and yet, already you speak of having more children?" Cahil embraced his wife as he handed her their child without truly seeing her delicate features.

He could admit to himself that he wanted a strong son, like any man that hoped to raise a son as a hunter of the great land. However, he was also thankful that his wife was healthy and whole and their child rested against her mother's breast, suckling contentedly.

He envisioned their future as Lily slept beside him with their child sheltered in her arms. They survived the long duration of the cold season and the land was already yielding to the warmer temperatures that would bring a time of renewal to the land.

The beginning of the warm season could also prove to be a time of hunger, food caches were emptied and hunting was scarce, but Cahil joined together with Simoi and Gisik to ensure that they would have enough to eat. The days were longer and the nights were less cold. Already, the people looked to him for guidance and direction. With the birth of their first child he realized that he was already looked upon with favor by many of the men that chose to leave the scattered bands of the great land and join the Krahnan village.

The people were persuaded to remain with them and erect permanent lodges. Cahil was not ignorant of the threat posed by Umak, a strong warrior in his own right. He was a man with the backing of a strong band comprised mostly of warriors, but Cahil knew that Umak could not hold back the changes sweeping over the land.

He expected Umak to confront him the moment that he made the announcement that he would take his place as the leader of the Krahnan village. He kept his hunting spear close by his side as his wife slept in his arms with their child pressed against her heart. He would defend what was his, even if that meant that he would be forced to fight to keep his rightful place.

Cahil dreamed that he was burning. There was fire all around and he could not break free. With a gasp, he opened his eyes and he was immediately aware of his surroundings. Lily slept beside him with their child wrapped in a warm swaddling blanket. He added a few pieces of dried wood to the small fire, where the coals smoldered and then crackled to life.

There was no fire and he assured himself that it was only a dream, although he had been certain that a fire blazed at his side. Cahil breathed a sigh of relief and reached out for his wife. He turned to Lily and saw that sweat rimmed her brow while her lips were chapped, the skin broken and raw.

"Lily." Cahil shook his wife as he swept a hand over her brow and found that her skin was hot to the touch.

"Lily!" He called her again as she moaned and her arms fell open. He quickly lifted the child from her chest and rushed out into the night. A light dusting of snow was falling and he did not realize that he wore only his loincloth as he ran to Simoi's lodge.

"Simoi!" Cahil called out before he reached the dwelling. "Simoi!"

"Cahil, what is it?" Simoi's eyes swept over Cahil and the child in his arms as Saghani, Gisik, and Anuk rose from their sleeping places.

"Lily's skin burns hot to the touch. Come quickly!"

Saghani reached out for the sleeping child as Simoi urged Anuk to go and wake Nisku's wife. Cahil ran back his lodge as Simoi kept step with him, they were both aware that they did not have a healer within their village, nor was their one amongst the gathered bands. Cahil groaned low in his chest as Simoi placed a bracing hand upon his back, before entering their lodge.

Over the next two days, Lily's fever broke and returned despite their efforts to draw the sickness out of her body. There were moments when she was lucid and alert, but her eyes were fever bright as she told her husband that she loved him and their daughter.

"Her name is Che-no-nura." Lily murmured as Cahil urged her to drink water. He even brought snow in to try to cool the burning of her body, but she was racked with chills that made her shudder and it was an agony to watch.

"Lily." Cahil could barely speak. He feared that he was watching his wife fade before his eyes and there was nothing that he could do to help her. "Do not leave me, I need you."

"I know." Lily murmured as she drifted off to sleep.

Cahil sat by her side, speaking to her, begging her to remain with him and she would wake to stare at him sometimes without comprehension.

On the third day, Simoi and Takotna threatened to drag Cahil from Lily's side if he would not at least eat and drink. Cahil forced food that he did not taste past his lips and drank long swallows of water as Lily battled for her life. He sat by her side, singing to her the songs that would keep her spirit with him even as she struggled mightily. He could see the distress upon her face and when she next opened her eyes, he was there, he was right there with her.

"Cahil." Lily's voice was a whisper. "Bring me our child."

Cahil summoned Anuk and the young man ran to get Saghani who had been nearby with the baby. Aniag began nursing the child, having recently given birth herself, but Cahil couldn't look at the baby while his wife was ill.

"Lily?" Cahil pressed his hand against Lily's chest, relieved to see that she still breathed and he was hopeful that she was recovering, now that she asked for their child.

"You know the song in my heart." Lily murmured as Cahil nodded, unable to speak as Lily weakly reached for the small burden that Saghani handed to her.

He watched as Lily inhaled the scent of their child and for the first time in several days, she smiled brightly. Saghani drifted away and Cahil was not even aware of her presence as he watched Lily with their daughter.

"Che-no-nura. The little blue bird that flies in the sky over a land filled with green." Lily looked to Cahil and he repeated her words exactly, knowing that it was important to her that he acknowledge their child.

"Lily, I need you to stay with me."

"I know." Lily struggled to swallow as her eyes welled with tears. Precious liquid that she could not afford to lose seeped from her eyes. "You were all that I ever wanted. Do you remember when we crossed the river and I feared that it would sweep me away?"

"Yes." Cahil was quick to reply. He saw that Lily struggled to speak and he hoped to make it easier for her.

"You took my hand and do you remember what you said?"

Cahil struggled to remember, it seemed so long ago that he tucked Lily against his chest and held her, breathing in the fragrant scent of her hair.

"I said, you have to be brave, take courage."

"Yes." Lily sighed as she kissed their daughter's round cheek with the last of her strength. "I need you to be brave, take courage. I will always be by your side, but I need you to be brave enough to let me go."

Cahil wanted Lily to swear to him that she would recover. He wanted to laugh with her over the way that she laid his soul bare with the sickness that nearly threatened her life.

"I can't." Cahil shook his head as Lily watched him steadily from the brown eyes that he loved. "Please Lily, you are the woman of my heart."

"Cahil." Lily's lips barely moved as she clasped his hand, expressing all that she felt for him with the searing heat of her gaze.

Tears blurred his vision as Lily silently begged him to release her and he knew that he held on to her by sheer force of will and he would have continued to do so if she did not tremble with pain and fatigue.

He would have given anything to keep her with him, he would have given his life so that she might live, but he wasn't given a choice. As he watched, Lily's chest rose and fell, only to rest still and silent. He pressed his ear against her lips and an animalistic moan of despair rose into the air as he realized that she no longer breathed. He lay with his lips against her neck and their child pressed between them as nearby, someone shouted in despair.

CHAPTER THIRTY-SEVEN

Saghani and Simoi heard the guttural cries that came from Cahil's lodge and they both ran toward the sound. Tears flowed freely from Saghani's eyes as she watched Simoi enter Cahil's lodge without hesitation. Simoi returned with the baby, which he quickly handed to Saghani. The quick shake of his head told her that Lily, her friend and dearest companion, was gone.

Saghani pressed Lily's child against her breasts as ragged sobs erupted from her chest. The child was small and fragile, but she watched the world around her with bright eyes. Saghani turned away as Simoi, Takotna and Gisik moved forward to sit outside of Cahil's lodge.

Ashish and Suntar came forward and stood silently as they waited for Cahil to allow them near. His grief was terrible to hear and the people gathered close as Ashish and Suntar took up the beating of their drums. It was a steady beat that soothed the spirit, though it acknowledged the searing pain suffered by their leader.

Aniag offered to keep Che-no-nura with her until the worst was behind them, but Saghani shook her head.

"Please feed her and return her to me." She needed to have the child in her arms, if only to release the vise of grief that welled in her heart.

Saghani sat beside Simoi and Gisik, along with Anuk as the drums announced the death of Cahil's wife. She felt as if she would never stop crying as Cahil came out of his lodge with Lily in his arms. The look of devastation upon his face was something that she would never forget. Cahil carried his wife away from the sound of the drums as the others watched. They did not speak as he walked past them with Lily pressed against his heart.

Aniag came forward and she offered the child to Saghani, who opened her arms readily. "I am sorry little one, your mother rejoiced at your birth and I know that she would have lived if she could have done so. She would have lived for you and your father."

Saghani and the others watched Cahil until he disappeared into the distance.

Simoi trembled with the strain of containing his sorrow as Ashish and Suntar led him into the chant of an undulating song that would allow them to mourn. He once vowed to protect and watch over Lily from the day of her birth and as Saghani handed Lily's daughter to him, he swore that he would watch over her child all the days of his life.

Time drifted past in a blur as Cahil grieved for his wife. Saghani and Aniag shared the care of his daughter, while Simoi and Anuk stayed close to Cahil.

At times, Cahil acted in a reckless manner, taking life threatening risks and Simoi was concerned that Cahil hoped to die so that he could be with his wife. His heart stopped several times when Cahil threw himself into the hunt without regard for his life. He kept his own counsel, though he was deeply concerned.

Saghani pled with him to do something to help Cahil after she learned that he walked over ice that was far too thin. The other hunters were not willing to follow Cahil out onto the ice for fear of falling into the frozen river, but Cahil dared.

Simoi listened to Saghani's concerns even as he willed strength to Cahil and waited in silence for him to shake free of the despair that held him in its grasp. Finally, when a late snowstorm blanketed the land in white and Cahil wandered into the distance with only his loincloth and spear, Simoi realized that he would have to speak to him or risk finding Cahil's body.

"You seek to end your life." Simoi did not soften his words as he stared at Cahil. His eyes were dark and lost as he stared into his intrepid gaze. "You do not fear death."

"No." Cahil shrugged his shoulders as Simoi shifted closer so that he was forced to look at him. "I do not fear death."

"I know." Simoi agreed readily. "You fear life."

"No." Cahil denied as Simoi scoffed and looked away from him in disgust.

"You care nothing for the grief of others." Simoi continued, despite the warning glare the Cahil sent his way. "She was my niece! I wiped her tears when she was a child. I learned when to be stern and when to relent. She was the light in my eyes."

Cahil listened to Simoi as rage built in his chest and he kept silent when Simoi shrugged his shoulders and threw his hands into the air. "You will die if you continue to live in such a reckless way. What will happen to your daughter if you die? What will happen to Anuk?"

Some of his rage diminished as Cahil thought of Anuk. The young man's natural exuberance diminished and he was quiet, a shadow of his former self.

Cahil barely noticed Anuk over the past several moons. He barely noticed anyone at all. His grandfather approached him several times, but he waved him away. He had been unable and unwilling to accept comfort from anyone.

Shame washed over him as he realized that he did not know where his daughter was, he couldn't bring himself to look upon her face since the death of his wife.

He shook off the feeling of shame. He preferred to let blinding numbness drown out the shame.

Simoi looked down at Cahil. "Your people need a leader that will not simply throw his life away because he does not have the will to live. Umak no longer tries to kill you, have you noticed? Do you know why? Because it is obvious to all that you have given up and if you continue the way that you have been then you will almost certainly bring about your death."

"She was my wife!"

The words were spoken with bitter force and agony as Cahil bent to one knee while grief swelled within him, drawing rage and anger from his chest.

"She was my wife." He repeated as soon as he could draw breath into his straining lungs.

"You are not the only one that knew joy because of her existence. I once mourned the loss of a woman that matched the fire in my soul. She died at the hands of my enemy and I mourn her still." Cahil did not lift his head as Simoi turned and walked away.

He settled upon a log as he buried his head in his hands, but he did not weep. He lost the strength to weep for his wife, long ago.

After a time, a sound caught his attention and he lifted his head as Saghani came forward.

He noticed the lack of mischief that normally danced in her eyes and he wondered if she still caused Simoi to fling his hands into the air with frustration. Memories of Lily hovered at the edges of his mind, but he quickly turned his thoughts away from his wife. It hurt to think of her, it hurt to remember her gentle spirit and kind ways.

"Here is your daughter. Simoi says that I can no longer keep her in our lodge. Aniag will continue to feed her until she is weaned."

Cahil was speechless as Saghani deposited the writhing bundle on his lap and walked away.

He did not see the tears that streaked down Saghani's face as she handed Lily's child over to him. Cahil held the child away from his chest as she chortled and squirmed. He could not bring himself to look at her and he simply closed his eyes as he willed himself to see nothing at all.

CHAPTER THIRTY-EIGHT

Throughout the night, Cahil learned that he could not simply ignore his child. She whimpered and cried until he was forced to remove her from the tightly wrapped blanket and check her body for injuries.

The low flickering firelight barely prepared him for what he would see. He ran one finger over her arms and legs which appeared tiny to him, but he knew that she was a good size for her young age. Her legs kicked with strength as he saw that her padding was wet and he used the supplies left in his lodge by Saghani to see to her care.

His fingers were clumsy and unskilled, but she did not seem to notice. In the darkness, he saw that she pressed three dimpled fingers into her mouth and suckled with relish.

During the middle of the night, Nisku and Aniag appeared at the entrance to his lodge. Nisku stood with him outside as Aniag nursed the child and handed her back to him without a word.

He could not find his voice and he was glad that Nisku remained silent. There was nothing that the other man could say that would draw Cahil from the edge of despair.

He fell asleep with the child at an arm's length from him and he awoke to her cries. Once again he checked her swaddling and placed fresh padding under her bottom. He wasn't certain how babies were wrapped, but he simply removed her wrappings and then wrapped her in a similar way.

Aniag appeared at his lodge entrance and he silently handed the child over as she went to sit with Saghani and several of the other women. He knew that Aniag fed his child, but he never watched her and a lump formed in his throat as his daughter latched onto Aniag's breast and suckled lustily.

"Che-no-nura." Cahil murmured as he spoke his daughter's name for the first time since the loss of his wife. He felt that he would break as he tried to contain the pain that flowed inside of him as he spoke her name. He took measured steps away from the village and then when he was outside of the prying eyes of his people, he ran.

Simoi and Anuk hurried to catch up to Cahil as he broke into a run. They followed at a distance until they were certain that he would not cause himself harm. Cahil fell to his knees beside the place where he once set stones over his wife's body. He bent his head and covered his face with his hands as Simoi beckoned Anuk to return to the village with him.

"Will he be well now?" Anuk suffered the swells of grief along with Cahil, though he kept him at a distance.

"It is too soon to say." Simoi answered, though his voice was filled with hope.

"I have never seen anyone grieve so deeply." Anuk cleared his throat as he thought of Cahil's grief.

"Death is a part of life. You would do well to learn this now so that you can face each day with thanksgiving in your heart." Simoi took Anuk under his wing during Cahil's darkest moments and he admitted to himself that Anuk's ebullient demeanor helped him begin to heal. He led the way back to the village with a sure step as Anuk kept up with him, walking in his footsteps.

"Simoi, I have been meaning to talk to you about Gisik." Anuk said as Simoi turned to look into his eyes.

"I am listening."

"Gisik has behaved strangely for a long time. Saghani first mentioned it to me, long before the first caribou hunt. Now we are approaching the time when the people will gather to hunt the caribou again and I cannot keep silent."

"What is it that he has done that you find strange?"

"Do you remember the necklace that Cahil always wears?" Anuk asked.

"Yes."

"I saw Gisik do something that I cannot understand."

"Go on." Simoi prodded as Anuk hesitated.

"Cahil removed the necklace when he lost his wife and I saw Gisik enter their lodge and take Cahil's necklace for himself."

Simoi's expression darkened as he tried to imagine why Gisik would have any interest in the necklace. It was valuable only to Cahil, whose father gave it to him, long ago.

"Have I done the wrong thing by speaking of it? Perhaps Cahil gave Gisik permission to wear the necklace and I should not have mentioned it to you." Anuk's voice was hopeful.

"You did the right thing by speaking of it, but do not concern yourself with Gisik's actions. He has his own ways and I will speak to him about it."

Anuk nodded in ready acceptance. "Good."

Simoi urged Anuk to run ahead so that he could remain alone with his thoughts. He turned his mind over Gisik's strange behavior and the scowl upon his face only deepened as he thought of the actions taken by his friend.

As the weather warmed and the village bustled with the arrival of new bands, Cahil welcomed distant relatives into their village. He accepted the vows of loyalty given to him by men that were once born to the Krahnan band, but drifted away over the changing of the seasons.

He began to organize the upcoming caribou hunt as Umak once again made his presence known.

"Your daughter is the image of your wife." Umak sneered as he stepped forward with his spear held low at his side. "I knew your wife when she was a child."

Cahil felt as if someone took sharp rocks and scoured them across a wound as he struggled to breathe normally and Aniag came forward to take his daughter from him.

"Umak, why is it that you and your men remain here, drawing off the resources that belong to the Krahnan village? It has come to my attention that you are not related to anyone here and the women in your band are not from the Krahnan village."

"All bands are welcome to join the caribou hunt and enjoy the spoils brought about by strong hunters." Umak's eyes gleamed menacingly as Cahil stood to face him.

"Perhaps. But as the leader of the Krahnan village, I will decide which bands will take the first wave of the hunt. The caribou herd travels from afar and they will do so again this season. It would serve you well if you decide to follow the herd and move on." A flicker of interest lit Umak's gaze as Cahil narrowed his eyes in threat.

"If I decide not to move on, what will happen?"

"I find it interesting that you remain unaware of the threat to your life."

"You?" Umak scoffed, "Do you threaten my life?"

"I have not given your death much thought." Cahil's voice left no doubt that he considered the option. "But someone else has."

"Umak." Simoi stood with his spear near at hand as Umak whirled to face him.

Cahil nearly grinned as Umak whipped around and then checked over his shoulder to confirm that his men were armed and nearby. It did not escape Cahil's notice that Umak and Simoi were evenly matched. They were men of a similar age and they were both muscular and lean, strong hunters each.

"If you seek me out again, Umak, I will know that you have issued a challenge that I will not be able to resist." Cahil opened his right hand and showed Umak his palm which was completely healed. "I am no longer injured by a weak man that would stalk an unarmed man during the darkest part of the night."

Simoi stepped away from Gisik angrily as the battle-scarred warrior spoke to him.

"Gisik, why is it that you defend Umak so forcefully?" Simoi questioned loudly as several of the people turned to watch Gisik speculatively. Simoi nodded once to Cahil and then he stalked away in the opposite direction of Umak and his men.

Cahil accepted the weighty bundle handed to him by Aniag and he thanked her for feeding his daughter.

"She is warm and dry and I think that she will sleep throughout the night." Aniag smiled softly as she hurried to catch up to her husband.

He held his daughter close as she gurgled and chortled contentedly. Something about his confrontation with Umak bothered him and he realized that he was ill at ease simply because Umak had been close enough to see his daughter's face.

"Your daughter is the image of your wife."

Cahil held his daughter at arm's length as he removed the blanket from her body and really looked at her. He inhaled sharply as his vision blurred.

He had been unaware of the strong resemblance between his daughter and his wife. Perhaps he unconsciously refused to peer into his daughter's eyes out of fear of what he would see.

"Che-no-nura." Cahil whispered as his daughter looked directly into his eyes and smiled.

His heart lurched as he was captivated by the dark fringe of her eyelashes which swept over brown eyes flecked with shards of amber. She looked so much like Lily that he forgot to breathe.

Only as he looked into his daughter's eyes was he aware that tears coursed down his face. He shook his head as memories of Lily came to him unbidden and his daughter squirmed against his chest.

He nestled her closer to the heat of his body as he closed his eyes and drifted off to sleep and in his dreams, he walked with Lily.

"Remember your promise." Lily's laughter tickled his ears and he knew that he would never tire of the sound.

Cahil ran his hands over the long fall of her hair and the soft curve of her cheek as she smiled into his eyes.

"Our daughter was born healthy and whole, remember that you promised to honor the ways of your father before the next caribou hunt."

"I want only to remain with you, Lily." Cahil held his wife in his arms as she sighed in contentment.

"I am always with you, I know the song in your heart." Lily kissed his lips as she turned away from him and he was powerless to stop her as she walked into the distance. "Thank you for letting me go. Remember to share my stories with Che-no-nura so that she will grow to be brave and strong."

"I promise." Cahil said as he blinked and opened his eyes. "I promise."

He felt the gentle weight of his daughter as she rested against his chest. Her lips were pursed together and her long eyelashes rested upon softly rounded cheeks. She was safe and sound, resting peacefully in his arms.

"She has your eyes." Cahil said to the fading dream as he tried to recapture the precious moments with his wife. His daughter's quiet breathing lulled him back to sleep, though he kept one hand upon the place where Lily once slept at his side.

CHAPTER THIRTY-NINE

Cahil was awake well before dawn and he gathered enough supplies to see him on a long journey. The night seemed endless as he thought of the past and future, meditating deeply upon his promise to his wife. He found Simoi sharpening his weapons outside of his lodge. The older man acknowledged him with a glance as Cahil greeted him.

"I need you and Saghani to watch over Che-no-nura while I am away." Aniag handed the child to Saghani after feeding her in the middle of the night and Cahil saw Saghani hold the baby on her lap as his daughter tested the strength of her legs.

"You know that you have only to ask, but I admit that I am curious. Where are you going?" Simoi questioned.

"I promised Lily that I would honor the ways of my father and I have yet to keep my promise." Cahil glanced toward the horizon that beckoned him. Takotna walked forward and he met him halfway.

"I will walk in my father's footsteps and seek out the dancing lights."

"It is good." Takotna's eyes shimmered with pride as he watched Cahil.

Simoi walked with him back to his lodge as he gathered his carrying sack along with enough provisions to last several days. His hunting knife was in its sheath at his waist and his hunting spear was in his hand.

"Do you think that it is wise to travel into the unknown by yourself?" Simoi asked as he considered Umak and the threat that he posed.

"I have traveled into the unknown before. This is not the first time." Cahil's gaze strayed to his daughter as walked over to Saghani and lifted the child into his arms. He felt the same surge of protectiveness that he always felt with Lily as he looked into the eyes of his daughter. If possible, the feeling was enhanced because of his daughter's complete dependence upon him. Cahil jostled his daughter in his arms as he accepted her slight weight.

"Watch over my daughter." Cahil entrusted his daughter's care to Takotna and Simoi. Both men readily agreed as he handed the child to Saghani and backed away.

Saghani thought of Lily and the silent promise that she made to her friend. "I will tell you stories of your mother while your father is away." Saghani whispered into Che-no-nura's ear as the baby pumped her chubby legs.

Takotna stood near Simoi as Cahil disappeared into the distance.

"How does he know where to go?" Anuk asked.

"It is simple," Takotna replied. "He will follow the seeking star until he reaches the dancing lights and then he will honor the ways of his father." Anuk lifted his eyebrows in silent question as Takotna answered. "He will seek a blessing from the heavens, an assurance of prosperity and good things to come."

Simoi sought out Gisik as the day waned toward sunset. His friend had been recalcitrant and obstinate on matters that affected the Krahnan village and Simoi became suspicious.

He noticed that Saghani no longer pined after the other man, though he was not certain if she truly lost hope that Gisik would respond to her or if she simply set her sights on another man entirely. Gisik began sleeping outside under the stars, though Simoi offered to help him build his own lodge. Gisik declined and no more was said between them on the matter.

Long ago, Gisik had been the war leader of their band and the scars that he carried upon his body were won in battle. Having broken off from their band, Simoi thought that they solidified their friendship, but the past few moons managed to test their solidarity. He was constantly on guard against Umak, especially since Cahil became the Krahnan village leader, asking him to stand as his war leader, should he ever need one.

Simoi thought that Gisik was merely unhappy that he wasn't honored with the role, but something about the man's furtive manner caused him to feel a sense of growing alarm.

He walked a far distance, having been told that Gisik preferred to sleep in a quiet meadow, where others rarely traveled. When he arrived it was to see Gisik standing close to Umak as he gestured toward a young woman. Simoi couldn't say why he decided to watch without announcing his presence, but he remained still and unmoving as Gisik stared hard at Umak. It was only as Umak turned that Simoi noticed that Cahil's necklace now hung around Umak's neck.

Anger seared Simoi's soul, but he realized that there was more to the matter when Gisik lifted his gaze, met his eyes and looked guiltily away. Umak left without a backward glance and Simoi wondered where the other man hurried off to so quickly. It was not like him to leave before he could claim a victory and having somehow turned Gisik against him, there was much to claim victory over.

"What have you done?" Simoi asked as the young woman lifted tear filled eyes toward him. "Who is this young woman?"

"Her name is Ashlu." Gisik ground out as he sighed heavily. "She is my niece."

Simoi looked between the tearful young woman and Gisik, but he saw no resemblance.

"She was my brother's child." Gisik gestured toward Umak's retreating form. "My brother's wife was ill and she perished."

"I thought that they both died long ago." Simoi responded as the young woman twisted her hands and shifted from one foot to another. Gisik didn't respond. He stared hard at Simoi as both men regarded one another. "What have you done?"

The matter between them was not over, but Gisik took the girl by her arm and turned his back on Simoi, sending ripples of shock down to his core.

"I have betrayed you and Cahil." Gisik's voice held a note of finality. "But you must understand that she is all that I have left."

"Gisik!" Simoi shouted as Gisik walked away with the girl at his side. "What have you done?"

Cahil traveled by star light and moonshine as he kept his footsteps turned in the direction of the seeking star. He did not know how far he would need to go before he found the dancing lights spoken of by his grandfather and Simoi.

Thoughts of Lily came to mind and at times he glanced up expecting to see his wife walking by his side. In his heart, she was there. He reached up to touch his necklace and forgot to breathe as he realized that in his hurry to leave, he left the necklace in his lodge where it rested ever since his wife's death.

As he glanced around, he was astounded by the beautiful landscape that swept outward in all directions, as far as the eye could see. He saw rolling hills of verdant green and granite cliffs in the distance. He recognized aspen, birch, spruce and alder stretching toward the sky as clouds drifted overhead.

He ate meager portions of dried meat and small bits of agutak left over from earlier in the warm season as he walked. He thought of Lily as the sweet delicacy touched his tongue and he smiled at the memory that the agutak elicited. Lily once promised him that he would love the taste and he did. One day, he would tell his daughter everything he remembered about her mother.

There were a few moments when he was unsure of the direction that he should travel and he searched the heavens at night for the seeking star and continued onward. He walked over ice that was newly formed and snow that dotted the land. As he thought of the hunters that waited on his return, he hurried along, certain that he would find the dancing lights the next day.

Moments of quiet despair caught him unaware and he would bend one knee and sink to the ground as he struggled to remember his purpose. Memories of his father, Nanuq, came to him unbidden and he realized that he was following Nanuq's last footsteps. It never occurred to him to ask Takotna exactly how his father died.

It was never far from his mind that he walked in his father's footsteps and his paternal grandfather before him. The journey itself helped him to come to terms with the shadows of his past and for the first time he felt as if he knew exactly who he was. With the birth of his daughter, he saw clearly how his father would have felt upon learning that his child had been taken away by an enemy.

"I will protect you, Che-no-nura."

Cahil spoke his promise on the wind as he crested a hill and spied movement down below. Far in the distance, a grizzly bear raised its head and regarded him steadily. The animals that he encountered were fattening up for the season ahead and he was careful not to drift too close to any of the larger predators that he stumbled upon.

During the night, he heard the howling of wolves and the yipping cries of coyotes, but he kept his fire supplies replenished and if he traveled by night he carried a torch to light the way.

As the days passed, he grew weary. Traveling such a great distance without a fixed destination in mind, would wear upon anyone and Cahil was no different from other men. He missed the comforts of the Krahnan village and he yearned for the familiar sights and sounds of home. The morning brought an icy wind and he decided that he would press hard throughout the day, but as he started to get to his feet, he thought of his wife. Lily often prayed to the Great One of All Things and though he didn't join her, he respected her willingness to believe that they were not alone, cast adrift in a land that was both harsh and beautiful.

Cahil bowed low to the earth as he spoke in earnest entreaty. "I seek only to help my people. Please show me the way to the dancing lights and when I ask a blessing, I beg of you to hear me."

He watched the great domain of blue sky overhead as he lifted his palms to the heavens. "Please hear me!"

He sat quietly for a long time as a shiver of awareness traveled over his backbone. Lifting his carrying sack with one hand, Cahil clasped his spear and continued on his journey. Whether for good or bad, he would walk until his legs gave out and then he would be forced to return to his people so that he could join the caribou hunt.

In the distance, Cahil saw that the land changed, shifting from lichen and drying grass to a barren platform of rock and stone. He moved forward tiredly as he searched the heavens for a sign. The sun was setting in the distance, but he saw something that struck a chord within him, urging him forward.

He stumbled a few times as fatigue caused his breathing to become harsh and strained while his legs began to tremble. Darkness swept over the land and for once, Cahil was not prepared with a torch or the dry wood needed for a fire. He assured himself that there was enough time to gather firewood, but as he glanced around he saw that there were not any trees or flowing streams where driftwood would collect. He sighed heavily as he struggled to find the strength to keep moving.

He caught himself as he fell to his knees, bracing his body with one arm. When he raised his head to look into the sky in search of the seeking star, he blinked as he struggled to clear his gaze. He could not see the heavens for the blazing trails of radiant light that moved in the sky, flashing forth with riotous streams of color. From deepest red to palest blue the drifting apparition called to Cahil, renewing his flagging strength and sending his heartbeat into a furious rhythm.

Cahil opened his mouth, but he found that he could not speak. He was stunned into silence by the beauty of the lights dancing overhead.

"Hayaia!" Cahil shouted in triumph as he lifted his palms to the heavens. "I ask that the Krahnan village return to a time of prosperity and good fortune. Help me lead our village in the way of my father and his father before him."

Lily's face appeared in the heavens as Cahil's eyes blurred and he swiped his hands over his face. Her image faded away as the lights shifted, sending a multicolored river dancing across the sky. Cahil mourned her loss, but the pain was made bearable as he realized that she was with him, in his heart and she lived on in the spirit of their daughter.

"Hayaia!" Cahil called as he crested a hill, set down his spear and raised his hands to the sky while the wind whispered over the great land and the lights danced in the heavens. He followed the seeking star until he found the barren lands and just as he hoped, he found the dancing lights.

"I will honor the old ways." Cahil promised, just as a voice behind him caught his attention.

"You will not live long enough to honor the old ways!"

Cahil turned to stare at the man that followed him from the Krahnan village, keeping to his trail over the last several days. He questioned whether he was imagining things when he sensed eyes upon him during the day, but now he knew that his instincts had been correct.

"I would have taken your life last night if you would have stopped walking long enough to sleep." Umak's face was grim as he stepped upon Cahil's discarded spear.

Cahil did not speak, he was filled with wonder at the immensity of all that he saw and he was also plagued by a terrible rage that caused his hands to tremble as he stared at Umak.

He asked himself what drove Umak to follow him. He set a punishing pace and most men would have waited for him to turn around and confronted him at that time, but not Umak. He was a man that sought glory and power for himself, these were the things that he treasured.

"Have you been here before?" Cahil asked, as Umak stepped closer, balancing his spear upon the top of his right hand, testing the weight of the weapon.

He saw that Umak wore his treasured necklace upon his chest and his hands clenched in anger. Fear for his companions and his daughter's life drove him to seek a deadly calm.

"Of course." Umak agreed as his face contorted in rage. "Long ago, your father decided that he would honor the old ways of the Krahnan band and he sought out the dancing lights, just as you have."

Cahil remained silent as Umak edged closer, close enough for him to see the thrill of victory in his eyes.

"I watched your father die at the hands of Kusug." Umak smirked as Cahil took a step back in disbelief.

"No."

"I followed Kusug when he came to my band, seeking food and shelter while he plotted his revenge upon Nanuq, your father."

"You speak the names of the dead in a sacred place." Cahil warned as Umak edged closer. He felt as if his heart was ripped from his chest upon learning that Kusug killed his father, but he controlled his response by sheer force of will.

"I do not fear the spirit world."

"You should." Cahil responded. "You should fear that which you cannot see, that which you cannot touch or hear."

"You seek to lengthen your life, but your life has come to an end."

Cahil raised his head and laughed. "You are wrong. I do not fear death, not even a traitorous death at my enemy's hands. For too long I have feared life and living." His eyes were fierce as he stalked toward his enemy and Umak pressed his hunting spear against his exposed chest.

"The Krahnan village will be driven to its knees at your death. I hold the power!" Umak growled as Cahil continued to laugh at his expense. He ripped the necklace from his neck and held up the pendant so that it swung through the air. "You cannot stop me!"

"Perhaps not, but he will." Cahil peered past Umak as he spoke.

Umak spun around with his spear raised and he pivoted as he realized that no one stood behind him. He raised his spear to attack, but in one swift motion, Cahil blocked his spear thrust and drew his knife across Umak's throat from ear to ear.

He bore the weight of Umak's body as the man slid to his knees while his blood flowed freely from the gaping wound at his throat. He stood silently by as Umak shuddered in search of air before his body gave out and death claimed him.

Cahil did not spare Umak's body another glance as he turned to face the sunrise, picked up his hunting spear and reverently placed his necklace over his head, tying it end over end. The pendant rested against his chest as the dancing lights moved overhead and Cahil threw back his head and released a primal shout to the heavens.

"Hear me! I am Cahil, the leader of the Krahnan village! The people of the great land have vowed to honor the old ways forever into the sunrise! I seek a blessing for my people!"

He remained standing in one place with his face lifted to the heavens and his arms spread wide as his voice echoed over the land and a sense of knowing spun loose in his spirit and he knew without a doubt that his request would be answered.

With a shuddering breath, he turned away from the dancing lights and began the long journey back to his people.

As he crested a hill, he was surprised to see two familiar figures hurrying toward him. Simoi and Anuk. He knew that they would have much to say to him, but he also recognized loyal friends and he was heartened by their support. The path would not be easy and the way would not always be clear, but he knew that his life mattered. The people of his village waited for his return.

His daughter needed him and he would keep his promise to his wife and set her footsteps along the path that she should walk. Everything that he was and everything that he would ever be belonged to Lily and he knew in his heart that he would see her again. Until that time, he was determined to live life to the fullest.

The seeking star faded away as light filtered over the land and Cahil walked ever forward into the newly risen day.

Six seasons later…

A small girl sat on a large boulder overlooking her village as the men returned from the caribou hunt. She shivered in the chill wind as she raised her fur hood, covering her blue-black hair. She closed her eyes and pretended that her father's arms were wrapped securely around her.

"Che-no-nura, where are you?" Saghani called as she ran forward and caught sight of the little girl and called her by the shortened form of her name. "Nura, I worried about you when you ran off from the other children."

Saghani's heart caught in her throat as she saw that Nura was in tears. "What has happened that you should cry?"

"I miss my father." Nura sniffled as she allowed Saghani to comfort her. "I am afraid."

"And why should you know fear?" Saghani's eyes glistened with unshed tears as she thought of Nura's mother, Lily. "Your mother would not be pleased if she knew that you were afraid."

"She wouldn't?" Nura asked, as she lifted familiar brown eyes flecked with amber shards to peer at Saghani.

"No indeed. After all, you were named after the little blue bird that flies high in the sky over a land filled with green." Saghani smiled as Nura's tears dried and she leaned forward with interest. "Long before you were born, your mother knew your name."

"I am Che-no-nura and I do not know fear." She repeated as Saghani told her the story as given to her by her mother.

"Come with me now, Nura. Your father and the other men have returned from the caribou hunt and there is much that we must do."

Nura took Saghani's hand until they reached the lodges that marked the Krahnan village. Anuk worked to build the village central fire and he waved as Saghani and Nura went by. There were more lodges than Nura could count and in the center of the village was her father.

"Father!" Nura called out as Cahil turned away from his conversation with Simoi and Takotna to open his arms to his daughter. Nura ran to him and the men laughed indulgently. They knew without question that Nura was the light in Cahil's eyes.

Cahil welcomed his daughter just as he always did, with arms that were ready to accept her slight weight and lift her into the air. Nura's smile was Lily's smile and her eyes were Lily's eyes. When he looked at his daughter, he saw her mother and remembered his promise to her. He would set his daughter's footsteps along the path that she would walk throughout her life.

"Be brave, take courage. I will always be by your side." Cahil heard Lily's voice in the silence of his mind as he embraced his daughter and spun her around until her laughter filled the air.

Author's Note:

I hope you enjoyed reading *The Seeking Star (Book One).* As always, I appreciate positive reviews and the kind encouragement from readers everywhere. Please post a review on Amazon.com and let other readers know what you loved about the story!

I would like to sincerely thank the readers that enjoy the stories that I live, breathe and dream. To join the mailing list please email Karah.quinney1@gmail.com

Thank you!

Karah Quinney

Read on for an excerpt of the sequel:
Shadow of the Moon (Book Two)

Thousands of years ago…

The need for vengeance filled his soul completely, giving him enough strength to journey into the freezing cold. Keluk had spent several days watching the people of the village, and it was easy to identify the one that would repay the blood debt called for by his band.

The village leader's daughter was given the respect of a highly favored woman. Keluk watched each day as the young woman rose early and went to refresh her waterskin at a nearby stream. He saw the way the other women were eager to shadow her movements, and his heart was glad.

The village leader was a man called Cahil, and Keluk wanted to make him suffer greatly. Vengeance required that Keluk take the village leader's daughter and deliver her to a slow death at the hands of his band.

This thought alone drove him to focus all of his strength upon his goal. He wouldn't rest until his people had been given an offering that would appease the wrong done to them by Cahil and his warriors.

Keluk watched as the young woman left her dwelling and walked the snowy path that led to a small stream. He didn't feel the cold hand of the wind as it roared over his body, instead he felt the fire of revenge which gave him power.

He stalked the young woman as she bent over the stream. She was early to rise, and she walked alone. It was a good thing. His blood surged within his body as he drew close to her. The white paste that he had applied to his sun burnished skin made him almost invisible against the snow.

The woman rose gracefully with two waterskins in her hands. As she turned away from the bubbling spring, he was instantly upon her. He held his hunter's knife to her throat as he whispered to her in the language of their ancestors.

"If you scream, I will slit your throat and kill your father as well. My people demand vengeance for the blood that was shed by your warriors. The choice is yours."

The young woman tensed in his arms as a sound caused him to scrape the surface of her neck with his knife. The serrated stone knife was well sharpened and could easily kill her with one powerful swipe.

When the woman held herself rigidly still, he knew that she would go along with him without a fight.

"Do you know fear?" His words were a raspy growl as he turned the woman to face him and quickly bound her hands. She remained silent, unwilling to answer his question or risk her life by doing so.

The time for words was at an end. Keluk gagged the woman so that she couldn't cry out and then he looped a rope over her hands and bound them to his waist. He gathered both waterskins and removed all sign of their presence. He wanted her father to worry about his prized daughter.

Keluk felt the last remnants of his heart shrivel in the grasp of immeasurable darkness as he pulled the woman along after him. He carefully took in his surroundings, ignoring the panting sounds that came from behind the woman's gag.

He knew that she was terrified, yet her wide eyes refused to give him the satisfaction that he craved. The air felt just as cold as the ice under his feet, but he was determined to put distance between them and the Krahnan Village.

Keluk gave no thought to the woman's suffering. The pain that was in store for her when they reached his band would nullify anything that she would endure during their journey. His foot coverings were enough to shield him from the icy chill of the water for now, but they couldn't travel this way much longer.

His purpose would only be accomplished when the woman's death was reported back to her father. Only then would Cahil come to know the same pain that now ravaged Keluk's spirit.

CHAPTER ONE

"Your death will not be quick." Those were the only words that Keluk spoke to the woman as he tied her hands to a young sapling tree.

They had reached the forest that edged the land claimed by the woman's village. Keluk eyed the young woman, and he hardened his heart against the bruises on her wrists where he had grabbed her. He saw that her legs trembled with fatigue, and it was obvious that she was not accustomed to traveling long distances in the freezing cold.

A sound from the forest alerted him to the presence of another. Keluk spun just in time to avoid the impact of a spear as it buried itself in the ground where he had been standing.

He heard the woman's muffled scream, but his gaze was focused upon the lone hunter that ran toward them. Somehow, he had been discovered.

"You have taken our leader's daughter!"

The hunter ran forward, certain that he could overtake Nura's captor.

Chilled by the cold, his ravaged heart was filled with a sudden sense of calm.

He had known from the outset that his journey might end with his death. The Krahnan hunter was caught unaware as Keluk spun and drove his right elbow between his neck and shoulder. As his opponent's hunting knife dropped harmlessly to the ground, Keluk flipped his weapon so that the stone handle met his adversary's skull. The hunter slumped to the ground, falling at Keluk's feet.

Nura used her shoulder to work the gag free. "You killed him!"

Keluk eyed the fallen hunter and then he looked into the distance without comment.

"Sule!" Nura struggled in futility as he dragged her away from Sule's prone body. For his part, Keluk never looked back. He set a fast pace, stopping only when necessary and as they traveled, he took advantage of an opportunity to kill a hapless rabbit. He cleaned the rabbit skin quickly, hanging it upon his traveling pack to dry. He made new foot coverings for the woman with the use of the remaining skins that he had collected since the outset of his journey. She wouldn't be able to walk without proper foot coverings, and he refused to carry her. He roughly removed the gag that the woman wore, reluctantly handing her a waterskin.

"Why have you taken me from my village?"

Nura could barely find her voice as she faced the man that held her captive. She spoke in the language of the ancients, just as he did. Throughout the day she had studied her captor as he plodded along. Pride alone kept her from falling at his feet when they stopped, and she was still shaken by Sule's death.

Nura saw that her captor wore a warm buckskin parka that was carefully stitched and turned fur side in. His muscular legs were covered with animal skin leggings and his feet were encased in moccasins. Such things spoke of his status within his own band.

As he washed the white paint from his body and removed the black paste from his eyes, she noticed a single black feather hung over one eye, which marked him as a hunter. Hunters often wore a feather tied by a band that would shade their eyes from the blinding sun during the day.

The man's black hair was as dark as a raven's wing and worn longer than most. The barely visible markings on his chest spoke of his lineage. Although she couldn't understand the symbols, she knew what they signified. He was a hunter and a warrior.

His eyes were narrow and long, offset by a broad forehead and strong chin. His mouth hinted at fullness, but remained set in a hard line as if his lips had never softened into a smile. All day they walked, never stopping until the sun rested.

Words of complaint didn't burst forth from her mouth, not even when her feet began to pain her as they continued their journey. Nura didn't flinch when the man stopped walking only to cut her treasured bracelet from her wrist and tie it upon a stake, which he drove into the frozen ground. Though the sight of his hunting knife frightened her, she hid her fear. She quickly realized that his actions would tell those that searched for her that she had been taken by force.

She marveled at the man's restraint, for he could have left such a sign by the watering hole or on the outskirts of her village. Instead, valuable time would be lost before her father and his men knew that she was missing. Even more time would be wasted before they realized that she hadn't left on her own.

Though she was a valued daughter of her village, her father would wonder if she ran from the arranged union that he sought to force upon her with the war leader of her village, Sarik. Deep inside, where the eyes couldn't see, Sarik was scarred by an unquenchable thirst for power and glory.

Nura was resigned to her fate despite her misgivings about Sarik. She was a dutiful daughter and she would honor her father's wishes, even though what he asked of her would surely crush her spirit.

As she thought about how her captor had hidden in the snow, she trembled anew. She had never been so afraid in her life. At the first sight of him, she had taken a breath to scream, but the intense look of hatred in his gaze stunned her into silence, and his words chilled her blood.

She realized instantly that he would have taken her life without question if she gave in to her terror by screaming. Not only would he carry out his threat, but she knew with one glance that he would find her father's lodge and do away with him, just as he threatened.

Each morning, Nura left her father's lodge to seek a moment of silence and peace. She held on to those precious moments and if she was given a choice, she would have chosen to remain within that time forever. But the days continued to slip away and before long, she would become the wife of a man that she despised.

As the village leader's daughter, she was bound by the will of her father. Cahil wished to see her joined as lifemate to a strong man that would give her sons. In this way, her father's name would be made known forever.

Nura protested her father's choice of a lifemate and when her protests were ignored, she pleaded with her father for more time. She knew that in the end such a request wouldn't matter. It was well past the time that she should have become a wife, and long ago, Sarik had asked to take her as his lifemate.

In the beginning, Nura couldn't identify the reason that she didn't wish to join with Sarik, she only knew that his eyes lacked warmth and kindness. He looked at her as if he already possessed her, and he made her yearn for safety and freedom. These were things that she never thought to seek for herself.

Nura knew that her father loved her and wished only to see to the security of her future. Sarik was a skilled warrior and a fine hunter. He would provide for the wife of his lodge and the children that came to his hearth. Any children born to Nura would have the right of leadership over the Krahnan Village. One day, when Cahil no longer walked upon the great land, Sarik would make a strong leader for their village.

Such things couldn't be denied and yet there was a hidden cruelty that only Nura seemed to sense in the man. She knew that it was wrong to disobey her father, but she couldn't seem to stop her heart from yearning for freedom.

Her father had chosen not to take another lifemate after the shattering loss of her mother. Even though her father expected her to abide by his decision without question, Nura knew that he loved her above all else. She shuddered at the thought of how he would feel when he realized that she had been taken. There were simply no words to express the grief that he would feel. This she knew well.

"Dear one?" Cahil called out for his daughter as he forced himself to move. He glanced around at the caribou skin walls of his lodge, and he noticed the familiar ceremonial masks, seal skin drums, carrying baskets, and sleeping blankets that had been carefully organized by his daughter.

Each season, he grew older and more tired. His spirit would rest easier when his daughter was good and properly joined to the man of his choosing.

Nura was early to rise and often returned from the cooking fire with a strong tea that would ease the aches within his body. He knew that she was truly unhappy with his choice of a lifemate for her, but he also knew that the daughter he raised wouldn't defy him.

As Cahil rose, he felt the creaking of his bones with every step that he took. His weathered features were set off by wise eyes and an aquiline nose, which gave way to a mouth that turned down at the corners as he proudly lifted his chin.

He left his lodge, which was adorned with the furs of the many animals of the land. His home bespoke his status as the leader of the Krahnan Village, they were people of the great land. His garments and walking stick were well crafted and even his daughter stood out amongst the other young women.

Nura's thick black hair and amber flecked brown eyes were highly praised amongst the women. She had the look of her mother, Lily. At the thought of his wife, Cahil's heart warmed. Lily had carried the same name as the flowers that bloomed freely in the land of her forefathers. It was a land that she had spoken of often and even now, the older women of their village were able to relay the stories to Nura, much to her delight.

Nura had her mother's high cheekbones and gently rounded face. His daughter's eyes were the same as her mother's, slightly slanted and darker than the night, but able to rival the sun in their beauty. Cahil remembered Lily with fondness, for she had been a gentle woman, full of kindness and strength. Though the hard edge of grief had dimmed over the passage of time, the love that he felt for his wife was still strong.

Nura reminded Cahil so much of Lily that it pained him greatly at times. He couldn't deny that he would always be grateful to his wife who died shortly after giving birth to their only child.

It didn't escape Cahil's notice that the other men of the village boasted over their sons that would carry their stories to future generations. Cahil regretted each day that he didn't have a son to call his own.

It was this desire that drove him to push Nura into a joining that she didn't want. By urging his daughter to accept Sarik as her mate, he would secure her future and that of their village. One day, Nura would present him with the son of her hearth, and his heart would rejoice.

"Have you seen Nura this day?" Cahil called out to one of the young women that usually accompanied his daughter.

"No, Great One, she is usually at the watering hole or on her way back by now." The young woman inclined her head respectfully after he thanked her.

As she walked away on footsteps that barely touched the ground, he recognized that old age held him in its strong grip. He couldn't remember moving with such agility in his youth, though it must have been so, for he was well known for his fighting and hunting skills.

He spoke to each person that passed him by and finally, he drew the attention of Sarik. The man was usually the first to greet him each day as he was eager to please the father of his future lifemate.

For some reason, the man's eager manner bothered him, but he couldn't identify the reason why this should be so. He felt a slight pang of guilt for ignoring his daughter's distaste of Sarik. However, he set aside any misgivings as Sarik approached him.

The young man was fierce in appearance and confidant in his abilities as a warrior and hunter. Nura would do well to join with a strong man that could provide for her long after Cahil breathed his last breath. With this sound reasoning in mind, Cahil greeted Sarik as the man glanced around.

"Cahil, are you searching for your daughter?" Sarik's voice was polite as he greeted his leader.

"Yes, have you seen her?"

Cahil knew with one glance that Sarik hadn't met with Nura this morning, and Cahil wondered if she would actually go so far as to hide from him. The thought concerned him, but he brushed his unease aside. He was certain that he had made the right choice for his daughter's future wellbeing.

"I was on my way to your lodge when I caught sight of you. Perhaps the young women that accompany Nura have seen her." Sarik pointed out the obvious, turning away to search the village with his dark gaze.

Cahil grimaced with impatience. He didn't allow himself to grow angry with the young man. Sarik meant well, and he didn't realize that Cahil had already walked through the village without finding Nura.

"I will check the watering hole where she goes to gather water each day. Perhaps she is only gathering plants or some other foolish thing." Sarik's jaw clenched in barely concealed irritation as he mentioned Nura's habit of seeking out the various plants that grew along the small spring.

Cahil knew that Sarik didn't agree with Nura's interest in such things. His daughter constantly tried to understand how the plants and roots that grew nearby could aid those that suffered various ailments. Cahil didn't think that Sarik would go so far as to forbid Nura from doing the work that she enjoyed. It was possible, but he reasoned that if the young man wished to win Nura's affection he wouldn't alienate her.

Cahil felt certain that the two young people would soon share affection for one another, if not love. He was also certain that once

Nura gave birth to her first son, she would grow to appreciate Sarik's strength all the more.

It was selfishness that kept Cahil from offering his daughter before this day. He knew that when she joined as a lifemate to Sarik, she would leave the security of his lodge, and he didn't wish to part with her. Yet, Sarik wouldn't be put off any longer.

Cahil's daughter was in her seventeenth season and as Sarik pointed out, most women of their village were joined with little ones riding upon their hip by that time. Only Nura remained free. Cahil had run out of reasons to delay the match between the pair, much to his daughter's despair.

Sarik called a halt to the morning's work as he told each villager to look for his future lifemate. Cahil ground his teeth when Sarik did this without first asking his permission. Concern for Nura kept him silent, although he told himself that he would address the man's actions later. His heart fairly stopped in his chest when Sarik reported that Nura couldn't be found.

"We will send out men to scout the area. Perhaps she wandered away while searching for useless plants and inedible roots." Sarik expression turned sullen and angry as he began to wonder if Nura had run away.

He quickly dismissed the thought. She wouldn't dare cast shame upon him or her father. He lowered his eyes so that Cahil wouldn't see the anger lurking within his gaze. Nura's inability to hide her aversion to him was part of the reason that he wanted her for himself.

He hungered for the day that Nura entered his lodge as his wife. He looked forward to forcing the glare of defiance from her eyes. She would learn to obey him in all things.

Cahil thought that his daughter was meek and easily molded, but Sarik sensed the challenge in her, and he reveled over the thought of breaking her spirit.

He was careful to hide his thoughts from Cahil, less the man back out of their agreement. Yet, he was unable to completely hide his secret thoughts from Nura. She saw what she should not, with dark eyes that boldly held his gaze.

Sarik told himself that she would come to know her place before long. He would see to it. Once Nura was his lifemate, he would stand in the place of Cahil and rule as leader over the Krahnan Village.

Nura shivered in the cold night air. She grieved the loss of Sule, and she wondered how her father faired. He would be sick with worry, she was certain. The man that held her captive said little to lend her any more knowledge as to the reason for her capture, and she feared for her life.

At times, she thought that he watched her with eyes that had foreseen her death. Undeterred, Nura strove to keep her jaw clamped tight so that she wouldn't shiver. She kept her eyes downcast at all times, lest she provoke an attack.

It was rare that any woman was taken with violence within her village, though such things were whispered to have occurred in the past. Nura would have remained ignorant of the violence that drove men to overpower women if not for Yonni, a young woman of their village who was a servant and would never be a wife. Yonni was taken in at a young age, when her first band died of a fever sickness. She was the only one to survive.

No one had been willing to adopt the foreign girl into their lodge as a daughter of their hearth, but several families offered to take the girl as a servant.

Nura didn't think that such a thing should have been allowed to happen, but it was not for her to decide. It was only recently that she and Yonni had formed a secret friendship that no one knew about except for the two of them.

One evening, Yonni came to Nura with tears in her eyes and explained that Sarik was not the man that Cahil thought him to be. Nura seized the chance to confide in someone about her feelings on the matter. As she drew closer, she noticed the bruises on Yonni's shoulders and arms.

"What happened to you? Did you fall?" Nura reached out her hand to touch one of the bruises that colored Yonni's arm.

"I didn't fall." Yonni's words were bitter, and Nura was rendered silent as Yonni spoke about walking to the stream to gather water and being cornered by Sarik.

"He attacked you?" Nura never imagined that Sarik was capable of such a thing. Yet, there was something dark and cold hidden behind his eyes.

"He will kill me if I tell you." Yonni's desperate whisper was answer enough for Nura.

"Are you hurt anyplace else?" Nura asked. "You will let me see." Nura grew weak when Yonni reluctantly showed her the bruises on her legs and thighs.

"Why did he do such a thing?"

Sarik carried himself like a beloved son of their village and until that moment, Nura hadn't witnessed anything to tell her differently. She thought that it was some defect in her that made it impossible to love the man that her father had selected as her future lifemate.

Nura shivered even as her teeth began to chatter, despite her promise not to feel the cold. Out of the corner of her eye, she saw the man move toward her. She tensed in expectation of violence. She was certain that he would try to violate her, and she vowed that she would fight him, though he was strong, and she had no weapon. She was no match against his superior strength, and she knew that fighting him would end in dismal failure.

CHAPTER TWO

Cahil stood mute, for only now did he begin to fear that something was truly wrong. Nura was not one to linger overlong, and she always returned quickly from her stop at the watering hole. Even though she was angry with him for ignoring her wishes, this was unlike her. Nura saw to his morning brew of herbs because she loved him, and she knew that without it he ached all day.

Sarik's thoughtless accusation that Nura had simply wandered off rang hollow. His daughter wouldn't do such a thing. One of the men returned with a stricken look upon his face, and Cahil took several steps back in denial. He didn't wish to hear the fateful words.

The man's breath hitched with every step, and Cahil knew that he had run a long distance. He was distracted by the thought that Sarik had sent scouts much farther than necessary without his permission. Cahil's face held a stricken expression as the man struggled to speak.

"Sule was found beaten and barely conscious. It appears that he saw your daughter in the company of an unknown warrior, and he was injured when he tried to intervene." The man struggled to catch his breath. "We searched further and at the outskirts of our land, we found something that belongs to Nura."

Cahil groaned deep in his chest as the man held up Nura's bone bracelet. It was always with her and never was she without it. It was one of the few items passed down to her from her mother. Small bits of bone were pierced through and linked with strands of sinew. Dark crimson streaks of blood now graced the length of the bracelet.

"She has defied you!" Sarik spoke bitterly as he grabbed Nura's blood smeared bracelet out of the runner's hand. "She ran to escape our joining."

Those nearby gasped in shock and dismay as Sarik threw Nura's bracelet to the ground. It was a shameful thing that a young woman would disobey her father in such a way, and he made his displeasure known.

"You cannot say for certain what has occurred. You have not found a trail. Go, find my daughter, and bring her back to us!" Cahil wanted to defend his daughter's honor, but he held back the words.

He couldn't be certain that she hadn't fled. He only hoped that such a thing couldn't possibly be true.

Sarik left to gather men for his journey, and Cahil stood alone looking out over the village that he led. Nothing mattered anymore. What chance was there that his daughter would ever return to him?

"Nura! Nura!" Cahil fell to his knees upon the ground as he clasped his daughter's bracelet in his hands. Agony unlike anything Cahil had ever known speared through his chest, heightening his grief.

Although Cahil hadn't ordered it, he knew that Sarik took it upon himself to tell other bands not to hunt within the boundaries set by their warriors. He didn't know the extent of the damage caused by Sarik's bloodlust.

In truth, he had ignored Sarik's cruel way of dealing with the smaller bands that dwelled nearby. Cahil felt guilt consume him. His daughter was alone upon the great land, and he knew that if others found her, she would be in grave danger.

He ripped his outer garments as pain speared through him. "What have I done? Oh, Great Father Above, what have I done?"

Cold surrounded him. Keluk felt the thrill of success that was shared by the other hunters. His younger brother, Denali, stood beside him, basking in the glory of their successful hunt. The women of their band worked to prepare the seal meat for the evening meal, but there was more than enough to share for many days.

The men celebrated amongst themselves, thrilled that they had been successful after so many days of hunting.

"You realize that you almost made your first kill." Keluk teased his brother.

"I know, Keluk, but next time I won't fail." Denali shrugged boyishly, his smile wide as he stared at his brother with a worshipful gaze. "Thank you for allowing me to accompany you and the other men."

Keluk grunted. He had been stricken by the urge to deny Denali's pleas to join him and the others, but he had reluctantly given in. He ruffled his brother's windblown hair affectionately.

A shout from one of the hunters would have gone unnoticed, but it held a frenzied pitch that was at odds with the air of triumph that surrounded them. Keluk whirled to find that their small settlement was surrounded by men from the Krahnan Village.

There were no words offered by the Krahnan warriors before they attacked. Keluk clearly saw the face of the man that led the attack, and he threw himself in front of Denali as a warrior ran toward them with his spear raised. All around them, women and children screamed in terror.

Keluk barely avoided being skewered by a warrior's surprise attack. He clenched his hand around his hunting knife, sinking the stone edge into the man's exposed neck as he turned to assure himself of his brother's wellbeing. What he saw nearly stopped his heart.

"Denali!"

The whirl of a war club sounded through the air, and he watched his brother fall from a blow to the head.

"Denali!" Keluk's raw scream broke the silence. His heart pounded as if it would explode from his chest, and his fists clenched and unclenched in remembered helplessness and rage.

The dream was always the same.

Each time he broke away from the memory of Denali's last day of life, he felt a renewed sense of vengeance and anger take hold. Grief wedged itself in his chest and his throat worked as he struggled for control.

He glanced at the shivering woman resting beside him, fully aware that she had heard him shout his brother's name. The moon was full and for a moment, he peered into her large, doe shaped eyes, and he saw fear and doubt lingering there. He couldn't risk a fire, but he needed to ensure that she lived through the night.

He vacillated between leaving her to suffer the harsh hand of the elements and tossing his cold weather parka over her huddled form. His blood thundered with anger as he removed his parka and tossed it toward her.

Bitter words caught in the back of his throat as she whispered softly, "Thank you."

He turned his eyes away from her as she expressed her appreciation. He almost told her that he kept her alive only to make certain that she was capable of withstanding the slow death that awaited her at the hands of his people. But in the end, he kept his thoughts to himself.

If she knew what awaited her, she might decide that it was better to die now from exposure to the cold than live to greet the torturous death that awaited her.

Honor demanded that he return to his people with an offering that would appease their sense of justice. Keluk wouldn't fail to avenge the wrong done to his band. With that thought in mind, he hardened his heart and firmed his resolve to keep his distance from his captive. Her fate had been determined by the actions of men that chose to harm innocent people and kill without cause. In his eyes, and in the eyes of his people, she was already dead.

"You will stand with me as we go on this trek to bring my woman back. If Nura is found by any other band, they will kill her in repayment for our raids upon them. We will kill those that think to seek vengeance. They don't deserve vengeance, for it was their error that caused them to tread upon our hunting grounds." Sarik drew the men together as one and gave them orders that they swore to follow. The warriors that he left behind would guard the village with their lives, of this he was certain.

Sarik glanced at the two men that readied themselves for the journey ahead. They were eager to prove themselves to him, their war leader. "We are brothers, united in a common goal. We will not stop until my woman has been returned!"

Cahil watched the proceedings as he sat outside of the fire circle. Sarik was filled with an anger that was awesome to behold, but he wondered again what had caused Nura to flee.

Cahil felt grief well up inside of his heart anew. In his quest to have his name known forever amongst his people, he might have erred irreparably by refusing to heed his daughter's tearful request. She had only asked that he allow her to choose her own mate, but he had denied her even that much.

He felt the chill night air surround him, and he shuddered at the thought of Nura alone upon the great land. His daughter didn't have the necessary skills needed to survive the cold and snow on her own.

To his knowledge, Nura didn't even know how to build a fire on her own. Cahil's breath hitched in his chest as he thought of his beautiful, defenseless daughter alone in the cold, surrounded by darkness. Grief tore at him, and his heart was laid upon the ground.

Nura barely slept. She drifted in a place of cold and frigid air only to wake at the slightest sound or movement. As the sun started to rise, she decided that she would sleep despite the danger the man posed. If he planned to attack her, she thought that perhaps he would have done so by now.

She knew it was possible that he was waiting for her to grow too weak to fight him, but if so, that time had already come and gone. If anything, her captor seemed to hate her so fiercely that he only touched her when he was forced to do so.

Her mouth watered as she remembered the tempting smell of rabbit meat that drifted her way over the small cooking fire. She hadn't taken her morning or midday meal, and she was ravenous.

Her people believed that it was meat that gave the body warmth. If she didn't eat, she would weaken and die. She didn't know if she could walk at the same pace that her captor set yesterday, not without nourishment of some kind.

"Eat." The man walked on feet that were silent, startling her by his sudden appearance beside her. Cutting her hands free, he extended a piece of meat upon the blade of his hunting knife. She wouldn't flinch in fear if he decided to end her life now. Instead, she took the food that he offered, chewing hungrily.

Her jaw ached from the way he had grabbed her face at the stream near her village. She realized now that he had lifted her chin with bruising strength so that he would have better access to her throat with the serrated edge of his stone knife.

The lethal way that her captor moved told her that he would have followed through on his threat if she had screamed. She was almost certain that he would have ended her life instantly if she had uttered a sound.

He roughly hauled her to her feet as soon as the last morsel of food disappeared, quickly binding her wrists together before tying the length of rope to him. Nura didn't tell him that she had to relieve her bladder.

She sensed without knowing why that he would lash out in anger if she spoke even one word. This time, she didn't drink from the proffered waterskin even though her mouth was full of thirst.

She had no doubt that she would shame herself in front of him if she drank even a drop of water. When she steadfastly refused to drink, he studied her bowed head with an intensity that left her trembling.

With a deft movement of his fingers, he untied her wrists and motioned for her to walk a few feet away. Nura immediately took care of the needs of her body.

She couldn't help glancing back to see if the man watched, and she couldn't explain her sense of relief to see that he had his back turned.

For a brief moment, she considered trying to run. But she realized that he could outpace her in three steps. If she ran now, she would only ignite the rage that simmered within the man's heart.

Nura couldn't bring herself to signal that she was ready to be tied up again. Instead, she walked back to his side and silently waited.

Her captor tied her wrists once more, after grudgingly allowing her to use the water to wash and drink. Nura took small sips of water as she took in their surroundings. She had never traveled this far outside of her village before.

Stories of the men and women that died alone upon the ice and snow ran through her mind. She decided that she would watch carefully the next time the man made a fire. Such things were always done for her in the Krahnan Village.

As the daughter of the village leader, Nura knew that she was privileged in ways that other women were not. Until now, it had never occurred to her that she was almost completely helpless without the knowledge needed to survive alone upon the great land.

She watched as the man took the waterskin and tied it to his belt. He showed little concern for the amount of water that she drank, and she wondered if perhaps she should have fully quenched her thirst. Why had she thought to save the precious liquid when he had given her a chance to drink her fill?

Snow was all around them. If they needed more water, he could simply pack more snow into the waterskin and press it against his chest until it melted. Surely he lost valuable body heat each time that he warmed their water.

They set off at a pace that quickly drained her strength. He stopped suddenly, and Nura almost ran into his back.

The man turned to face her, and for the first time, she saw his features up close. His dark eyes were fringed by thick black eyelashes while high cheekbones were offset by a broad nose and lips that were held in a thin, unmovable line. The stark coldness in his eyes nearly took her breath away and Nura jerked her gaze away from his face as he took a menacing step toward her.

She quickly lowered her eyes and looked at the ground. How many times had she noticed Yonni avoid eye contact with those that she called master? It didn't shame Nura that she was forced to resort to the same tactics as a servant.

It was true that she was the daughter of a village leader, and her blood was that of village leaders from time before memory, but she was not within the safety of her village any longer. She was alone with a fierce man that challenged her with each searing glare, and she reminded herself that her strength was scanty in comparison. She would do well to remember it.

Keluk searched the distance for any sign of pursuit and seeing none, he remembered the reason that he had stopped walking. From his carrying pack, he withdrew the moccasins that he had made the previous night. He was not skilled with a bone awl and neat stitches, but most hunters were not concerned by such things. He threw the moccasins at the woman's feet and grunted when she only stared at them with an expression of terror.

"Put them on." His voice was a raspy growl.

Nura glanced at the man and then looked at the massacred rabbit fur that he flung at her feet. She was not certain where he wanted her to place the mutilated fur upon her body. She quickly bent and gathered the two pieces awkwardly in her hands. She lifted them up, quickly discerning that they were to be worn on her feet.

As she removed her thin foot coverings and replaced them with his offering, she immediately felt a sigh of relief well up from deep in her chest. Yesterday, she had tried to avoid thinking about her cold feet.

It was obvious that she hadn't planned to set foot outside of her village. Most of the women in her village didn't have the need for sturdy foot coverings. But here upon the great land, she needed some type of protection against the ever changing ground.

"Thank you." Nura voiced her appreciation quietly as any sound from her seemed to infuriate the man.

He tugged on the ropes that bound her wrists, and she quickly rose and started to follow him.

Nura winced in pain, but she didn't speak or try to draw his attention in any way. At times, she hoped that he would simply forget that she was there at all.

CHAPTER THREE

Keluk was troubled by the woman. She didn't act or react in the way that he thought a captive should. The vengeance that pushed him to fulfill the blood debt owed to his band surged forward. They still had many days of travel ahead of them before they reached his band, and each day seemed to last longer than the last.

He could feel his captive's eyes upon him constantly, and he was surprised that she would look at him as if he were a man like any other man. Her people had treated his band as if they were no better than animals. Yet, she didn't seem to do the same.

At midday, he stopped and found the place that he knew was well protected and would offer adequate shelter against the cold.

"Take them off." Keluk nodded toward her moccasins, but the woman wouldn't look at him. He knew very little of her language, and he didn't wish to learn more. Yet, the language of the ancients was sacred, and he refused to use it unnecessarily.

Nura froze.

The man spoke in her language.

Shock rippled through her as he gestured to her body. He wanted her to remove her garments, but she couldn't bring herself to disrobe. She wouldn't. Nakedness was not something that she hid, yet in this case, the man sought to do her harm. If he meant to kill her then she wouldn't aid him, she would fight.

Keluk waited, but the mutinous glare of defiance in her brown eyes brought an end to his patience. In an instant, he pushed her down into the snow, tearing the icy moccasins from her feet. He didn't have time for childish games.

Nura didn't scream as she fell. For a moment, she understood fully the restrained power held by this man, this warrior.

How else could she explain the lightening quick movements that he claimed as his own? When he yanked the moccasins from her feet, she took a shaky breath. He inspected her feet before shoving the moccasins toward her.

"Good." The man spat the word as if it was distasteful.

Keluk was glad to see that the woman's feet showed no sign of the ice sickness. If a person became too cold, fingers and toes were the first to suffer harm.

He couldn't afford to let the woman sicken and die here upon the great land. He vowed that he would make certain that she was whole and able to withstand the torture his people would inflict. They wouldn't allow her to have a quick death. Not by any means. This he knew well.

Nura had never been so cold in her life, but her captor plodded along as if he didn't feel the chill wind that blew over the frozen land. She stubbornly refused to give him any cause to strike out at her with the anger that burned in his soul. She knew that she couldn't endure a beating, not when her every movement took all of her will.

After a time, the man stopped walking and untied her bonds. He motioned for her to sit, and Nura tried to stiffen her legs so that she wouldn't fall to the ground in relief. She watched as he walked away without another word.

All around her was ice and snow.

Before long the man faded away into the distance, and Nura began to wonder if she had been left to die. Tiredness lashed at her, and she forced her eyes to remain open. She knew better than to fall asleep without a fire in the freezing cold.

All day long, she had tried to ignore the cut upon her leg, but now that she sat still, she could feel the pounding of the wound.

Nura wished for her bag of herbs so that she could make a poultice for the deep gash.

She quickly lowered her leggings and looked at the wound, wincing at the sight of her exposed flesh. The injury wasn't excessively deep, but it needed to be treated.

She couldn't hope to do anything other than clean the wound and make certain that it didn't bleed again. Nura gasped as she cleaned the injury with fresh snow. She bit her lip to keep from crying out.

Already, her upper thigh was stained red with blood. She could only hope that one of the wild animals that walked the land wouldn't catch the scent of her injury. Her captor had to know that they were attracting predators with their every step. She wondered suddenly if he had purposely abandoned her to die.

Nura settled back into place carefully. Such thoughts only caused her to shiver with fear and cold.

"I am Che-no-nura, daughter of Cahil, leader of the Krahnan Village. I am Che-no-nura, that is my secret name, given to me by my mother. I am the little blue bird that does not know fear." Nura continued to repeat the words that bolstered her courage over and over again.

After a time, the wind no longer cut through her fur parka and leggings with such ferocity, and fear no longer hungered after her soul.

Keluk watched the woman from a distance. She didn't seem to sense his presence, and he hadn't found any sign of pursuit when he backtracked to check for danger. But he was certain that the young woman's father wouldn't rest until he knew her fate.

He hadn't been successful at finding an animal willing to come to his arrow or spear, and he returned to the woman with the intention of sharing some of the seal meat that had sustained him on his journey thus far.

"Wake!" Keluk spoke sharply when he saw that the woman's eyes continued to drift closed even though she fought sleep.

Nura jerked awake, shaking her head to clear it. Her heart trembled within her chest as she realized how close she had been to falling deeply asleep. Without food or warmth to sustain her, such a careless mistake could prove fatal.

"I will do better." She promised herself in a low murmur.

"Eat." The man tossed a small amount of meat her way, and Nura forced her hands to obey the command of her mind. Her fur encased hands were like blocks of ice, but she ignored the discomfort and quickly chewed the seal meat.

"Thank you." Nura whispered her thanks though she wondered if she should do so. The man flinched, but he didn't glance at her and for that she was grateful.

Keluk cast his eyes forward. He sought the familiar shape of the large mountains of ice that they would need to cross in order to reach his band.

Men that crossed the ice mountains often tied themselves to the man in front of him and still another. Yet, on the journey here, driven by his need for vengeance, Keluk had crossed the ice mountains alone without the safety of having others near.

He urged the woman forward even as his heart sped up in rhythm as he contemplated the yawning crevices ahead of them. First, they would have to climb the ice mountains, then they would face the crevices that could easily swallow them whole, burying them under a world of ice.

Keluk kicked his foot into one toehold after another and carefully made his way up. The woman seemed to understand what was expected of her because she imitated his movements exactly. He stopped when they were finally above the crest of the ice and snow.

When the woman started to scoop snow from the ground and press it to her lips, he stopped her. His movements were harsh and jerky, as he held her small wrists within his grasp. Her bones were small and fragile like a snow bird. He snatched his hands away from her wrists as soon as he had her attention.

"Do not eat the snow." Keluk ground the words between clenched teeth and pressed the waterskin into her hand after shaking it free of snow.

Earlier, he had filled the waterskin with snow and warmed it against his chest during the climb. He didn't stop to tell the woman about the painful snow blisters that would appear upon her lips and inside of her mouth if she swallowed too much snow.

It was obvious that she had never been in a situation where she was forced to survive. Keluk felt his anger grow as he realized that he and the others in his band fought daily against the challenges of the great land. Yet, the young woman before him had never known such hardships.

He narrowed his eyes at her when she carefully tied the waterskin and handed it back to him. He released the knot that kept her wrists pressed together and gathered the rope around her waist.

He heard her sharp gasp when he unsheathed his hunting knife and tied the end of the rope to it. Her eyes were wide and dark with uncertainty, but he refused to offer any words of reassurance. They were in a dire situation. One wrong step and they would plunge into the icy depths below. He wouldn't tell her otherwise.

He thought for a moment that perhaps she would seek her own death as some might, to avoid torture. But the determined gleam in her eyes told him that she wanted to live, if only for a little while longer.

Keluk would see to it that she survived long enough to be delivered to his people. Only then would the blood debt be repaid. This was the way of his band since time beyond memory, and there was nothing that he could do to change such a thing, of this he was certain.

Shadow of the Moon (Book Two) – **Available Now!**

KENNEDY PUBLISHING
TITLES BY KARAH QUINNEY:

The Whale Hunter
Pillar of Fire (Book One)
Sacred Fire (Book Two)
Sacred Path (Book Three)

The Great Land
The Seeking Star (Book One)
Shadow of the Moon (Book Two)
Light of the Sun (Book Three)

Sundancer
Legend of the Sundancer (Book One)
The Last Sundancer (Book Two)

Warrior
The Warrior's Way
Daughters of the Sun
The Cloud Forest – New Release

KARAH

QUINNEY

Made in the USA
Middletown, DE
11 August 2022

71172340R00166